WAYNE STINNETT

FALLEN PALM

A JESSE MCDERMITT NOVEL

◆·◆·◆·◆

Caribbean Adventure Series
Volume 2

DOWN ISLAND PRESS, LLC

2019

Original Copyright © 2014
Published by DOWN ISLAND PRESS, LLC, 2019
Beaufort, SC

Second Edition Copyright © 2019 by Wayne Stinnett

Library of Congress cataloging-in-publication Data

Stinnett, Wayne
Fallen Palm, Second Edition/Wayne Stinnett
p. cm. - (A Jesse McDermitt novel)

ISBN-13: 978-1-7322360-8-0 (Down Island Press)
SBN-10: 1-7322360-8-9

Cover photograph by Goran Jakus Photography
Graphics by Wicked Good Book Covers
Edited by The Write Touch
Interior Design by Ampersand Book Designs

This is a work of fiction. Names, characters, and incidents are either the product of the author's imagination or are used fictitiously. Any resemblance to actual persons, living or dead, businesses, companies, events, or locales is entirely coincidental. Most of the locations herein are also fictional, or are used fictitiously. However, I take great pains to depict the location and description of the many well-known islands, locales, beaches, reefs, bars, and restaurants throughout the Florida Keys and the Caribbean, to the best of my ability.

FOREWORD

I used artistic license to move the location of the wreck of the Confederate blockade-runner, *Lynx*, from Wilmington, NC, to Fort Pierce, FL, one of my favorite dive spots. I've spent a lot of time in The Keys, fishing, diving, sailing, boating, and of course drinking, and have tried to convey the island attitude in this work as best I could.

In my late twenties, back in 1988, I wrote three short stories about a young, rough-and-ready Marine veteran-turned-fishing guide who lived in the Florida Keys. From the dozens of query letters sent to publishers and agents, my submission got a handful of rejection letters. Most recipients didn't even bother to reply. Twenty-five years later, while cleaning out the garage, I came across the floppy disc that those stories were saved on. With encouragement from my wife and others, I updated the character, brought the three stories up to present time, compiled them, and then completely rewrote the manuscript as a single novel. This, my first novel, is the result. The main character, Jesse McDermitt, in both the short stories and in this novel, is now an older and wiser man. Maybe a bit slower, too. But aren't we all?

I'd like to thank the many people who encouraged me to pursue this project, especially my wife, Greta. Without her encouragement, motivation, support, and the many ideas she's given me along the way, this novel would never have been completed. Thanks also to my youngest daughter Jordy, for her contribution in naming many of the characters. Also, thanks to our other kids, not only for their support, but also for not laughing at this old truck driver for thinking he could write a novel.

I'd also like to thank Captain Marty Williams and his son, first mate Jimmy Williams, of the sport fishing charter boat Wide Open out of Whale Harbor, Islamorada, in the fabulous Florida Keys, for their help in detailing life and work on a modern charter fishing boat. Times have changed.

Thanks to fellow Marine Ted Nulty, of the Long Rifle Institute, for his contributions in detailing modern Marine Recon small unit tactics and weaponry.

Many thanks to my friend Donna Rich for her proofreading and to my editor, Marsha Zinberg.

Lastly, I'd like to thank Colonel Roy Shelton, USMC, retired, for putting the crazy notion into my head that I could write a book in the first place.

If you'd like to receive my twice-monthly newsletter for specials, book recommendations, and updates on coming books, please sign up on my website:

WWW.WAYNESTINNETT.COM

Jesse McDermitt Series
Fallen Out
Fallen Palm
Fallen Hunter
Fallen Pride
Fallen Mangrove
Fallen King
Fallen Honor
Fallen Tide
Fallen Angel
Fallen Hero
Rising Storm
Rising Fury
Rising Force

Charity Styles Series
Merciless Charity
Ruthless Charity
Reckless Charity
Enduring Charity

Don't forget to visit the Gaspar's Revenge ship's store.
There you can purchase all kinds
of swag related to my books.

WWW.GASPARS-REVENGE.COM

DEDICATION

Dedicated to Jordy,

whose vibrant enthusiasm and unabashed innocence
remind me of a day and time, long since gone.
We should all stop sometimes to look at
ourselves through the eyes of our children.

"In the sense of movement, a boat is a living thing.
It is a companion in the night.
Each boat has its own manner and character."

Travis McGee, **1985**

MAPS

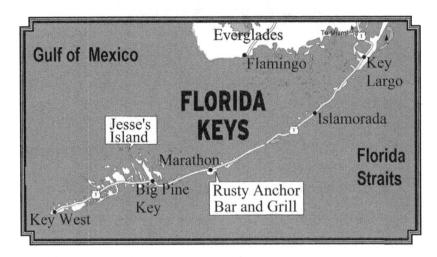

The Florida Keys

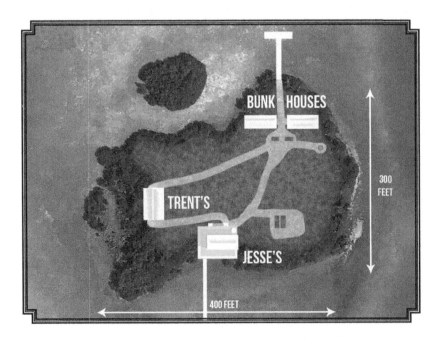

Jesse's Island

CHAPTER
ONE

Lester Antonio was having a hard time coming to grips with his recent good fortune. Things were finally starting to go his way. He'd lived a hard life, 25 years and counting. He was born in Philly, the son of a crack-addicted street prostitute who couldn't even guess at who Lester's father might have been. His childhood wasn't pretty, and the continuous visits by rough-looking men to the dingy one-room motels he grew up in didn't provide any ideal male role models. Before reaching puberty, Lester had had more than his fair share of encounters with the law.

At thirteen, as part of his initiation into a street gang in North Philly, he'd stolen a Toyota. The theft hadn't gone unnoticed for long. While sitting at a stop light at Broad and Cherry in Center City, a cop pulled up right beside Lester's boosted Corolla. Kensington, his hood, was to the north, so he put on his right-turn signal, tried to sit up taller in the seat, and look cool. But the cop saw right through his attempted façade to the nervous thirteen-year-old kid at the wheel.

When the light changed, Lester had turned right and stomped his foot on the gas, heading toward the Convention Center. But it was a one-way street and he was going the wrong way. The cop hit the lights and siren and came after him. Lester's big-time criminal career had lasted a whole two blocks before he was tangled in oncoming traffic with the cop car stopped right behind him, blocking any escape. That had cost Lester half a year in juvie.

Back on the block six months later, he'd tried other criminal enterprises—picking pockets, petty theft, drug dealing, and so on—with pretty much the same results. Lester just wasn't a very good criminal, though he aspired to be.

At eighteen, he was charged with drug possession and intent to distribute. All he was doing was carrying a box from a guy's house in Fishtown to another place a few blocks away. The local hard-ass would've given him a crisp C-note to do it, if the cops hadn't popped him. As it turned out, the package had contained two pounds of coke.

That got Lester some real time, six years in state lockup. It was rough, but he managed. With little else to do but play basketball or lift weights, he soon started putting on a little bulk. At a slim five-ten, he quickly added 50 pounds of muscle during his incarceration. When he left the pen, he tipped the scales at a ripped 220.

Leaving the industrially cold prison on a Monday, Lester didn't have a lot of options open to him. He'd heard through the grapevine that the guy who he'd been carrying the coke for blamed him for the loss of the two pounds. Kensington and Fishtown were out.

The prison bus dropped him at Jefferson Station in Center City and Lester stepped out onto the street a free man. But where to go? It was afternoon and he only had a few dollars in his pocket, not even enough for cab fare. If he even had a place to go.

Crossing the street, Lester joined the mass of people on the wide sidewalk and walked to the corner. There, he stopped and leaned against a building. He needed cash, and he needed it fast.

A pretty blonde in a short skirt walked by and he watched her with hungry eyes as she strolled down the sidewalk. Pushing away from the building, he began to follow her, walking slowly. Though her stride was enticing, her short skirt bouncing up and down, he was watching the men who hurried past him, knowing that their eyes would be on the blonde.

Two blocks later, he stopped on another corner and leaned against another building, peering up and down the streets. The blonde was gone, and the guy whose wallet was now in Lester's pocket probably wouldn't miss it for a while. He stepped inside the small store and bought a pack of cigarettes, very pleased to find several twenties and some smaller bills in his new wallet, along with a couple of credit cards.

Following his route back to the bus station, he stopped at a couple of stores, bought a backpack and some clothes, then returned to the corner and looked once more at Jefferson Station.

With the idea that maybe a change of climate would improve his luck, Lester crossed the street and bought a one-way ticket on the next southbound bus. There wasn't anything holding him in Philly. He was headed to the Sunshine State, with less than $100 and a couple of stolen credit cards in the stolen wallet. He really didn't have a destination in mind, so long as it was somewhere that didn't have dirty gray snow. That would be good enough for him.

After travelling through the night, the bus stopped on US-1 in the old town of St. Augustine. Lester stepped off to stretch his legs, leaving his bag in the overhead. By the time he'd walked around the building, the bus had disappeared. Complaining to the guy behind the thick glass wasn't much help. He offered to call the next stop and have his bag pulled off.

"Where's that?" Lester asked. The bus had stopped at more than twenty little towns already, so maybe it wasn't far.

"Daytona," the man replied. "About 45 miles south."

His wallet was in his bag, as was his bus ticket. Stranded in a beach town, he first tried panhandling, to bum enough money for something to eat and a ticket to Daytona. A St. Johns deputy sheriff picked him up and he was charged with vagrancy. Since he had no license, no money, and no bags, he spent another month in lock-up. Released from the county jail, he made a beeline for the interstate and stuck out his thumb.

He needed to get to Daytona fast and didn't want to try bumming or lifting a tourist's wallet. Staying in Saint Augustine was out of the question. Too small and too old. Bright lights and big city—that was where Lester wanted to be. He felt more comfortable surrounded by people. Daytona was big. Miami was bigger.

A car pulled to a stop on the ramp to I-95 and Lester trotted toward it. The driver was an old guy with dark hair around his temples but snowy white on top. He had a long, crooked nose, dark, pockmarked skin, and was driving an expensive-looking sedan.

The driver put the window down on the passenger side. "Where you headed, kid?"

"Anywhere but here, pops. Someplace with people that aren't all related to each other."

The driver opened the door and said, "I ain't your pops, kid. But I could use the company. I'm headed to Palm Beach. Get in."

Lester climbed into the air-conditioned comfort of the big sedan and the old guy pulled out onto the freeway. "Sorry for the pops thing, man. I just wanna get out of here quick is all."

"Name's Sonny Beech, kid. You ain't a druggy, I can see that. You ain't a queer, are ya?"

"No, I ain't no fag. For real, your name's Sonny Beech?"

"Yeah, kid," the driver said. "But with an *o* and two *e*'s. Grew up in Amish country and hated my first name. When I came down here, I picked up the nickname Sonny. Suits me better."

"I just spent some time with the county's finest on a bogus charge," Lester said. "Just need to get outta here is all."

Dammit, Lester thought, *I need to keep my yap shut. Dude's probably going to pull over and put my ass on the shoulder now.*

Sonny drove on in silence for half an hour and Lester said nothing more. He concentrated on keeping his mouth shut. The exit for Daytona was coming up. Lester wondered if there was any chance his stuff would be at the bus station. He decided it wouldn't. Besides, there was only twenty bucks left in the wallet, and the guy was sure to have cancelled the cards after more than a month.

Passing another exit for Daytona, Sonny asked, "You need work, kid? I could use some muscle. Someone that ain't afraid of getting his hands dirty, if you know what I mean."

So, Lester's career as hired muscle for a Palm Beach loan shark began. At first, Sonny had him doing menial tasks befitting his stature and lack of education. In other words, Lester worked under one of Sonny's thumb breakers, a weird dude named Walt.

In no time at all, Sonny had Lester performing more important jobs, picking up deadbeats who owed Sonny money and taking them for a meet. Sometimes, he even took them back to where he'd picked them up. Other times, he didn't.

During his days off, Lester trolled the shoreline looking for beach babes. It was already cold up north; he'd seen a weather report saying it was snowing back home. Lester smiled.

He got a lot of looks from some very attractive ladies, but as soon as he'd start talking to one, she'd drop him like a hot potato.

Lester wasn't the greatest conversationalist. One day, he noticed an old guy coming out of the water with scuba gear on. Even though he was a fossil, the guy was immediately surrounded by several bikini-clad young women.

"Gotta have an angle," Lester mumbled to himself.

Lester watched as the old guy smiled and talked to the pretty girls. Then he waved to them and started walking his way. As the old guy walked by, Lester asked him, "Is that hard to learn?"

"Scuba diving or picking up chicks?" he replied, laughing.

"The diving thing," Lester said.

"If you can swim, you can dive. You'd have to take a course and there's a little math involved, but it's pretty easy."

"What do ya find out there? Is the course close by here?" Lester asked.

"You can catch lobster during the season, or spear fish, or just look around at all the pretty fish," the old guy replied. "There's dozens of scuba centers all over town—just look for the red-and-white dive flags. My name's Russ."

"I'm Lester," he replied, shaking Russ's hand. "Hey, what's that long thing ya carrying? Don't look like no spear gun to me."

"Oh, this?" Russ asked, as he lifted a contraption that had a box with some dials and meters on it at one end and a round plate at the other. "It's an underwater metal detector. Sometimes I find things that people lose off their boats."

Lester noticed he was wearing something on a chain around his neck. It was gold, but oddly shaped with a cross on it and some symbols in the four parts separated by the cross. He couldn't make out what they were.

Has to be some kind of treasure, he thought. *Dude is looking for more than some old lady's wedding ring, that's for sure.*

Several weeks later, Lester spotted Russ at the same beach again. Approaching, he said, "Hey, I'm taking one of those diving courses. Maybe you can show me how to look for stuff when I get finished with it."

Russ said, "Yeah, I can show you a few things once you're certified. I don't dive here a lot, though. I live up in Fort Pierce."

A month later, Lester had his Open-Water certification and had asked around about Russ. Turned out he was right—Russ was a kind of amateur treasure hunter with a reputation for skirting the salvage laws.

Although Lester didn't do well with the ladies despite his physique, he always managed to make friends with other men pretty easily. The next time he ran into Russ, they got to talking about his new diving certification.

"Where ya from, Russ?" Lester asked over a beer at a Palm Beach tiki bar.

"Originally, I'm from Philadelphia, but I haven't been back there in over twenty years."

"No kiddin'? I'm from Philly, too! Kensington."

"Grew up in South Philly—Packer Park."

"Small world, ain't it?" Lester said. "I just moved down here a few months ago."

After talking about their neighborhoods over a couple more beers, Lester finally asked, "Say, Russ, besides looking around, or spearfishing, can a guy make any money doing this scuba diving?"

Russ seemed to think it over for a minute, motioning the waitress to bring another round. Finally, he looked intensely at the younger man in front of him and said, "With a lot more classes, you could be a dive master and earn just about enough to buy this next round. The tradeoff is, you get to live in paradise. But yeah, there's money in the water." Russ paused, then added, "You just gotta know where to find it."

"Money in the water? You mean like finding old ladies' rings and what not?"

"No, kid. I mean *real* money." Russ leaned closer, inspecting Lester's eyes. "You see, over the last three or four centuries, hundreds, maybe even thousands of ships have sunk during storms right out there on that reef. It runs from Key West to Fort Pierce, over 300 miles. A lot of them were headed back to Spain, carrying gold and silver. If a person knew where to look, he might find some of it." Russ leaned in closer and stared harder at Lester, as if trying to read his morals through his eyes. "Of course, sometimes it's not exactly legal to look in some places, and the State of Florida wants a cut of anything found legally."

"Well, Russ," Lester said, grinning, "the way I look at it, nothing's against the law till ya get caught."

"I could use a dive partner on some of my dives," Russ said. "A guy with your strength could come in handy. Could involve you coming up to Fort Pierce on occasion. Interested?"

With that, Lester became a part-time treasure hunter—at least, until he could find out where the old man kept his trinkets hidden. Then, well, maybe the old-timer might join those guys that Lester didn't take back to where he'd picked them up for Sonny Beech.

Several weeks and a dozen dives later, Lester and Russ were once more out on his boat. Russ had used Lester to carry the heavy gear, move stuff around on the bottom, and just provide muscle in general.

"Ya sure this is the place, Russ?" Lester asked.

It was Lester's only day off. If it were up to Sonny, he'd be working seven days a week, but Friday was Sonny's day at the track, so it became Lester's day off. And Russ wasn't paying him anything. Just teaching him stuff and cutting him in on anything they found. So far, that amounted to nothing.

"Hell no, I ain't sure, kid. That ship was sunk near here by a Union warship over a hundred years ago, toward the end of the Civil War. Likely it broke up and is scattered over a mile-long stretch of bottom. You see the bottom on the depth finder—there's something down there, all right. No way to tell what it is till we get down there, though. For all I know, it could be a '64 Impala with a couple of gangbangers in it."

Russ had made it clear to Lester that he hadn't been greatly impressed with Lester's mental acuity over the last couple of weeks. Lester wasn't sure what acuity meant, but figured that Russ thought he was dumb, like everyone else.

But he'd also said that Lester was stronger than a bull and did what he was told. Russ liked his work ethic. He'd been looking for some sign of this particular wreck for over a year and this was the thirteenth pile they'd dived together in three weeks. Probably nothing, he'd said. But he had to check.

Lester could only come along on Fridays, but they did squeeze a couple of night dives in on sites that were nearer the shore. When they weren't checking out Russ's hot spots from the depth finder, Russ was busy poring over charts and internet sites.

"Look, kid," Russ said. "The *Lynx* was a blockade runner and was reported to be carrying $140,000 in gold bars."

"You been looking for this boat for years, you said?" Lester asked. "Seems like a lot of work for only 140 grand."

Russ grinned at him, "Yeah, ain't inflation great? Look, during the Civil War, gold was about $170 an ounce. Know what it is today?" Lester shook his head. "Today, that same gold would be worth nearly ten times that amount. The *Lynx* was carrying twelve gold bars, each weighing ten pounds—that's almost 2000 ounces. At today's rate of $1400 an ounce, it'd be worth over two-and-a-half million bucks. Even more than that for its historic value."

Not that Russ was interested in the history. He'd told Lester that his man in Fort Lauderdale would pay him 70 cents on the dollar for the melt weight of anything he found. He'd melt down anything from gold coins to bronze cannons. Just one of those gold bars would give him a heck of a payday. He and Lester had agreed on splitting anything they found 80/20.

"You ready, kid?" Russ asked as he put on his mask.

Lester replied with a nod and they both fell backwards off the boat on opposite sides. Each of them had a spear gun and a goodie bag to make it look like they were just a couple of spear fishermen. The bags were oversized, and each held a small underwater metal detector capable of finding something as small as a nail buried up to two feet deep.

Once they reached the bottom, they located the ridge the depth finder on the boat had pointed out. Swimming along the bottom of the ridge, it looked like it was going to be yet another false hit. Lester was about ten feet out from the ledge, as they'd agreed on earlier, and Russ was just a few feet out. They swung their detectors back and forth as they followed the ridge, but whenever Lester looked over, Russ seemed to be studying the ridge itself.

After about 50 feet Russ saw a nice-sized grouper hiding out in a hole and speared it. Putting it in his bag, he looked over at Lester, who gave him a thumbs up with his free hand. Just then the metal detector in Lester's hand went off. He looked down and waved it back and forth, the meter swinging wildly as the machine made an audible whir-whir sound.

Lester pulled out the little garden shovel that each of them carried in their bags and started digging. While he was doing that, Russ swam over, continuing to study the ridge. When Lester paused and glanced at what Russ was looking at, he noticed the ledge seemed to have a symmetry that he hadn't noticed earlier. Lester resumed his digging.

After a moment, the steel garden tool struck something solid, and Lester started digging with his hands, uncovering several large links of chain. As Russ had instructed him, he began to tap his tank with his shovel, and when Russ glanced over, he waved frantically for him to come and see what he'd found. Lester was sure it was important.

Russ swam over to take a look. In the hole that he'd dug, Lester pointed out the unmistakable shape of several large chain links.

Working together, they uncovered more and more of it and soon they could see five feet of a large, rusted anchor chain, heavily encrusted with long-dead barnacles. Each link was about six inches long and three inches wide—the rings were at least three-quarters of an inch thick.

Russ pulled out his writing slate and penciled the words, "anchor chain."

Lester nodded and took the slate from him, writing, "From the ship?"

Russ only shrugged, then motioned Lester to follow him. They swam back to the ledge, where Russ pointed out some straight lines in the rock. Russ checked his gauges and motioned that it was time to surface. They'd only been down 35 minutes but had burned up more than the usual amount of air from the exertion of digging up the anchor chain. Russ swam back over to the chain, tied the lanyard from his dive flag to it, and started toward the surface.

Once above the water, they saw that they were about 100 yards from the boat. They started toward it, swimming on their backs and using only their fins.

"Ya think that might be a chain from the ship we're looking for, Boss?" Lester asked. Lester had never called him boss before but wanted Russ to know he respected him.

"It might be," Russ said. "The size of those links is the same as the anchor chain used on the blockade runner. Let's get back to the boat and you can swap out our tanks while I start her up and move closer to the flag. Then we'll go back down and look around some more with the detectors."

About a mile away, Russ saw a boat turn so that it was headed straight toward theirs. A few minutes later, he could tell it was a Florida Marine Patrol vessel.

"Lester, take my detector and yours and put them both in your bag. That's a patrol boat heading our way. When we get near to where the anchor is, drop the bag. Be cool now—I have a grouper in my bag and it's legal size. They'll probably just check our fishing licenses and make sure it's legal."

"Oh, man, those guys are like cops, aren't they?" Lester asked nervously.

"Yeah, they are cops. Carry guns and everything. Just be cool and let me do the talking."

Lester managed to get both detectors in the bag, but his hands were shaking, so it took a moment to break them down. The patrol boat was nearly on top of them when he rolled over and put his snorkel in his mouth to look for the anchor. Once he spotted it, he wasted no time in dropping the bag with the expensive detectors in it.

CHAPTER TWO

The marine patrol boat arrived at Russ's boat just as they were slinging their masks and fins aboard. Russ looked up as they came alongside on the far side of the boat and said, "Afternoon, officers. Nice day to be out on the water, even if you're working, huh?"

"Afternoon, sir. I'm Lieutenant Briggs, FMP. Just stopping for a random check. You're not after lobster, are you? They're out of season, you know." He was looking over Russ's boat, not missing anything.

"Lobster? No, we're spearfishing. Got a nice grouper here in the bag." Russ tossed the bag to the far side of the boat so the cop could reach it.

"Saw a few snappers and tied off the dive flag over there to bring the boat closer," Russ continued. "We were almost out of air when we found them."

Briggs picked up the bag and handed it to his driver, saying, "Check it, Doug."

Russ and Lester moved to the back of the boat and were climbing aboard, getting their tanks and weight belts off and equipment sorted.

"Can I see your fishing licenses, sir?" the cop said. "Both of you."

"Lieutenant," Russ said. "I was a Marine staff sergeant and a grunt. Calling me sir just don't cut it. Name's Russ. Russ Livingston. Our licenses are in the console. You want to tie off?"

"That's all right, we won't be that long," said the lieutenant. Russ went forward and pulled both of their fishing licenses and wallets out of the console, handing Lester's to him. Quickly, Russ drew his driver's license out of his wallet and handed it, along with both their fishing licenses, to the lieutenant. Lester pulled out his own brand-new Florida driver's license and handed that over, too.

The patrol boat driver had measured the grouper and told the lieutenant, "Checks out good, Eltee. Looks like you boys are gonna eat well tonight."

Russ smiled and said, "Told the wife to have the smoker fired up and the mesquite soaked by 1600. We should be able to add a couple of snappers to the menu before we gotta head back in. Lester, go ahead and swap those tanks out so we can get back down there, okay?"

"You got it, Boss," Lester replied, a little too enthusiastically.

The lieutenant handed the licenses back to Russ and said, "Looks like Doug's right—you gentlemen enjoy your meal. I can see you have all the required equipment. Always leave it out on display like that?"

"Lieutenant, like I said, I'm a Marine. We called it a *junk on the bunk* inspection. Anything to make things operate more efficiently, I do it. You guys be safe, okay?"

With that, the lieutenant nodded at his driver, who put the patrol boat into gear and idled away from Russ's Grady-White. A minute later, they were up on plane and moving away fast.

"You know where you dropped the gear?" Russ asked.

"Almost on top of the anchor, just like ya said to," Lester replied, "That was close, huh?"

"Always be prepared, son," Russ said. "Just remember the Seven P's. *Proper prior planning prevents piss poor performance.* Those guys are just doing a job and all they saw was exactly what I wanted them to see—a couple guys diving for their supper. Get down there and grab that gear while I get the anchor up. It's only twenty feet—you won't even need your tank."

"Sure, Boss, but I don't know if I can go that deep on one breath," Lester said apprehensively.

"Sure, you can. Just go hand over hand on the anchor line and pull yourself down. Just don't forget to equalize your ears on the way. If you don't think you're gonna make it, just kick to the surface and I'll do it. I'll wait until you're up before I pull the hook up. It's not hard. Hell, little girls in Japan dive for pearls in over 80 feet of water on a single breath."

Lester wasn't going to take a challenge to his manhood like that. "Okay, I'll do it." He put on his mask and fins, dropped over the side of the boat, and swam to the anchor line.

"Before you start down," Russ said, "take several quick deep breaths. That'll oxygenate your lungs and give you an extra few seconds. Then take as deep a breath as you can. You'll feel the pressure squeeze on your lungs in the first few feet, and you'll be able to hold it in easier."

Lester did as he was told, then started pulling for the bottom, kicking furiously. He was surprised that it only took him a few seconds to reach the anchor and when he looked around, he saw the bag just a few feet away. He swam over, grabbed it, and started kicking toward the surface.

Splashing out of the water with a huge grin on his face, he yelled, "I did it!"

"Wasn't that hard, was it, kid?" Russ asked.

"You were right, man. Was a lot easier than I figured. Hey, how deep can you go on one breath?" he asked, as he handed up the bag with the two detectors in it.

"I've made it to about 90 feet a few times when I was younger. Probably wouldn't try anything deeper than 70 feet today, though," Russ said, quickly transferring one of the detectors to the other bag. "Get in. I want to get back down to that spot where you found the anchor chain. Something about the wall of that ledge didn't look quite right."

Lester climbed up the dive ladder as Russ hauled up the anchor, coiling the line as he went. Holding the short chain that was shackled to the end of the line, he dipped the anchor in the water a couple of times to get the sand off, then laid it and the chain on top of the rest of the anchor rode.

As Russ started the engine, Lester asked, "Whaddaya mean, it didn't look right?"

"I don't know, it just didn't look natural," Russ replied as he gunned the engine toward the dive flag 100 yards away. When they reached it, Lester dropped the anchor over the bow as Russ backed away with the current. He killed the engine when he felt the anchor take hold, then quickly started getting his buoyancy compensator and tank on.

Lester did the same, sensing the urgency in the older man's movements. When they were both ready, they grabbed the two bags with the detectors in them, back rolled off the sides again, and headed back to the bottom.

Russ had told Lester about the ship he'd been looking for. He'd researched the *Lynx* for years. She was a long and fast paddle steamer with two masts, sunk by the slower Union warship, *USS Howquah*, with help from two other Union ships. She'd been hit eight times by the *Howquah's* big 100-pound guns, several balls hitting right at the waterline. More than likely, Russ had told him, she'd come apart and spilled her cargo over a large area.

When they reached the bottom, Russ went directly to the vertical wall of the ledge and dumped the air from his buoyancy compensator, so that he was kneeling on the sandy bottom, facing the ridge. Lester did likewise and looked again at the almost straight lines that appeared here and there.

Yeah, it was too symmetrical, he thought.

Lester didn't know much about the natural world, but what he'd noticed on all his dives was that nothing under the water was straight. He closed his eyes and cleared his head. When he opened them again, he could almost see the wooden planks of the old blockade-runner Russ had described. It was right there in front of him.

Russ pulled his slate out, wrote the word "planks" and showed it to Lester. He motioned to him with a sweep of his hand and pointed toward the top of the ledge. Once they began moving in opposite directions above the ledge, both men had hits on their detectors within seconds.

Russ dug up a rusted iron nail in one spot and a black rock that was shaped like an old pistol. Lester found a tin cup encrusted with barnacles and several objects that looked like flatware from the galley. Russ motioned Lester over and showed him the settings on his detector, moving the dial so that it would only register very dense metals. Then they moved apart and started sweeping again.

After twenty minutes, moving apart, then back toward each other along the top of the ledge, Russ was about to turn and head away again when his detector pinged. He waved it back and forth over the area and then started digging with his small shovel.

Lester heard the sound and, seeing what Russ was doing, swam over and helped him move the sand away. Russ swept the detector over the spot again and the ping was stronger. They dug deeper, until they were over two feet down. Then Russ's shovel hit something solid.

It was something like the sound Lester had heard when he found the chain, but different somehow.

They fanned the bottom of the hole, whisking the sand away, and there it was— a small rectangular object that gleamed like the day it was taken from the mold and cooled.

Gold.

Monday morning, Lester arrived at Sonny's office early, so he could talk to him privately. He had no qualms about what he'd done and had been trying to think of what to do next for two days. Trouble was, he didn't know anyone with money. Except Sonny.

"Hey, Boss, you got a sec?" Lester asked as he entered Sonny's office.

The old loan shark was at his desk in the back office of a junkyard he owned on the outskirts of West Palm Beach. He'd bought the yard, just off US-1, ten years earlier, mostly as a front for his other enterprises, but also because it had a dock on a canal that went straight to the water.

"Got nothing but time, kid. Did you ever find that deadbeat Joseph Whatshisname?"

"Had a line on him in Riviera Beach on Saturday," Lester replied. "I waited around where he was supposed to be all afternoon and he never showed. I'll find him, though. Look, I got this problem and I don't know what to do about it and I was thinking maybe you could help me out." Lester's gaze was fixed on a picture of a naked girl on the calendar by the door. It was dated 1975, but she was still hot, he thought.

"Whatcha need, kid? An advance?" Sonny opened a drawer in the old metal desk and pulled his wallet out. "I can probably give you a couple C-notes..."

"No, Boss, nothing like that," Lester said. "See, it's like this. You know I took up scuba diving, right? Well, I found something the other day and it's pretty valuable. But I don't wanna go to a fence I don't know and was wondering if you might know someone that could maybe handle it for me."

"Hmm, yeah, I know some people," Sonny said thoughtfully. "Been down here for over forty years. Not too many people I *don't* know in this town."

"Thing is, Boss, well, this thing is maybe more valuable than anything I could ever find. I don't wanna get took by anyone." With that, Lester closed the office door, opened the green gym bag he was carrying and pulled out a towel. He set it on Sonny's desk with a heavy thud and unrolled it. "It's a solid gold bar, Boss."

Sonny couldn't believe what he was seeing. It sure looked like gold, and he reached to pick it up but misjudged its weight and it dropped back onto the towel with a heavy thud. Using both hands he picked it up again. Lester had been amazed when he'd weighed it; it was ten pounds.

"Where the hell did you find this, kid? You didn't knock over a Brinks truck, did ya?"

"Found it in the ocean, Boss," Lester replied. "Found a few other things, too."

Lester unrolled the towel the rest of the way. There were four gold coins, one mounted and hung on a necklace, and a gold cross with three big green stones on it.

"Holy shit," Sonny said. He recognized the gold doubloons. He'd seen a few of them before. Mostly in museums, but once he'd seen a guy wearing one on a chain around his neck, like the one that was mounted here. "You mean to tell me that you was swimming in the ocean and just found all this stuff?"

"Not exactly, Boss," Lester said, not sure how much to tell Sonny. "Well, the bar, I found in the ocean, yeah. The other things turned up later. Any idea how I can get rid of them and how much they're worth?"

Sonny thought for a minute, rolling the doubloons in his fingers. Then he picked up the cross and looked closely at the stones. There was a setting for a fourth one, but it was missing.

"Well, I'm pretty sure I can help ya fence it," Sonny said. "But it'll cost ya. You work for me, so I'm gonna take a big cut. That bar's gotta weigh at least ten pounds. I'd guess it's worth two hundred thou by itself. The coins are sometimes called doubloons. They're two-escudo cobs—that's Spanish money— and worth maybe a thousand bucks each. But this gold cross might be worth more than all the others combined if it wasn't missing a stone. And if these are real emeralds. Saw one like it in a museum and they said it was worth a million bucks. With a stone missing, I'd guess maybe half that."

Sonny put the cross down and looked up at Lester. "But, ya gotta unnerstand, kid. My fence ain't gonna pony up full price, and the price will be just what the metal and stones are worth, so the cross might bring ten grand. Best guess is he'd do about 50 cents on the dollar. So, you're looking at about $100,000, maybe a bit more. I'll take thirty percent. That fair to you?"

Lester arched his brows, thinking. Math wasn't exactly his strong suit, so Sonny added, "That'd be seventy thou to you and thirty to me. Give or take a few grand."

"That's more than two years' pay for me, Boss. Sounds more than fair. But I'd like to keep the necklace—it's cool-looking. How soon ya think ya can get the money?"

"Tell ya what I'll do, kid. I was about to go downtown for lunch anyway. Let me carry this to a guy I know. Once he verifies it's the real stuff, I'll give you your cut outta my own pocket when I get back. I'll prolly have to wait a day or two to get the money from him. Why the hurry? You ain't gonna cut out on me, are ya?"

"No way, Boss. I got it good here. I think I might wanna buy myself my own car. Not that I don't like tooling around in your de Ville, but I think I'd kinda like something a little sportier."

Lester fidgeted. He trusted Sonny, but this was big. "I also kinda found a Ford truck, but it's old and pretty beat up."

Sonny laughed and said, "Found a truck, huh? Look, kid, ya need to just torch that, okay? Sportier car, yeah. But with a clean title. You'd look good with a red Mustang or something wrapped around ya. Look, I ain't gonna pry about where this stuff come from. But is there anything else you wanna tell me?"

Lester thought it over and said, "It's like this, Boss. I also found this book. It was after I found the coins and the cross. The guy that owned it wrote down a lotta shit in it. I think he's a treasure hunter. Lots of dates and numbers. I got no idea what they mean."

"What kinda numbers?"

"Long ones," Lester replied. "Too long to be a phone number or anything. They all start with the same group of numbers, but some in the middle and end is different."

"You say this guy's a treasure hunter? They're prolly GPS numbers he saved for places he found stuff."

"Yeah! He had one of those GPS things," Lester blurted out.

"So, you know this guy? Is he gonna know you got this stuff? Maybe come looking for it, or call the cops?"

"No, Boss, he ain't gonna be callin' the cops. We found the bars together, but the rest of the stuff, and the book, I got out of his apartment. I also got the GPS thing off his boat, too."

Sonny looked up at the man. "You tellin' me that you and him went out in his boat, but only you came back?"

"Boating accident," Lester replied.

"Anything else in this book, kid? Anything at all?"

"I got it right here, Boss," Lester replied, pulling a small leather-bound book out of his back pocket. He opened it to the first page. "The dates go back to 1990. Only thing other than dates and numbers is this one name. See here? Says 'Jesse McDermitt' and it's repeated a few times further on."

The next evening, Sonny sat in his car, idling in a parking lot in North Miami Beach, the air conditioner turned up to full blast. *Middle of October*, he thought. Still hotter than middle of August back in Pennsylvania. Well, there were tradeoffs in everything. At least he didn't have to worry about getting snowed in down here.

Elijah Beech had been born Amish. But at eighteen, Amish kids were sent out into the world and they either came back, or they didn't. He didn't. He found his way to south Florida, liked it, and stayed. The hoods he ran with had given him the name Sonny, because he was a real son of a bitch. Over the years, he'd had less and less contact with his parents back on the dairy farm. Last time he'd contacted them was almost ten years ago.

A Miami-Dade police cruiser pulled into the nearly empty lot and slowly drove straight toward Sonny's Caddy. *About damn time*, he thought. The cruiser rolled up to his driver's side and both the cop and Sonny lowered their windows. The officer extended a file folder, which Sonny snatched from his hand.

"Okay, Mister Beech," the officer said. "We're square now, right?"

"Yeah, Stimmel, we're square. That is, if this is all good information."

"It's good, Mister Beech. You can count on it."

"I'll be the judge of that, kid," Sonny said. "Now beat it, before someone sees us."

The cruiser pulled out of the lot and drove away. Sonny opened the file and read the information on the first page. Then he put the car in gear and pulled out of the lot, heading north on US-1. When he got to the Palm Beach city limits, he picked up his cell phone and dialed a number. Once connected, he barked, "Meet me at my office in thirty minutes. We got a fishing trip to plan." Then he ended the call and smiled. *Yeah, a fishing trip.*

Twenty minutes later, he was pulling into the junkyard in north Palm Beach. He drove around to the back of the large garage, parked his car, and entered his office through the back door. A few minutes after that, he heard a car pull up outside and four doors close. Lester walked in a few seconds later, with three of Sonny's other employees, Walt, Benny, and Tomas.

"What's up, Boss?" Lester asked.

"We finally got the scoop on that guy we were talking about, Les," Sonny said. "You know, that Mick down in the Keys?"

"And what Mick would that be?" asked Walt sarcastically. Walt O'Hara was Sonny's most senior collector. He was a strange-looking man—totally bald, and not just on his head. He had no hair anywhere, and the lack of eyebrows and lashes made him appear like an alien or something.

"Sorry, Walt," Sonny said. "Didn't mean anything by that. The guy's name is Jesse McDermitt and he lives on a boat down in Marathon."

Truth was, Walt bothered Sonny. He was hard to control and had been known to go to some extreme measures on his collections. "I want you four to go down there, hire him for a fishing charter, and then bring him back up here."

"Boss," said Tomas, "you not been listening to da news? Dere's a hurricane heading dat way."

"Hurricane?" asked Sonny. "No, I don't watch no damn TV. That's what I got you guys for, to tell me these things. Okay, when will this hurricane be past the Keys?"

"Last I heard, *Jefe*," Tomas replied, "it'll make it past dere by next Monday."

"Good," Sonny replied. "You guys get down there Tuesday. Here's the scoop on where he lives on this boat of his." Sonny handed Walt the file folder. "Schmooze the guy. Get him to take you out fishin'. I want this guy up here no later than Thursday. Got it?"

"No problem, Boss," said Walt. "What if he don't wanna come along?"

"Do whatever you need," Sonny said. "Just get him here."

After considering who he was talking to, Sonny added, "But he's gotta be able to talk when he gets here, okay?"

CHAPTER THREE

One Month Later

The banging continued incessantly. At first, I thought I was just dreaming. Hangover dreams were always strange. Gradually, as the fog in my brain started to lift, I realized it wasn't a dream. Was someone pounding on the door?

"Go away," I mumbled irritably.

Opening one eye took some effort. But little by little my right eye slowly transitioned from the inky blackness of unconsciousness to dark red, then to pink, finally cracking open just enough so I could see the floor, slightly fuzzy, through my eyelashes.

It sounded like the noise was coming from below the floor—a floor that looked very familiar. The wood was dark and burled, the planks of varying lengths and widths. Even through my alcohol-induced haze, I realized that it was what's called *palo santo*, or "holy wood," in South America. Here in the Florida Keys, we called it lignum vitae—a gnarled type of brushy tree that some-times grew to 30 feet.

I know that board, I thought. *That's my floor.*

Apparently, I was in my own house, lying face-down across my own bed. The dark burled floor plank looked familiar because I'd cut it myself from dozens of gnarly pieces and several large trunks a friend had brought out to me. I'd shaped it, sanded it, and installed it myself, along with every other board in my little stilt house.

Well, if this is my house, I thought with a groan, *that can't be someone knocking on the door.*

I lived alone on an otherwise uninhabited island, in a group of uninhabited islands.

Then a second pounding started, and I knew exactly where this one was coming from. Inside my skull. It competed with the banging that came up through the floor, until I felt I was literally surrounded by a cacophony of noise.

"Yeah," I moaned, rolling over onto my back, "you got one hell of a hangover, McDermitt."

Slowly, I sat up, the pounding in my temples growing louder. What the hell was I thinking, going toe-to-toe, or was it shot glass-to-shot glass, with a bunch of sailors almost half my age?"

Slowly, the memory of the night before began taking shape. After a long day on the water putting up with four loud-mouthed fat-asses from Ohio who'd chartered my boat, *Gaspar's Revenge,* for a day of dolphin fishing, I'd finally put them off at *Dockside,* a bar in Boot Key

Harbor, Marathon, Florida. After cleaning up the barf, beer cans, and blood, I'd turned over the job of hosing down the rest of the boat to my part-time first mate, Jimmy Saunders. I'd told him to catch up with me at the *Rusty Anchor* to collect his pay when he'd finished cleaning the fish for the Ohioans.

Jimmy was a decent guy, though he tended to smoke too much pot. I hated that he'd had to put up with those guys. But in his typical laid-back Conch fashion, he'd not only taken good care that they stayed baited, with cold beers in hand, but kept them out of my hair. I don't get along well with most people, and definitely not with fat-ass northern bubbas. They couldn't fish for shit, and had it not been for Jimmy's help, they'd never have boated a single fish.

My favorite little hole-in-the-water bar, the *Rusty Anchor Bar and Grill*, owned by my old friend Rusty Thurman, was a short distance from *Dockside*. The *Anchor* wasn't a tourist place. There were no hyped-up billboards proclaiming paradise. In fact, Rusty didn't have an ad in the phone book. Not even a listing with the Marathon Chamber of Commerce, for that matter. It was a *locals-only* kind of beer joint and restaurant and that's just the way Rusty liked it. Unless you lived in the Middle Keys, you'd never heard of it.

I remembered climbing into my rusted-out hulk of a '73 International Travelall 4x4 and starting the perilous one-mile drive. An old girlfriend had christened my ride *The Beast* a couple of years back and it was just that. A short, one-mile trip in *The Beast* could easily turn into a harrowing adventure. A couple of minutes later, I'd pulled off the Overseas Highway behind the Lower Keys bus, affectionately called the *Magic Bus*. A couple of local fishermen were about to board it and had stopped me to ask if I wanted to go with them to Key West—or, more to the point, to drive them there to save the five-dollar bus fare.

"Thanks for the invite, guys," I'd told them, "but Key Weird's not for me. Too many tourists."

They waved as they boarded the *Magic Bus*, and it coughed and chugged as it pulled back onto the highway, barely missing an RV with Indiana tags that was headed south. I'd driven on down the crushed-shell driveway, through the arched tangle of gumbo limbo and mangrove trees, into what passed for a parking lot at the *Anchor*.

The driveway was sandwiched between two residential roads, and it looked pretty much like any other residential driveway in the Middle Keys. There were no signs saying otherwise, so it was very rare that anyone not known to me ever came in.

As I rose and went to the head to relieve my swollen bladder, the memory of the night before became clearer. I'd recognized all the pickups in the *Anchor's* lot as belonging to local fishermen, but one grey Ford sedan had looked out of place.

Obviously, it had been a rental car. How they'd found the place was anybody's guess. I'd only planned to have a couple of beers at the bar and get caught up on the Coconut Telegraph with Julie while I waited for Jimmy.

Julie was the bartender at the *Anchor* as well as the accountant, the busser, the chief bottle washer, and Rusty's one and only child. After visiting with Julie, I'd planned to drive back to *Dockside*, jump in my skiff and head home.

"Well, look what washed up with the tide," Julie'd said, smiling as I'd walked in and taken a stool at the bar. "Thought you'd run off to Miami or somewhere else way up north. Hey, Jesse."

Julie, like her parents and their parents before them, going back at least 100 years, was a true Conch. Born at Fisherman's Hospital in Marathon, she'd only been north of Key Largo a few times in her 23 years. She was a pretty girl, with wavy auburn hair usually tied in a loose ponytail at the base of her neck. Always ready with a smile for a friend, she was all business behind the bar.

Her dad, Rusty, on the other hand, was a man of the world. He and I had first met on the bus to Parris Island, a little island off the coast of South Carolina, near Beaufort. It's a place where boys were first turned into men and then into Marines. Rusty and I were in the same platoon in boot camp, and since we were the only two from Florida, we quickly became good friends. Later, we'd served together in a few far-flung places around the world. We'd stayed in touch by mail when we weren't in the same unit.

Rusty had left the Corps after four years, but I shipped over and made a career of it, finally retiring at the age of 37; a gunnery sergeant with no skills and two failed marriages. It was often joked that if the Corps wanted you to have a wife, you'd have been issued one.

Rusty had married his high school sweetheart when he went home on leave a year after boot camp. I'd taken leave at the same time and served as his best man. But just before his first tour ended, Rusty's wife had died giving birth to Julie at home. The baby had stayed with her paternal grandparents until Rusty left the Corps on terminal leave, and then he'd raised her the only way he knew how. She was tougher than the limestone rock that most of Florida was made of.

"Hiya, Jules," I'd said. "You oughta know better than to curse your elders like that. Miami? Hell, if I thought *The Beast* could make it that far, I'd go ahead and pay the toll to take the Sawgrass around that hellhole and just keep on going."

I remembered looking around at everyone in the bar, as I always did. I'd nodded to a couple of shrimpers I recognized sitting at the bar, who'd nodded back. Then I'd glanced back at a table where three very serious-looking young guys with crew cuts sat huddled over their beers, talking animatedly.

When Julie had placed a dripping cold Red Stripe in front of me, I'd asked, "Where'd the sailors come from?"

On an island, even though you hadn't seen someone in weeks or months, you could pick up a conversation as

if you'd last seen them at breakfast. No need for pleas-
antries or greetings. I guess it's because even though you
might not see someone, they knew pretty much everything you'd been doing since they last saw you.

"Best guess? Key West NAS," she'd replied. "They've
been here a couple of hours. Said they were waiting for
you. The big blond dude says he knows you."

I'd slowly turned on my stool and given them a closer
look as I swallowed half of my cold Jamaican beer with
one long pull. The big kid had looked vaguely familiar,
but I couldn't place him. So, I'd just walked over, spun
the only empty chair at the table around backwards
and straddled it.

Remembering how the talking had stopped instantly
and I'd almost heard the click as three sets of eyes locked
onto and bored into mine, I should have known they
were a special part of America's military.

I'd glanced at each of them and paused on the bigger
man, a blond-haired, blue-eyed Scandinavian-looking
guy. Even sitting, I could tell he was close to my own
height of six-three, but probably a few pounds shy of
my 230.

"I hear you're looking for me," I'd said and took
another long pull of my beer, then motioned Julie for
a round.

"If your name is Jesse McDermitt, I am," the big Swede
had replied. "My dad was Russell Livingston."

Like a switch being turned on, the synapses in my
brain had made the connection. The kid had looked

so familiar because I'd known him when he was little, probably eight or nine, the last time I remembered seeing him. He looked closer to thirty now, but it was definitely Russ's son.

I'd served under Russ Livingston in Okinawa and Lebanon some years ago. Even though he was my platoon sergeant, we'd become fast friends, mostly because of our love of the ocean. We'd taken leave together several times and come down here to scuba dive, fish, and raise hell with Rusty. The kid looked just like Russ had back in the day. A little taller, maybe, but the eyes and chin came directly from his dad. I recalled him saying once that his son had become a naval officer and joined the SEALs.

"*Was* your father?" I asked.

"Dad died last month," he replied. "The Coroner said he drowned. I'm Russell Junior, but everyone just calls me Deuce."

We'd shaken hands then, and I'd expressed my condolences. I hadn't seen Russ in a few years, and asked Deuce why he was looking for me.

"Dad's last wish was to have his ashes scattered on some reef down here," Deuce had replied, the news of Russ's death flooding back into my memory. "In his will," Deuce had continued, "he said you'd be the only one who knew where it was. We've been here two days and asked around, but I haven't found anyone who knows anything at all about it. Have you ever heard of Conrad Reef?"

He'd said that Russ had drowned, which just didn't fit into the character of the man I remembered. I'd told Deuce about how Russ and I had come to call the spot Conrad Reef. "Yeah, I know Conrad. Russ and I called it that, back in the day. We'd just come back from Lebanon, right after the bombing, and we came down here on a 96-hour pass. We were taking turns dragging one another behind my old skiff, looking for lobster, and we found it about three miles offshore. We anchored up and free dived on it the rest of the day and into the night. The batteries in his dive light finally gave out and he put a dead battery on his shoulder and dared me to knock it off. So, we called it Conrad Reef from then on."

Deuce gave me a puzzled look and I said, "Never mind, way before your time. Sure, I'd be honored to take you and your dad's ashes out there. He was a good man."

I looked at the other two and added, "But, nobody else." I didn't know these guys, and a good lobster honey hole was something you kept secret.

The other two at the table started to protest, but one glance from Deuce shut them down. He introduced me to a wiry black guy named Tony Jacobs and a short, muscular white guy named Art Newman just as Julie arrived with a tray of beers.

"Hey, Jules, is your old man around?" I'd asked her.

"He's out back," she'd replied. "Been tinkering all day with an old Evinrude he picked up at a yard sale. I'll get him for you. Everything all right here?"

Julie was like a den mother to all the regulars. Never mind that nearly every shrimper, diver, fisherman, and boat bum who came into the place was at least a decade older than her. The younger guys, after striking out with her, kept to the more upbeat places like *Dockside* or the *Hurricane*. She was much older than her years, had grown up around boats, boaters, and boat bars and looked after her patrons and friends.

"Yeah, we're fine. Yell at Rufus in the kitchen and if he has any fresh hogfish, I could use a sandwich." Turning back to the table, I'd asked, "You guys eat yet?"

The black guy, Tony, had asked, "What's a hogfish?"

"Make it four plates, Jules," I'd told her with a grin. "It's a local fish, Tony. Tastes just like bacon."

Julie had rolled her dark brown eyes at the old joke and turned to go back to the kitchen, which wasn't really a kitchen because it only had one wall—the back wall of the bar. It was just a deck out the back door where Rufus, who was older than anyone on the island, performed magic with little more than a large deep fryer and a couple of gas grills. Mostly, though, he sat in the shade of an umbrella and read old paperbacks, as the *Rusty Anchor* was more beer joint than restaurant, and few people ordered anything more than a fish sandwich or cheeseburger. Rusty let him live in a little cabin on the back of the property in exchange for the occasional meal order.

Rusty had come through the side door, and you'd think the whole place tilted just a little as he carried his portly, 300-pound frame across the room, stopping to grab a cold Bud longneck from the ice chest. Rusty was a short guy and had been the brunt of everyone's jokes in the Corps. But he'd been solidly-built back then, and more than one Marine had underestimated both his strength and his tenacity. With a head full of bright red hair, he was christened "Rusty" in boot camp and the name had stuck ever since. These days, he was nearly as big around the middle as he was tall, with a shiny head and a thick red beard that was going gray.

"Jesse, you old barracuda!" he'd roared. "You need to get off that damned swamp you call an island a bit more than once in a blue moon and drag your sorry ass down here. How the hell ya been?"

As he'd approached the table, I'd asked my old friend if he thought Deuce looked familiar. Deuce had stood and shaken hands with Rusty, who'd studied the younger man's face for a moment. If there'd been a hunk of charcoal between their palms, they would have turned it into a diamond. Rusty was twice the weight he'd been in the Corps, but he was still stronger than a Missouri mule and three times as stubborn.

Finally, Rusty's face had lit up and he'd said, "Sumbitch, if he ain't the image of old Russ. You remember him, Jess. He was our platoon sergeant over to Oki, back in the 80's."

I'd introduced Deuce and the other two men and Rusty had grabbed Deuce in a big bear hug, nearly lifting the taller man off the ground.

"How's your old man doing these days?" Rusty had asked, after releasing the surprised younger man.

Deuce went on to tell the story of his dad's passing and last wishes again.

"Real sorry to hear about that," Rusty'd said. "Russ saved my ass quite a few times when I got falling down drunk at Whisper Alley on Oki. Anything I can do for you, son, you just name it."

Rusty had then looked around, studying all three men the way only someone who'd once been one of them could, and said, "You boys got hair too short for civilians, but too long to be Marines. Stationed down at Key West?"

"No, sir," the white guy, Art Newman had replied. "Dam Neck, Virginia." He'd offered nothing further. But nothing more was needed.

Rusty and I had eyed one another, then both nodded as Rusty said, "Nuff said about that, then."

Dam Neck was home to some of the Navy's finest warriors, SEAL Team Six, now known as Naval Special Warfare Development Group, or DEVGRU for short. They were a very tight-knit bunch who'd seldom socialized outside their team and rarely spoke of their jobs.

Rusty had snagged a bottle of Pusser's Navy Rum from behind the bar and returned to the table with the bottle and five glasses. We'd toasted Russ and other lost warriors, and then the sea stories had started. After Rusty and I had told the three men a little about our own backgrounds in Marine Force Recon, the three SEALS had relaxed somewhat.

By midnight, Jimmy had come and gone, and there were two empty bottles on the table and five fairly drunk special operators sitting around it. I'd learned that Deuce was a lieutenant commander and Tony and Art were both petty officers, first class. Equal in rank to a Marine major and staff sergeants.

Sometime after midnight, Rusty had blurted, "You know, Jesse here earned a Bronze Star and Purple Heart when he and your dad was in Lebanon."

I remembered rolling my eyes at my old friend, but there'd been no stopping him. "Jesse'd just been promoted to sergeant and transferred back to One-Eight, up to Lejeune, and they got deployed to Lebanon. Took a bullet in the shoulder but kept his men in the fight all the way to the barracks."

"Dad talked about that a few times," Deuce had said. "He always said it was one of the most terrifying times he had while he was in the Corps."

The sea stories went on and on, until Julie had finally called it a night for us at 0300. By then, the bar had emptied out. Somehow, I'd managed to find my way back to *Dockside*, where I kept my new flats skiff. I kept it there when I came down to take out a charter or cavort with the locals.

Miraculously, I'd made it home. The trip was either fifteen miles across skinny water, or nearly twenty miles if I'd followed the main channel without becoming a permanent part of the Seven Mile Bridge or Harbor Key Light. At least, this was what I thought must have happened. I didn't remember much after leaving the *Anchor*, but I'd somehow made it back.

After washing up, I returned to my bedroom to change for the coming day but couldn't help plopping down across the bunk again. The pounding outside would have to wait until the floor stopped moving.

My house was little more than a shack on stilts, just over 1000 square feet, with a large combination living room, dining room and kitchen in front and a bedroom and head in back. But it was solid, and it kept the summer rain and winter wind out. As far as solitude, it was better than sleeping on the boat, though not nearly as luxurious. I'd built this place by hand on an island in the Content Keys, northwest of Big Pine Key. This group of islands was mostly uninhabited scrub-and-mangrove-covered marshes and sandbars. My nearest neighbor was an older guy who was a bridge builder by the name of Woodson. He lived about three miles away.

When I retired, I'd used up nearly all the savings I'd scraped together for over twenty years while in the Corps, supplemented by an inheritance from my grandfather about six years ago, to buy *Gaspar's Revenge* and this tiny island. It was no more than two acres in size at low tide and had a very small beach on the west side. The water around it was so shallow you could walk to most of the neighboring islands and not get your shorts wet.

It took me a whole winter and spring to hand-dig a little ditch in the shallows from Harbor Channel, just deep enough for my little skiff to get to the island. There

I'd carved out a part of it and spent that whole summer building my stilt house above the little ditch. I'd planned to make the channel wide enough and deep enough to get *Gaspar's Revenge* through it, but it proved to be too much work to do by hand. One day I would rent a dredge and do it, but for now I'd keep running back and forth in the skiff.

I'd gone up to the commercial docks in Miami during that summer and scrounged through the discarded piles of pallets. There were lots from South America and I managed to find a lot of mahogany and oak planks, along with other hardwoods rare in the States, but plentiful down there. Rusty had located quite a few discarded lignum vitae posts, which became floor beams and planks, wearing out a number of table saw blades. The exterior siding of my house was weathered mahogany. The roof was corrugated steel I'd scrounged from the naval air station in Key West when they'd torn down some of the old Quonset huts that had been there since before World War II. The floor was fourteen feet above the narrow channel at high spring tide, just enough room for the *Revenge*. The floors, studs and beams were solid lignum vitae and it was through these heavy boards that I could still hear the constant banging noise. My little house could withstand anything Mother Nature could conjure up, but something down below was trying its best to knock it down.

Finally, I gave up trying to ignore the noise and the pounding in my temples. I slowly got up from the bed. It was hot.

Too hot to be morning, I thought.

I walked out onto the deck and saw that I was right. The sun was directly overhead, and though it was looking like another hot October day in south Florida, there was a strong wind blowing out of the southeast, churning up white caps out on the flats as far as I could see. The shallow waters north of Big Pine Key were normally flat in late summer and fall. Usually there wasn't even enough wind to make a ripple, unless a squall blew in from the Gulf. I figured there must be a storm brewing, and the pounding I'd been hearing must be my skiff banging against the dock below.

When I went down the steps to the dock area, I found that the skiff looked like it had been tied up by some rookie sailor, and it was indeed banging against the pilings. My boat was an eighteen-foot Maverick Mirage, with a 150-horsepower Yamaha engine under the poling platform. It was a fast little boat and could handle the skinny water around the back country and Florida Bay with ease.

"Jesse," I addressed myself again, "you really outdid yourself this time. Lucky that old skiff ain't halfway to Cape Sable by now."

I tightened the mooring lines, then went back up to the house to get some water, aspirin, and food for my growling stomach. The pounding in my head finally subsided a little as I wondered how I'd gotten home. It wasn't like me not to remember a fifteen- to twenty-mile boat ride. But I must have made it as there was nobody else on the island. After three bottles of water, four aspirin, and a ham sandwich, I felt nearly human again and thought back to the events of the previous evening.

Russ Livingston had drowned? It was a stretch to think that'd be how Russ would leave this world. The man had practically lived in the water. He was an accomplished diver, as was I. We'd once swum completely around the island that Hammocks Beach State Park, near Camp Lejeune, was situated on—a distance of some six miles, half of it in open ocean—just on a dare.

In the fall of '82, Russ and I took leave together and had been diving for lobster off Fort Pierce when we found something far more interesting. The whole area of ocean from Saint Lucie Inlet to Sebastian Inlet was where the 1715 "Plate Fleet," twelve treasure-laden ships, had sunk in a hurricane. While trying to get at a really big and exceptionally stubborn lobster, I'd pulled out a big black rock from under a ledge. Once the lobster was in the bag, I turned and found Russ examining the rock I'd pulled out. It was nearly two feet long and about a foot square, black and heavily-encrusted with barnacles and tube worms. Even underwater, it was very heavy. I'd almost dislocated my shoulder dislodging it to get at that lobster.

I remember swimming over and tapping Russ on the shoulder, giving him the universal "what's up?" sign with my hands out, palms up and a shrug. He replied by rubbing his thumb and first two fingers together in the universal "money" sign. When we got back up to the boat, Russ said, "Jesse, I think that might be silver." We'd rigged a line around the rock and hoisted it into the skiff. Out of the water, it was even heavier.

Since the whole coast was still an active salvage site of the 1715 fleet, we knew we had to keep our find on the down low. Russ said he knew a guy who could help us out. Turned out, we'd found 256 silver bars, all crusted together and enveloped with barnacles. Each bar was about four inches long and one-inch square. They must have been in a chest and the wood had just rotted away over nearly 300 years, since it was wedged under that ledge. Each bar weighed about ten ounces, giving us a total of over 160 pounds.

Russ's friend had paid us $100,000 dollars in cold, hard cash, no questions asked. Russ, being Russ, hadn't wanted a share of it at first. "You found it, Jesse. It wouldn't be right for me to take any money."

"Russ," I'd said, "I found a big black rock, trying to get at a five-dollar lobster. You're the one who recognized it for what it was. Half of this is yours. No more argument."

Russ had been hooked, though. He'd just been promoted to staff sergeant earlier that year and was due to reenlist again in the spring. But after that experience, he'd decided to pass and left the Corps after twelve years to devote his time to hunting treasure. And that's just what he'd done, up until his recent, untimely death.

Well, we're not getting any younger, I thought.

Russ must have been in his early fifties at least. But still, something kept gnawing at the back of my mind and I just couldn't let it go.

CHAPTER FOUR

I t was early afternoon and I hadn't accomplished much of anything since waking with a hangover at noon. While heading down to Boot Key Harbor yesterday, I'd noticed that the engine on my skiff had a bit of a sputter at three-quarter speed, when I'd crossed Bahia Honda Channel. So, I spent the afternoon rebuilding the Walbro carburetor on the Yamaha outboard.

I'd always liked working with my hands. It allowed my mind to wander as my hands worked. I took the carb up to the house, where I have a large built-in work bench. The window above it overlooks the rest of the island.

Last spring, I'd cleared a large area of sea grape, wild coffee, buttonwood, and saw palmetto in the middle of the island, with the crazy notion of growing some vegetables. After two weeks of cutting, digging, and scraping, I had a fairly round patch cleared that measured 150 feet across. I left a single coconut palm standing in the middle, it being one of only three coconut palms on the island.

Reality sank in shortly afterwards, when I borrowed a tiller from a friend on Grassy Key and found out that the sandy soil on the surface was only a few inches deep and below it was limestone and ancient coral. Then there was the problem of irrigation. Salt water doesn't help vegetables very much. I figured that maybe if I brought in a few thousand tons of rich topsoil, I might be able to make it work. Another project put on hold.

As I sat at the table, I looked out across the clearing past the mangroves and gumbo limbo trees on the northeast side of the island into the Gulf of Mexico. My island was just thirty feet off of Harbor Channel, which ran northeast to Turtlegrass Bank, then turned north in several natural cuts, leading to the deeper waters of the Gulf. Out there, I could see several pelicans diving on bait fish, just south of Upper Harbor Key. To the west, I spotted a pair of herons wading through the shallows along Content Passage while several others sunned in the mangroves and banyans along eastern Content Key.

It was relaxing up here, away from all the distractions in the many towns and villages that made up the Keys. I didn't really need a lot of human interaction and it seemed there were just more and more tourists down there lately.

A year ago, there was one human I enjoyed interacting with. Her name was Alex. We were only friends and occasional workout partners when I lived on my boat at *Dockside*. She was very striking in appearance, tall, with a swimmer's broad shoulders, long blond hair, and a pretty face. But she'd left last year. Flown back up to Oregon to take care of a sick brother.

After finishing with the carb and finding only some gunk in the float bowl that seemed to cause the float to stick a little, I headed back down to the dock to reinstall it on the engine. I was just putting the cover back on when I heard a whining sound coming from the southeast.

I climbed back up to the deck to look out over the tree canopy and saw that a small flats skiff was heading my way across the choppy water. After grabbing my binoculars from inside, I trained them on the boat. After a few minutes, I could make out the driver's auburn hair tied back and flying behind her and recognized the skiff as the one Rusty had bought a few months earlier.

Julie was coming to see me? Not that she'd never been out here—she had. But the last time was more than six months ago, when she'd ferried out some oak lumber for me that Rusty had found at a yard sale on Duck Key. Rusty had known I'd probably want the lumber and had sent Julie to deliver it.

I climbed back down to the docks and was waiting for her when she slowly made her way through the mangrove-covered channel to my house. "Dammit, Jesse, you need to answer your phone. Dad's been calling all morning and finally sent me way out here to check on you."

"Sorry to waste your time, Jules. No idea where my phone is, probably here in the skiff." I stepped over onto my own skiff and grabbed the line she tossed, tying it off to a cleat on my boat. Then I looked in the console and sure enough, there was my phone—right where it'd been for the last three days. I powered it up and saw that I had six missed calls, all but one from Rusty. The other was a Virginia area code, probably Deuce.

"Maybe you should invest in a radio, too," she said sarcastically. "There's a big storm coming. Guess you hadn't heard about that?"

I took her hand and helped her step over onto my skiff, then onto the dock. She had a strong, firm, dry grip, as always. Most self-assured women did.

"I have a radio. Was just listening to a jazz station out of Miami while I rebuilt my carburetor. I already guessed a storm was coming, just by looking at the water. How bad is it?"

"Remember that Cat-5 storm that hit the Yucatan a few days ago? Well, it's a Cat-3 now and headed this way."

I looked through the tunnel created by the trees hanging over the channel. The water had churned up since earlier in the day, and the flag on my pole was beginning to snap in the stiff breeze. The winds were out of the southeast and gusting to maybe fifteen knots.

Why hadn't I recognized it?

All the signs were there and yes, I had heard about the storm hitting the Yucatan while I was out on the water with the Ohioans just the day before. I'd assumed it would cross the Yucatan and head into the Gulf of

Mexico, maybe threaten Texas or the other Gulf Coast states.

"Hurricane Wilma?" I asked. "I thought for sure it'd continue straight into the Gulf. Where's it located now?"

"It's 50 miles northeast of the Yucatan and headed northeast. They downgraded it to a Cat-2 when it crossed the Yucatan, but it's gathering strength and headed our way. The Weather Channel says it will most likely pass north of here and make landfall again on the west coast of the state. Jesse, they've issued an evacuation."

"Evacuation?" My mind was already moving toward preparations. "What're Rusty's plans? Never mind— he's gonna ride it out, right? Those three sailors we were drinking with—have you seen them around any today?"

"Yeah, they're still around," she said. "The bigger one came by and asked for you a couple of times. I just told him you were out here. Who were those guys? Every time I came by the table last night, y'all either stopped talking or started talking about something else."

"Jules, I don't know how much of our past your dad has ever shared with you, so let's just say that those three guys picked up where he and I left off, okay? The less you know, the better." I started toward a storage closet and to change the subject, I asked, "Do you have time to help me out here? We can go back to Marathon together. I just need to secure the house."

"Sure. What do you want me to do?" she asked. I opened the storage closet and showed her the corrugated steel covers for the windows.

"Each of these panels fits over a certain window," I said as I grabbed one. "The first one here goes over the little window below the cistern. The others go over the other windows, working around the house counter-clockwise. Each panel has four holes in it—see here? Each window has corresponding bolts threaded into the wall studs, with nuts and washers on them. Just remove the nuts and washers, put the panel in place and put the nuts and washers back on. Shouldn't take us more than a half hour."

I was close—it only took twenty minutes. Julie was a fast learner and an even faster worker. She hung four of the panels to my three. Once we were done, we went down to the dock and I showed her the lift system I had installed. After I untied her skiff and tied it off to the other dock, I lowered the cables at the stern of my skiff. The cables were connected to a three-inch nylon strap. Then I went forward and lowered the other lift in the same way.

Julie looked up at the floor of the house and smiled. I took the starboard side and she went around to the other dock on the port side. Together, we worked the straps under my skiff until they were in the right place. I showed her how the forward crank assembly worked, and I headed to the aft assembly. Usually, I'd do this myself, raising the bow about eight inches, then the stern, alternating back and forth.

But working together, we were able to raise the skiff quickly, until the wind screen nearly touched the floor boards. My Maverick was now completely inside a box made of the very oak planks she'd brought out two years earlier.

The last chore involved a long piece of corrugated steel that needed to go under the skiff and be bolted into place. I had two planks that fit across the railing of the two docks. These allowed me to walk the piece of tin out to the middle and lift it in place while Julie snugged the bolts, both of us standing on twelve-inch wide boards seven feet above the water.

"So that's what those heavy oak boards I brought out here were for," she said. "Pretty cool."

"Yep, my skiff's completely protected now," I replied. "I'll be right back."

All that was left was to lock the doors, and my little house would weather the storm with no problem. I ran back up, grabbed a bug-out bag I always kept handy packed with several changes of clothes and a Sig Sauer 9mm pistol inside a waterproof box. Also, in the box were four loaded magazines. I pulled a backpack out of the closet and stuffed it with a few other items I might need, and then ran back down the steps to the dock.

Julie already had the skiff untied and the engine idling when I stepped aboard. "If you back out to starboard, there's a turnaround I dug last month. No need to back all the way out the channel."

Julie piloted the little skiff like a pro and within minutes we were up on plane and heading southeast. "The wind's out of the southwest," I said, "so maybe we ought to stay in the lee of Howe Key and Big Pine, then shoot down Bogie Channel to the Seven Mile Bridge, instead of going straight across open water to Marathon."

"Yeah, that's the way I came, but it was still pretty rough that first seven miles, running alongside the bridge.

We rode in silence for a while. The wind was blowing clouds up from the southeast, which meant the storm was still well to the west and likely going to pass to our north. Still, there was a good bit of chop until we got to the lee side of Howe Key. The sun was shining, so we both just enjoyed the ride.

The Content Keys are a small group of islands on the northeastern edge of the Lower Keys, an archipelago stretching from Key West to Big Pine Key in the shape of a slice of pie. The water all around this area is very shallow, with natural and manmade channels cut through it. Very few of the more than 700 islands in the Lower Keys are inhabited. Mine has a population of just one, making it the most inhabited island for some distance around.

Passing between Cutoe Key and Howe Key, the water was only about two feet deep, so it was very calm. Cutoe Key is part of a group of islands that were once known as the Buttonwood Strips. Nobody knows exactly how it came to be called that, though. Both it and Howe Key, just to the west, are mangrove- and palm-covered islands, with no real beaches. Both are uninhabited, even though they're much larger than my little island. Howe Key's interior is sandy, with nothing much growing there. South of these two islands are Annette Key, also uninhabited, and Big Pine Key, home to about 5000 people and about 800 Key deer. They're really small compared to their white-tail cousins. A full-grown buck is no bigger than a Labrador Retriever.

From there, all the way down to Spanish Harbor and the Seven Mile Bridge, it was fairly calm, so Julie opened up the big Johnson outboard. We skimmed across the flat water with nothing but the sound of the engine and the spray of the water for distraction.

"Alex is in town," Julie said. "She stopped by this morning. That was another reason Dad was trying to reach you."

Alex? Back in Marathon? Though we considered ourselves friends, we had dated a few times while I was still living aboard the *Revenge* before I built my stilt house. She was a flats fishing guide—a very good one, actually. She had a knack for putting anglers on fish when every other guide in the Middle Keys was skunked. She came from a small town near Salem, Oregon, and was an accomplished fly fisherman there. She'd come to the Keys to try her hand at bone fishing, fallen in love with the place and stayed on. She'd had her only sibling, a brother six years younger, sell her house for her.

Their parents had been killed in a car wreck when she was just 23 and she'd taken over as his guardian, getting him through high school and into college. She'd pushed him hard and he'd graduated with an MBA in just five years and opened his own accounting firm.

Three years later, just a year after she came to the Keys, her brother was diagnosed with cancer and she had to go home to care for him while he was undergoing treatment. We hadn't been seriously involved, or so I thought, but it was heartbreaking to watch her walk out of my life. Hard to explain, since we hadn't even spent the night together. We worked out every Tuesday and Thursday morning, either running or swimming in the ocean. She even got me to go to the local gym a few times. We talked on the phone occasionally after she left, but I was never big on phone calls, so they dwindled down to almost nothing. Things just devolved over time. But every woman I'd met in the past year, I subconsciously compared to Alex, and they all fell far short. One woman, Savannah Richmond, had been a close second. Dating wasn't a high priority these days, so I mostly stayed at my little house, working on clearing the island of dead wood and trash.

"She say how long she was going to be in town?" I asked, trying not to show any emotion.

"She didn't say," Julie replied. "I was busy, and Dad talked to her while I was working. He didn't say anything else but to let you know she was here." We rode on in silence, between Howe Key and Annette Key, then into the lee of Big Pine Key, as my mind drifted back in time.

CHAPTER
FIVE

I t was just a little over two years ago that I'd first met her. I'd seen her around a few times before that day in the middle of the summer. I'd been broken down on the side of A1A again, just south of Duck Key. My old Travelall had been showing me its weekly stubborn side. If it wasn't a clogged fuel filter, it was the air filter, or one of a million other problems that old truck would throw at me. If being stranded on the side of the road wasn't depressing enough, it'd been pouring rain on a hot and muggy August afternoon and I was soaking wet.

Alex was tall, with thick, shoulder-length blond hair, usually pulled back, or tucked under a long-billed fishing cap. Whenever I'd seen her, she was wearing khaki pants or shorts with an oversized long-sleeved shirt. But even dressed like that, I found her to be quite a beautiful woman. So, when she stopped next to my truck and I glanced over from my vantage point under the hood, all I saw was a bright yellow Jeep Cherokee and a pretty blonde driver wearing a crisp blue sundress, her hair shining like the sun. I didn't even recognize her.

"Car trouble?" she'd asked with a smile after the passenger side window went about halfway down.

I'd studied her face and it took me a few seconds before I realized who she was. There I was, rain pouring down, soaked to the bone, covered in grease, feeling totally vulnerable. I remembered just standing there, water pouring off my brow, mouth hanging open, and not saying anything.

I finally snapped out of it and said, "Uh, yeah. Truck won't crank. I think the battery's dead."

Smart comeback there, McDermitt.

"Give you a lift somewhere, Jesse?" she'd asked.

Huh? She knows my name? A lift? Yeah, I need a lift. I'm soaked and covered in grease. I was standing there with my mouth hanging open again. *She said my name. How'd she know my name?*

"Uh, yeah. But I'm a little wet and dirty," I'd said.

Oh yeah, real suave, McDermitt.

"We all get that way sometimes. Get in before I change my mind."

It was a great laugh. Not a little princess giggle, but a hearty, genuine belly laugh. Then the words she'd actually said got through my fog-addled brain. *We all get wet and dirty sometimes?*

Was there something to that? No, couldn't be.

Slamming the hood, I'd climbed into her Jeep and ratcheted the seat all the way back to keep my knees off the dash. She reached in back and handed me a towel.

While drying my face, I asked, "How'd you know my name? Have we met?"

"It's a small island, Jesse. I asked around about you and that big Rampage of yours."

Asked around? About me? Hmm, an honest, direct answer to a simple question, I thought. *I like that.*

"Do you have a destination in mind, or do you just want to sit here, dripping water on my floor boards?" Again, that hearty laugh.

"Yeah, um, if you could drop me at my boat, over at *Dockside*, that'd be great. Guess I'll wait out this rain and get my friend Rusty to bring me back after the engine's cooled. I think it's just a case of vapor lock. That's where—"

"Where air bubbles form in the fuel line when it gets hot, like today," she'd interrupted, pulling to the shoulder.

Okay, she knows a little about engines, I'd thought.

She'd made a sharp U-turn then, driving south toward *Dockside*.

"Or," she'd continued, "it could be a clog in the fuel return line to the tank. That'd mimic a vapor lock problem. Has it done this before?"

Okay, she knows a lot about engines.

"Only about every other day or so," I'd replied, looking over at her as she drove. She must have been coming from or going to a lunch date, or something. She'd been wearing a short blue print sundress with thin straps and what looked like pale blue and yellow flowers all over it. Smooth, bare, tanned legs and a pair of blue flat-heeled sandals. Her blond hair was styled, but not overly so, just a little wave in it. She wore no makeup, except maybe some lip gloss. A far cry from the woman I'd seen around the docks and on the flats, who was purported to be one of the best fishing guides around. She smelled faintly of jasmine and soap. Nothing overbearing, just a hint—probably not perfume, but more likely the shampoo she used.

"You should get rid of that beast and buy something built in this century, maybe. At least in the last quarter-century." She'd laughed again. "Hey, reach back there and grab me a beer, would you? Get two, if it's not too early for you."

Looking back, I'd seen a small fiberglass boat cooler, reached in, feeling around through the ice, and pulled out two icy cold bottles of Hatuey.

"Thanks for the beer," I'd said, twisting the top off and handing her one. "Beast, huh? Seems a fitting moniker for that old truck. I really don't need a truck and it'd be a waste of money to buy anything newer, as little as I drive it. Besides, it's kind of like me, old and cantankerous at times. Usually, if it won't start, I can just walk to wherever I'm going, or take my skiff. But today I was going up to Long Key to look at some new Fin-Nor reels a guy up there just got in. Guess that'll have to wait for another day now."

"My client for the afternoon canceled because of the rain," she'd begun. "I just came from meeting my attorney and I don't have anything else to do today. If you want, we could stop by my place on Key Colony Beach and I could change and take you to Long Key. I've wanted to look at some new tackle myself."

"I couldn't put you out like that," I'd told her, though I was really hoping she was serious. I could've listened to her laugh all day long.

As if reading my thoughts, she'd said, "I'm Alex, short for Alexis, but nobody calls me that. Really, I'm serious. This rain's not going to stop anytime soon and since my client canceled, I have absolutely nothing else to do today. And I really do need to replace one of my fly rods, and I should add a few different spinning rods and reels, too. You know, expand my abilities. I'm a fishing guide myself."

Without waiting for an answer, she'd turned into the K-Mart parking lot, turned around again, and started driving north, toward Key Colony Beach. I like a woman who's strong and decisive and this lady was a real take-charge kind of woman. Knowing that against a strong-willed woman like this, arguing would be pointless—not that I'd wanted to, anyway—I said, "Well, if you're sure, I'd enjoy the company."

Five minutes later, we'd turned into the Sunset Beach Apartment complex on Key Colony Beach. As we ran toward the overhang to get out of the rain, she'd said, "I have some shirts that will fit you, but I don't think you can get into my jeans."

That'd made me stop in my tracks. She'd laughed again and continued laughing all the way to the door of her apartment.

Inside, she'd disappeared down the hall and come back a minute later with a well-worn, long-sleeved denim shirt. "Give me five minutes," she'd said and disappeared down the hall again.

I'd pulled my T-shirt off, looked around and finally just deposited it in a trash can in the kitchen, pulling on the denim shirt she'd given me. It smelled faintly of clean girl.

I remembered spending a few minutes looking around the living room. It was functional, not at all girly or anything. There'd been three fly rods supported on hangers along one wall. A fly-tying table and chair sat under the window with several boxes of small hooks and assorted pieces of cloth and feathers. I'd found a few pictures on a bookcase. Her, several years younger, standing with a teenaged boy and an older couple. Family picture, maybe? Several pictures of her, fly rod in one hand, a trout in the other, with mountains in the background. There was another of her with the teenaged boy, probably taken a few years later, as he'd had a moustache in that one. She was in a black skirt and white blouse, with her hair longer. He was wearing the cap and gown of a graduate and she wore a very proud smile.

"My little brother, Mark," she'd said from behind me. Her sudden appearance startled me a bit, as I hadn't heard the slightest sound. "That was his college graduation. Our folks died when he was seventeen and I took over, helping him get through those tough years."

"I can see the resemblance," I'd told her, noting the tall young man in the picture had the same blond hair and high cheekbones as his sister. "Sorry about your folks."

She'd changed into more comfortable clothes, I'd noticed. A pair of khaki fishing shorts, a baggy, short-sleeved guayabera in light blue and her usual long-billed fisherman's cap.

"Shall we go shopping?" she'd asked. And without waiting for a reply, she'd headed toward the door.

CHAPTER SIX

J ulie and I were in Bogie Channel now, in the lee of
Big Pine Key. Soon we'd be in Spanish Harbor, near
Southeast Point. That's where Big Pine Key Fishing
Lodge was located.

"Stay over on the left side of the channel," I said. "In
the shallows there along No Name Key, it'll be rougher
than going along close to Big Pine, but not too rough."

"Good idea," Julie replied. "It's sure to be rougher on
the outside. If we have to, Dad can bring the trailer down
to the ramp at *Dockside* and pull the skiff out of the
water."

It was pretty rough crossing Bahia Honda Channel,
and trying to stay between the waves was difficult, but
Julie handled it like a pro. It calmed down quite a bit
once we passed Pigeon Key, and we were able to ride
in relatively calm waters toward Knights Key, on the
western outskirts of Marathon. But once we cleared
the jetty at Knights Key Campground, it really started
getting rough, as the wind was coming straight out of
the south. In no time, though, we were pulling into the

quiet waters of Boot Key Harbor. We were a little wet and a bit shaken up, but the ride wasn't too awful.

I stepped off onto the dock and told Julie I'd catch up to her at the *Anchor*, leaving her to tie off at the dinghy dock. First, I wanted to duck into the office at *Dockside* to let Aaron know Julie's skiff would be tied up in my spot until we could arrange to get a trailer over. Once that was taken care of, I went back to the dinghy dock, grabbed my gear out of her skiff and walked over to the end of the dock where *Gaspar's Revenge* was tied up.

Jimmy was there, as usual. Although I only took out one or two charters a week, sometimes not even that many, Jimmy stayed close by and had recently started sleeping aboard in the guest cabin. It was fine with me—in fact, I felt more secure knowing that someone was there, and Jimmy was at least reliable.

"What do ya think, Jimmy? We gonna have to take her down to Cuba to avoid the storm?" I asked, as I put my gear on the transom.

"Really, dude? That'd be too cool," Jimmy replied.

Sometimes Jimmy was just too gullible. "Just pulling your leg, man," I said, laughing. "We should be pretty safe here in the harbor." I looked around and added, "We'll need to tie her off better with more lines, but we can ride it out right here, unless the storm turns and comes straight for us. The south side of a storm is weaker. You have a place to stay?"

"Not really, *el Capitan*. My latest girlfriend sort of kicked me out a couple weeks ago. I been staying here on the *Revenge*. But I don't know about staying aboard during a hurricane."

"Well, I don't mind having you stay aboard—feel free to make it permanent. But the same rules apply right here on the dock as out on the blue, okay? Nothing, absolutely nothing, illegal on board. Let's head on over to the *Anchor* and see what Rusty's plans are, once we get her tied down."

We spent the next hour moving everything below deck that might get knocked loose and tied the *Revenge* down with several extra lines. The dock was pretty new, and the piers were heavy timbers punched down through the limestone. They would hold up well in a storm, I was sure. At least I hoped so.

After we finished, Jimmy and I walked over to the *Rusty Anchor*. The whole time we were getting the boat ready, I was nervous and apprehensive. Would Alex be there? What would I say? What would she say? I felt like a man approaching the gallows, not knowing what awaited on the other side. It was the longest mile I'd ever walked.

CHAPTER SEVEN

Jimmy and I were caught in a pouring rain before we got to the crushed-shell drive at the *Anchor*. Normally, I enjoyed being outside in the rain. Most people would rush for cover, but I'd learned a long time ago that the human body was waterproof, and clothes dried. As we walked through the nearly empty parking lot, I noticed a bright yellow Jeep among the few pickups parked there. My heart started racing. It was Alex's car.

When we walked through the door, everyone looked our way. But I only saw one person. Her hair was longer than I'd remembered. She was wearing designer jeans and a blue denim shirt, hair spilling over the collar and down her back. Even though I was expecting to see her, I stopped dead in my tracks. Jimmy almost knocked me over in his rush to get in out of the rain.

"*Déjà vu*, Jesse," Alex said with a laugh that seemed to light up the whole room. God, how I'd missed her laugh.

Again, just like that day more than two years ago, I was standing before her slack-jawed, speechless, and dripping wet. The way she'd said my name, it was as if we'd only been apart for an hour or two. But it's been over a year. How did the woman do it? How did she make me feel like a high school kid on prom night? I couldn't form words anymore. Sentences were way beyond my sophomoric abilities.

I looked down at my soaked shirt and jeans, then back up to her, and grinned. I took a step toward her as she rose from her stool at the bar. Then she ran toward me and wrapped her arms around my neck. I held her close and smelled that same jasmine scent in her hair.

"I've missed you so much," she whispered, and I could feel her crying softly into my shoulder.

I held her tighter. "You're really here? I've missed you, too." When she tilted her head back and looked into my eyes, I found the words I wanted to say. "If anything, you're more beautiful than I remember."

She stepped up on her toes then and kissed me. Not a sisterly peck, but a kiss with more passion than anything I'd ever experienced. I wasn't ready for that. We'd kissed before but only a peck at the door. In the year we'd known each other we'd become good friends, shared a few meals, worked out, run, and swum together. I'd fantasized many times about taking our relationship further, but my track record with women wasn't the greatest and I didn't want to lose one of the few good friends I had.

"I like the hair," she said, tussling it. "No more 'light and tight?'"

I laughed and corrected her. "It's 'high and tight.' Guess I've just gotten lazy."

"Well," she said, "I like it."

Suddenly, I heard and felt the presence of others in the room. Everyone was cheering and clapping, as if the star quarterback had just run the length of the field for the game-winning touchdown. I looked around and everyone was looking right at us. Alex's cheeks colored a little at all the attention.

I noticed the TV over the bar was on the Weather Channel. "Um, ah, where's the storm, Rusty?" I stammered.

"About 150 miles west of Havana and heading northeast," Rusty replied. "If it holds course, it'll probably make landfall on the mainland, maybe around your old hometown."

I was raised in Fort Myers, Florida, though I hadn't been home but a few times since I'd joined the Corps. I'd lived in many places while I'd served, but when I retired, there was no question where I was going to settle down. Rusty and Julie had put me up for a few days until I found *Gaspar's Revenge* about five years ago, advertised in a yacht trader magazine to be auctioned at a boatyard in Miami. Rusty had driven me and Jimmy up there in his old pickup to try and buy her.

Alex and I walked over to the bar and sat down. The Weather Channel was just giving the update on Hurricane Wilma.

"This is Shomari Stone in Marathon. Right now, the winds are starting to pick up. If you look at the palm trees, they are swaying a little bit, but it's not too intense. Marathon's in the heart of the Keys between Key West and Key Largo, and thousands of Monroe County residents have already evacuated. Twenty-seven thousand live in Key West and officials tell us it's too early to tell how many have left town. Now, many of them are concerned about the heavy rain, the wind, and the potential threat of a storm surge. If you look right over here, these waves continue to rise and they pound the, uh, the rock here and they're really expected to rise in the next 48 hours. Authorities expect it to rise all the way up this slope here and we'll just have to see how far they actually go up, depending on the strength of Hurricane Wilma. Now, just to give you a unique vantage point, to show you just where we are, if you look right over there, this is the Seven Mile Bridge. It's the only way to get out of Key West. This thing stretches from Marathon all the way to Key West, and a lot of the residents are headed north on this thing. Forecasters are expecting at least a five-foot storm surge. Now, I'm about six feet two inches tall, so that would come about to my shoulders, standing here on the seawall. Now, just to let you know, there's a gas station on the Marathon side of the Seven Mile Bridge and they are open, and they

have plenty of gas, but will close at five o'clock.
That's the very latest on Hurricane Wilma. I'm
Shomari Stone, for The Weather Channel."

"Well, that guy was real enlightening," Alex said. "The Seven Mile Bridge goes all the way to Key West? I bet the people in Big Pine, Cudjoe, Sugar Loaf and Boca Chica got a kick out of that." She turned to me and asked, "Will the surge really be as high as he says?"

I thought about it for a minute, recalling reports about the Labor Day hurricane of 1935. It had a storm surge of nearly twenty feet when it crossed the Keys, devastating virtually everything and killing thousands.

I shrugged. "Like the guy said, it depends on how strong it gets and how fast it moves."

Rusty made his way over and placed a beer in front of me. "It's a Cat-3 now and moving pretty fast, Jesse. A five-foot surge won't be much problem. We're ten feet above sea level here and the canal is a good seven feet below the sea wall at high tide. Whatcha gonna do with the *Revenge*?"

"Jimmy and I made her fast at the dock. She'll be okay there," I replied.

"But aren't there still a lot of boats anchored out in the harbor?" Alex asked. "What if one breaks loose from its mooring ball and hits your boat?"

Just then the door opened, and Deuce, Tony, and Art walked in. "Deuce," I said, "I figured you'd be halfway back to Virginia by now, what with this storm coming on."

"Storm?" Deuce laughed. "I won't let a little blow like this keep me from fulfilling Dad's last wish."

"We stick together," Tony added. "The commander tried to order us back to the base, but since we're on leave we pointed out that his orders didn't really hold any weight."

"Gentlemen, this is my, um, friend Alex," I said. "Alex, meet Lieutenant Commander Deuce Livingston and Petty Officers First Class Tony Jacobs and Art Newman."

Alex looked at me when I said the word "friend," then extended her hand to Deuce. "Pleased to meet you, Commander." Then she turned to Tony and Art, shaking their hands also as she added, "You too, Petty Officers. My dad was coast guard, out of Astoria, Oregon."

"We're Navy, ma'am. And please, it's just Deuce, Tony, and Art," Deuce replied.

"Okay, but only if you drop the 'ma'am.' It's Alex DuBois. Short for Alexis."

"*Enchanté de vous rencontrer, Mademoiselle DuBois,*" Deuce said.

Alex beamed and responded, "*Le plaisir est tout a moi,* Commander. Your French accent is excellent."

Turning to me, she said, "So, *friend,* what about your boat?"

Oops, I thought, *did I just screw up?* I thought she'd come back because of me, but a thousand other reasons instantly came to mind. Then she laughed that hearty laugh of hers and I knew I might at least be a small part of her motivation for returning.

"I'm having second thoughts now that you mentioned all those boats moored in the harbor. There must be forty or fifty out there," I replied.

Rusty placed three cold beer bottles on the bar for Deuce and his men and suggested, "Why not bring her up the canal and moor her here?"

"Here?" I asked, passing a beer to everyone. "Your canal isn't deep enough, Rusty. What is it, five feet deep? The *Revenge* draws four. I'd be too afraid it'd bounce off the bottom if waves wash up the canal."

"It *was* five feet. I dredged it to ten a coupla months ago. It's fifty feet across, too. And there's five concrete bollards on either side. Each one's poured fifteen feet down. She'd be snug as a bug here."

"You had it dredged? Who did it?"

"Did it myself. Bought an old backhoe and a barge last year. It's still out there in the canal," he replied.

"And you never mentioned this to me? I could have dredged my channel deeper and saved a ton of money on dockage. Thanks a lot, buddy."

"Hey, you never asked," Rusty laughed. "Anyway, I think the *Revenge* would be better off here than in the harbor. You should bring her over, and soon."

"Ready to get wet again, Jimmy?" I asked my first mate.

"Mind if we tag along, Jesse?" Deuce asked.

"The more the merrier. Alex, will you be here for a while?" I asked.

"Actually, Rusty and Julie were kind enough to offer me their guest room," she replied. "We were just talking about it before you got here."

"Okay, then, let's go, guys," I said, turning to the door. "I suggest we walk, Deuce. Might not be able to get back to get your car later."

"We'll take my pickup," Rusty said, coming out from behind the bar. "Gotta fetch that skiff back here, anyway. Finish your beers while I hook up the trailer."

Jimmy said, "I hope you dudes don't mind getting wet or seasick."

We all looked at Jimmy and started to laugh. That is, everyone except Alex and Jimmy himself.

"I don't get it," Alex said.

Between laughs, Tony managed to say, "We're Navy SEALS, ma'am—er, I mean Alex."

We walked back out expecting rain, but the sun was shining, and the wind was now coming out of the south-southwest. A good sign.

"What the hell?" Art said, looking up at the sky. "It was pouring just a few minutes ago."

"Welcome to south Florida, dude," Jimmy said, stretching his arms wide, and turning his shaggy face toward the sky. "If you don't like the weather here, just wait a few minutes."

We walked around to the docks in back. Just as Rusty had said, there was a Caterpillar 416 loader with a backhoe sitting on a 35-foot barge. On both sides of the canal were several large, round concrete bollards that looked like they could moor a battleship. The canal was straight as an arrow, going south-southeast into the Atlantic about 250 yards away. He'd enlarged what had been a depression at the end of the canal and turned it into a small turning basin. It was a good 70 feet across. Plenty enough to turn the *Revenge* around. I remember Rusty's dad telling me one time that the depression and shallow canal had been a thriving wrecker's marina in his grandfather's day.

"Man, I used to operate one just like that," Tony said, pointing at the loader. "Grew up on a farm in North Carolina. Tough piece of equipment, and you can attach all sorts of cool things in place of the scoop, even an auger."

Viewing the loader, I was already thinking about my channel. "Once this storm passes, Jimmy, maybe Rusty'll let me borrow that thing and you can come up to the house and help me deepen and widen my channel." Gazing south down the canal, I said, "It's rough out there, but the *Revenge* can handle it with no problem. We can bring her all the way in here and then turn her around. I want her bow into the highest wind when we tie off."

"Will this wind continue out of the south during the whole storm?" Tony asked.

"I sure hope not, *compadre*," Jimmy replied, as we climbed into Rusty's pickup bed. "'Canes rotate anti-clockwise. Say a 'cane's coming right at you from the west. The wind's gonna blow straight out of the southwest till it hits ya, gettin' stronger and stronger as it gets closer and closer. Then, *pow*! The eye hits and everything goes calm and serene, man. But once the eye passes over you, *crash*! The wind starts to blow from the opposite direction. But if it's blowing slightly from the southwest early on, like it is now, that means the storm is going to pass north of you. The more westerly the wind, the further north it is. The wind'll keep moving around the compass, blowing more westerly, then northwest, as it moves past. Just the opposite if it passes to your south."

I looked at Jimmy and nodded. "We'll tie the *Revenge* in the turning basin, with the bow facing southwest, and hope you're right, Jimmy. Any waves coming up the canal she'll take on the port beam."

CHAPTER EIGHT

We arrived at the dock and climbed aboard the *Revenge* while Rusty and Julie drove on to the dinghy dock. Once at the helm, I got the big diesels started while Jimmy and our new crew set about untying the lines from the dock cleats. The three SEALS didn't need any instruction at all—they seemed more at home on a boat than on land. Deuce joined me on the bridge, looked over the helm and said, "Fine boat, Jesse. What's she got for power?"

I studied Deuce for a second and thought, *What the hell? He's Russ's kid.*

"A pair of Caterpillar C-18E diesels, rated at just over 1000 horses each. I don't divulge that to just anyone, so I'd appreciate you not passing it along. Normally, the Rampage 45 is powered by smaller engines, but this one had apparently been custom-built for the drug trade. I bought it at a Coast Guard auction after I retired from the Corps. It'd been impounded in a drug bust."

"You were a gunny, right?" he asked.

How did he know that? I wondered. I knew which direction he was going with it, though. The military wasn't exactly the career choice for a person who hoped to get rich.

"Yeah, I was," I replied. "About a year before I retired, I inherited some stock holdings and land from my grandfather. I sold off all the assets and bought this boat and a small island up in the Content Keys. I think Pap would have approved, though."

"All set, Skipper!" Jimmy yelled from the cockpit.

Turning my back to the controls afforded me a good view of the stern of the boat against the dock. I put the wheel at the small of my back and nudged the controls into forward. Watching the stern until we were clear of the docks, I could steer slightly with my body, but mostly with the throttles. Once we were clear, I called down, "Y'all come on up!"

The bridge had two seats at the helm, a bench seat on the port side and another bench in front of the console. Once all three of them were up the ladder, I steered the *Revenge* along the channel toward Sister Creek. "Jimmy," I said, "seas are only about five feet on the outside, so I doubt we'll have any trouble at all. But once we turn toward the channel, we're going to have fast-moving following seas and I might have to come into the canal pretty hot to have any steerage at all, so stay on your toes."

Jimmy nodded and Deuce asked, "Is there anything we can do to help?"

"Not really. Jimmy'll keep an eye out forward as we near the channel. Extra eyes won't hurt, though. You can watch the port side as we come into the channel and if Tony watches to starboard, we'll be fine. The channel's a bit narrow, only about 40 feet across, and the *Revenge* has a sixteen-foot beam. That'll leave us a good twelve feet of channel on either side."

As we passed the end of the private docks, I turned sharply left into Sister Creek, which wound between Boot Key and Key Vaca, where the town of Marathon was located. Boot Key was mostly undeveloped and since the bridge over the mouth of the harbor had been closed ago, the only way on or off the island was by boat. A number of fishermen lived there in houses built before the bridge was closed, and the federal government maintained a broadcast tower there that sent propaganda in Spanish to the people of Cuba. It was called *Radio Marti*. The Cuban government blocked the transmission, though, so only people in the United States could actually hear it. Our tax dollars at work.

"Who's Gaspar?" Art asked.

"He was a pirate," Jimmy replied. "Jose Gaspar was his given name, man. But when he stole a ship called *Floridablanca* and left the Spanish navy, he took the name *Gasparilla*. He was one of the last of the buccaneers, bro. His base of operations was up in the Port Charlotte area where Jesse's from. He and his crew plundered ships all up and down the west coast of Florida, man. When he finally decided to retire from pillaging, he was about 65.

But as he and his crew were dividing up their booty, they spotted a fat merchant ship offshore flying the Union Jack. They just couldn't pass up the opportunity to add a bit more to their stash. So, they sailed out toward the merchant ship, but as they got close, she lowered the Jack and hoisted the American ensign. It turned out that the fat merchant ship was actually the topsail schooner USS *Enterprise*, a notorious pirate hunter. Gasparilla's ship was nearly blasted apart, man, and he went down with her, just off the island that now bears his name."

"Is that all true?" Tony asked me.

"Well, that's the way the story goes," I replied with a lopsided grin. "The fact is, a man who in his later years claimed to have sailed with Jose Gaspar lived into the early 1900s. My grandfather met him as a child. Whether the stories he told were true or not depends on the person hearing the story."

We were coming out of the last turn in the creek and about to move into open water. I nudged the throttles up to 1200 rpm and the *Revenge* dropped down at the stern, lifting the bow slightly higher, until the horizon was lost below the windscreen. In just a few seconds, though, the bow came back down as she lifted up on plane. I loved the feeling I got when my boat changed from a displacement hull to a planing hull. I added a little more throttle, bringing her up to about twenty knots as we left the creek and started to encounter wind-driven waves. The *Revenge* was a 45-foot Rampage convertible, which is one of the best offshore fishing boats available anywhere. The deep V-design cut through even the roughest water and the Carolina flare of the bow just knocked the spray out and down, so even in rough seas like we had now, it was always a dry ride.

My guests knew about boats, that I was sure of. You didn't make O-4 and E-6 in the SEALS without having a whole lot of time on the water in all kinds of crafts. I could see by their expressions that they were impressed with the *Revenge*.

"This is some boat, man!" Tony exclaimed. "I thought for sure this'd be a pounder."

"Pounder?" I asked.

Art looked over from where he sat next to Deuce on the port bench. "Most of the boats we use ride like a Sherman tank. This is more like a Bentley."

As I started to make the turn past Sister Rock Island, as if on cue, a large wave hit the starboard bow. All it did was nudge the bow slightly to port and we rolled gently into the trough, coming back on course.

"Now that's what I'm talking about!" Tony yelled.

Once clear of Sister Rock, I brought the *Revenge* on around to the left and started the run toward the channel leading to Rusty's canal. It was identified by just two markers in eight feet of water, tucked in close to shore.

Turning again, I lined the *Revenge* up with the canal between the two markers and nudged the throttles a bit more to 1400 rpm, as the swells were rolling behind us now. I didn't want to wallow in the trough, nor be passed up by the fast-moving swells. We were running a lot faster than I usually liked to go through a channel, making nearly 25 knots. We flew past the first marker and in seconds were less than 100 yards from the mouth of the canal. The swells were smaller now and moving slower, so I eased back on the throttle to 1200 rpm and the stern rose slightly as our wake caught up with us. Passing the rock jetty, there was only a slight chop to the water, so I dropped the throttles down to idle speed and we nosed into the canal just as the *Revenge* came down off plane and became a displacement hull again.

"You'd have made a half-decent sailor there, jarhead," Deuce said. Interservice rivalry was common, especially between Marines and Sailors.

"Sorry, squid," I replied, laughing, and waving both hands. "I only have two arms." But coming from a man like Deuce, I took it as a great compliment.

As we idled down the long canal, Jimmy, Art, and Tony climbed down to the cockpit. "Jimmy, go on up to the bow and I'll put you off on the port side as I turn her around. I can see Rusty and Rufus ahead on the starboard shore. They'll handle the port lines once I spin her around and you can handle the starboard ones." Jimmy scrambled along the rail on the port side and made his way across the expansive foredeck to the bow, where he unhooked the cable across the front of the pulpit and stood ready.

When we reached the center of the turning basin, I reversed the port engine, nudged its throttle just above idle, and spun the wheel to the left. The *Revenge* started turning sideways while still drifting toward the barge at the end of the canal. Then I shifted the port engine back to forward and goosed the starboard throttle. The *Revenge* surged slightly forward, and I brought the throttles to reverse idle. She stopped just a couple of feet from the western dock and started backing, just as Jimmy took a long stride and stepped onto the western dock with the starboard bow line in his hand.

Working the wheel and throttles, I again put the *Revenge* into a spin to the left, and as Jimmy tied off the bow line to the first bollard, she came to a dead stop. Tony and Art threw lines to Rusty and Rufus, who were waiting on the eastern dock, and after they made them fast on the furthest two bollards, I brought both engines to neutral and idled them for a minute before shutting down. We were tied up at a 45-degree angle to the canal, with the stern only a few feet from the barge.

"I take that back, Captain." Deuce said. "You'd have made a damn fine sailor."

"Thanks, Deuce," I replied.

Tony and Art were already throwing off more lines to the three men on shore and within minutes they had six heavy lines tied fore and aft to both sides of the turning basin. Alex was standing on the old barge next to an aluminum gangplank that was connected to the barge with a large hinge pin. She lowered the other end to Art at the stern, who was thoughtful enough to bungee a bumper to the underside of the gangplank to protect my finish.

I nodded down to the cockpit and said, "A good sailor is a reflection on his leader."

CHAPTER NINE

I climbed down from the bridge and walked across the gangplank after Deuce. "Power's out, Jesse," Rusty said. "I got the backup generator going, but it only gives enough juice for the house or the bar, not both. Got the bar powered up right now, but everything in the cooler's gonna go bad when I switch it over to the house. You guys hungry?"

Art and Tony joined us on the barge and Tony said, "If you got any more of that bacon fish or whatever it was, hell, yeah!"

After several people laughed, Alex asked, "Are you still pulling that hogfish joke on unwary tourists?"

"Only when I can find a gullible enough tourist," I replied.

Jimmy was walking toward us from the end of the canal and called out, "Here comes rain, man."

"Let's get inside," I said. "That squall's gonna be here in a few seconds."

Everyone ran to the door and made it inside just as the rain started pounding on the roof.

"Okay," I said, "we need to come up with some kind of a plan. Let's check the update on the storm on the TV first. Deuce, do you guys have a place to stay?"

"Yeah, we have two rooms at the Blue Water Resort, just down the road," he told us.

I looked at Rusty, who shook his head. "Might be better to stay here, Deuce," I said. "When the power goes out, it's usually the whole island. Plus, if Wilma stays on track, the north side of the island will get it worse."

"We have a guest room in the house," Julie said, looking at Deuce. "But we asked Alex to stay with us. I guess we can just all stay right here in the bar."

"Jimmy and I will bunk in the boat," I said. "It's plenty safe way up here in the canal. Way better than *Dockside*. The crew cabin has three bunks. Anyone want dibs on the couch in the salon?"

"That huge forward berth, for just you?" Alex asked. "Kinda stingy there, *friend*. Here's an idea. How about I bunk with you? The commander here can take Rusty's guest room and Jimmy can bunk in the crew cabin with these nice sailors. Maybe they can teach him to cuss properly."

That brought a huge laugh from everyone, but I was too busy looking at Alex. She smiled at me coyly and nodded, saying, "If that's all right with you, Captain."

"Well, um, yeah," I stammered. Turning to the others, I said, "Okay, so that's taken care of. What next? Rusty?"

Rusty was behind the bar and had turned on the TV. The Weather Channel was just coming out of a commercial and Rusty was setting beers on the bar, along with a bottle of ginseng tea for Jimmy. Though he smoked pot, he very rarely drank alcohol. Two local fishermen, Lefty and Diego, looked up at Rusty expectantly.

"I can make one forecast already," Rusty said, as the lights dimmed for a second or two. "No matter where Wilma goes, we're not gonna have power back tonight and the bar is gonna be closed up as soon as we know the storm's passed. So, drink up, people. Beer's gonna get hot before morning. On the house," he said, looking at the two fishermen. "Julie, you seen Rufus?"

"He went out to his cabin a little while ago. Want me to get him?" she replied.

"Yeah, let him know we got some fish to cook up," he said. "And anything else he has in the icebox. Sorry, Tony, the hogfish is all gone. But Rufus makes a mean blackened grouper."

Julie looked over at Deuce and asked, "Will you come with me? It's getting dark."

Deuce dutifully put down his cold Red Stripe and followed her to the door. I glanced at Rusty, who watched after them for a moment as they walked outside. He looked back at me and just shrugged. I raised an eyebrow in question. Julie knew every square inch of the property intimately. The house she and Rusty lived in had been her only home and the yard was where she learned to crawl and to walk.

"Hadda happen sooner or later," Rusty said, just loud enough for me and Alex to hear.

"Hey, turn that up, Rusty," Jimmy said. "They're about to give the update."

Everyone gathered at the bar, watching as the local weather guy came into focus, wearing a yellow slicker buffeted by the wind.

> *"This is Shomari Stone in Marathon, with the update on Hurricane Wilma. As you can see the wind has really started to pick up. Wilma has been upgraded to a Category-3 storm, a major hurricane, with winds clocked near the eye at a hundred and twenty miles per hour. It has increased forward speed and as of eight o'clock Wilma was centered 100 miles west-southwest of Key West, heading northeast at twenty miles per hour. Hurricane warnings are now up for all of the Florida Keys and southwest Florida. A mandatory evacuation has now been ordered for all of the Lower Keys, and a tropical storm warning has been issued for the rest of the state. Right now, here in Marathon, we're about 100 miles from Key West and the winds are coming out of the southwest at 30 miles per hour, with occasional gusts to 40. The rain's been coming down in sheets, as the outer bands come over the island. If Wilma maintains her current path and speed, it should make landfall somewhere south of Fort Myers in the early morning hours. We expect conditions here in the Middle Keys to worsen throughout*

the night, but it looks like the Keys may dodge this one. However, we know from past experience that even a glancing blow can have devastating effects. We should expect winds here to reach tropical storm strength in the next couple of hours and may even reach hurricane force before this is all over."

A cheer went up in the bar as Julie and Deuce came in through the back door, old Rufus following behind. Deuce looked up suddenly, scanning the room, his face reddening. Then he saw that nearly everyone was watching the TV, not the door.

"Rufus, you feel like cooking?" Rusty asked. "Power's out and I got the generator running, but when I switch it over to the house, everything's gonna go bad."

"Yes, suh, cook it all up? I go and fire up dem cookas."

"Yeah, all of it. Gotta be more than ten pounds of grouper in that cooler, plus about a hundred jumbo shrimp." Turning to his friends, Rusty asked, "Any special requests?" Without waiting for an answer, he turned back to Rufus and added, "No? Good. Blackened grouper and shrimp it is, Rufus. If you find anything else in that cooler, cook it up now. It's only gonna go bad if we don't."

"Aye, Mista Rusty," Rufus replied. "Got some corn an' stone crab claws in dere too, mon. Might could be di lass good food we get fah a coupla days."

Rusty came out from behind the bar and approached me. "Jesse," he began, "my skiff's still hooked to the pickup. Can ya help me unhook it and stake her down?"

"We'll get it," Art said, stepping away from the bar and tapping Tony on the shoulder. "Just show us where you want it."

"Thanks, son," Rusty said. "Follow me." They headed out the bar's front door, which the wind caught and slammed shut, but it looked like it'd stopped raining for the moment.

I turned to Alex. "Are you sure about this?" I asked her. I'd thought about taking our relationship to the next level many nights before she left. Many, many nights.

She looked me right in the eye and, as if reading my mind, told me, "I've been thinking of you every day since I had to leave. Thought about you quite a few nights, too. I know you wanted to take it slow last year. I thought that maybe you just weren't interested. Are you?"

Typical Alex—direct and to the point.

I took her hand, led her to a table and sat down next to her, "Interested?" I asked. *Yeah, a lot.* "I'll admit, I wanted to go slow. You'd become a good friend and those are hard to find. I've never had much luck with relationships, though. You know that. I just didn't want to risk losing a friend."

"Jesse, you spent a lot of time overseas, I know. Neither of your exes could handle that. They were weak women, if you ask me. Many women can't handle waiting. Too bad for them, though. Besides, your globetrotting warrior days are over now. Let's just sort of pick up where we left off last year, okay? No rush, no lifetime commitments, just one day at a time. But safe in the knowledge that we both want more from each other."

"I like the sound of that. Once this storm passes, I have a surprise for you. Do you remember that island I bought up in the Content Keys?" She nodded, and I continued, "Well, I cleared part of it, cut a channel and built a little stilt house."

"Really? You don't sleep on the *Revenge* anymore? The old man from the sea has a real house?" She laughed at her own joke. "I can't wait to see it. Do the snook still run through the pass up there? Does it have a kitchen?"

Typical Alex, I thought again. Always dreaming of her next big catch. I'd tried to get both my ex-wives to try fishing, but they were both too citified. Alex wasn't like that at all. This woman was born and raised in the Oregon wilderness.

"Yeah," I said. "I got an eight-pounder just last week. And yes, I have a galley and even a head. Nothing fancy, just a propane ship's stove and propane refrigerator, a few cabinets, and a small table. The lights are all twelve-volt and there's a solar panel and small wind turbine to keep the batteries charged. I'm pretty sure you'll approve."

I couldn't wait to show it to her. She'd mentioned once that her ideal home would be on or near the water, away from the rat race in the city. Every day, as I was building it, I was thinking of her, and what she'd like in a house. I never guessed she'd be back in my life, though.

Rusty, Art and Tony came back in. Deuce was talking to Julie at the bar but came over to the table when Rusty resumed his spot behind the bar. "You got a minute, Jesse?" he asked.

"I'll go out and see if I can help Rufus," Alex said. "I just love that little old Jamaican mon. His voice sounds like he's singing." She smiled at Deuce as she headed to the back door. I couldn't take my eyes off her as her hips swayed in those tight jeans.

Deuce sat down and handed me a beer. "To seafarers and the women who wait for them," he toasted, as he touched the neck of his beer to mine.

"I'll certainly drink to that. What's up, Deuce?"

"Suddenly, I have a number of things to talk with you about. Damn, where do I start?"

I looked over to the bar, where Julie was watching us. "Maybe you could start with that little bar wench over there?" I teased.

"Yeah, well, there is that. First, about my dad. You brought it up last night. I've really only known you a little over 24 hours, but I'm good at sizing men up, and I know Dad trusted you. You said last night that he was part fish, and I agree. Truth is, I have my doubts about that coroner's report, and I think you do, too."

I mulled it over for a minute. "We're all gonna leave this life one day," I said. "I just can't imagine any circumstance where a man like Russ Livingston would go out that way."

"Coroner's report said he'd gotten his tank fouled in his anchor line. Said he must not have been able to pull the anchor free and ran out of air. Dad never dived without at least one knife. He'd have cut that anchor line or ditched his gear."

"What did the cops say?"

"Big city. Too many murder investigations to handle. They seemed to accept the coroner's report, rather than have another investigation on their hands."

"Murder?"

"Dad wouldn't drown. We both know that."

I nodded. I'd been thinking the same thing. "You said big city? Fort Pierce is a small town."

Deuce shook his head. "It happened off Palm Beach. About a mile off the coast. I'd talked to him a few days before and he said he had some new information on a Civil War wreck he'd been searching for. I'm just not buying that coroner's report. Dad also said he had a new diver working with him, part-time. A muscle head by the name of Lester." He paused a moment. "Look, Dad had changed some since he left the Corps. He found a few things, sometimes in areas he wasn't supposed to be looking. Sometimes he turned a blind eye. He told me about what you and he found, back when I was still a kid living with Mom."

Russ and I had promised not to let anyone know about that. Was Deuce trying to feel me out? Did Russ really tell him? I knew he'd been skirting some laws.

"A hundred thousand in silver," Deuce added, confirming that Russ had told him. "He'd been drinking when he told me; I doubt that he remembered it the next day. Anyway, his and your secret is safe with me. We have to get back to the base, day after tomorrow. What I wanted to ask you was this: I won't have time now because of this storm, but if we can get out to that reef tomorrow, to fulfill his wishes, I'd appreciate it. Then, I'd like to impose on you to go up to Fort Pierce and box up his stuff and send it to my mom for me. I'm between places now. His boat's in evidence at the sheriff's office, along with his dive gear and everything else that was on the boat. Think you can bring it all down here and sell it? Whatever you get, you can donate to whatever charity you like. We have a mission coming up in about a month and I'll be way too busy training."

"Tell ya what," I answered, "we'll all go out to Conrad tomorrow afternoon and give Russ a Viking send-off. Then Wednesday, if I can borrow Alex's Jeep, I'll drive up and take care of his things. Knowing Russ, it won't take but a few hours. Now, what about that bar wench?"

Deuce colored a little and smiled. "That obvious, huh?"

"Well, considering that neither Rusty nor I have seen her take an interest in anyone, yeah, it kind of sticks out like a sore thumb. She's a great kid and Rusty likes you.

He might not always show it when he likes someone. I'd advise you though, to read up on the 'Rules for Dating a Marine's Daughter.'"

Deuce laughed so hard, I thought he was gonna spew beer out of his nose. "You know I have a sister, right?" he asked when he got himself under control. "Dad had those rules framed and hanging by the kitchen door when she started dating. I really felt bad for those guys. There's one other thing, though, that I wanted to talk to you about."

"Fire away but make it quick. I smell blackened grouper coming through that back door."

"I've actually left the navy," he said simply.

"Really?" I asked. "Why? Hell, you gotta be more than halfway to retirement."

"I resigned four months ago. I was offered a position where I can make a bigger difference. Our hands were getting tied tighter and tighter with new ROEs," he said.

I nodded my understanding. We'd been shackled with some very stringent Rules of Engagement during the first Gulf War, so I knew exactly what he meant.

"I can't really say anything more," he continued. "But I do know this. The people I'm working for now are looking for someone like you, too. I talked to my new boss, and he asked me to give you this." Then he handed me a business card with a name and phone number on it, nothing more. I looked at it for a minute. The printing was standard military-style block lettering, not embossed. But the card itself was heavy stock, with no rough edges.

"Deuce," I said, "I've been retired for over five years now. I like what I do and where I do it. Alex has just come back into my life after being gone for over a year and I'm going to take her up to my island, where I built a house over this past year. I'm not really interested in a nine-to-five job."

"Just call the guy," he said. "Doesn't have to be right away. Maybe I can tell you more tomorrow."

Just then, Alex and Rufus opened the back door and a gust of wind blew in, carrying with it the smell of some of Rufus's finest concoctions. "No promises, man," I said. "Let's eat."

The wind was getting stronger as we chowed down on some fine grouper, shrimp, and crab claws. Rufus had thrown over a dozen ears of corn in a steamer, too. It was nearly midnight and we were having a good time, but still checking the updates on the storm every fifteen or twenty minutes. At 0130, Rusty finally called it a night by saying, "Looks like a gator storm, y'all." Then he clanged the brass ship's bell hanging on the wall. "Last call! I gotta switch the power over to the house soon, or I'll lose everything in the fridge there. That's our breakfast and lunch for tomorrow. I think it's time we all turned in."

"You're absolutely right," Alex said, smiling at me. "I'm getting pretty tired anyway. It's been a long day. What's the latest on the storm?"

Julie had changed the TV channel from the Weather Network to a PBS station that only showed the most recent update scrolling across the screen. "Says its 70 miles west-northwest of Key West and still heading northeast. It probably won't get any closer than 80 or 100 miles of us to the north, maybe just before dawn." Then she faked a yawn and said, "Russell, walk a girl home?"

Deuce got quickly to his feet and together they headed for the door. Again, I looked over at Rusty behind the bar.

"They're adults," he said. "And Deuce seems like a nice enough guy. It ain't like they're gonna sleep together tonight, right under my roof."

"All right, everyone," I said, "party's over."

Lefty and Diego had left quite a bit earlier, as soon as the food was gone. Rufus had gone to his little cabin shortly after that. The former rum shack had withstood a lot of storms, including the infamous Labor Day Hurricane of 1935. If anything, it was stronger now. Besides, Rufus loved to watch the stormy water.

"Lock up, will ya, Jesse?" Rusty asked. "I'm gonna turn in and clean up in the morning."

Turning toward the door, Jimmy called out, "Come on, dudes, I'll show you where you're gonna bunk. I think there's still a few beers in the cooler." Together, the three of them headed out into the howling wind.

"Here's your chance, *friend*," Alex said, mocking me again. "You can run out that door and sleep under the bridge."

I grinned and took her in my arms. "No," I said, "I've been thinking about this for two years. Damn shame it's not a little better night. Gentle breeze, bottle of wine, stars all across the sky, you and me back at my little house…"

"I never pictured you as the romantic type," she said. "Let's go, Captain Romeo, before you change your mind."

Just then, the lights went out and it became pitch dark inside the bar.

"Guess Rusty's trying to hurry us along," I said, holding her, and enjoying the scent of her hair.

Alex wrapped her arms around my neck and stood once more on her toes to kiss me. A slow, passionate kiss, pressing her body tightly to mine. When we broke apart and I took her hand, I wasn't sure which way the door was.

Lightning flashed far to the south, briefly illuminating the inside of the bar, just enough to let me get my bearings, and we made it to the door without tripping over anything.

"Wait," Alex said. "My overnight bag is behind the bar, along with my purse."

"I'll get it," I said.

Getting to the bar in total darkness was easy since I'd done it so many times. I knew where Julie kept her purse stashed and that's where I found Alex's belongings. Once back at the door, I opened it and we stepped out into the gale.

The wind was howling, but for the moment, the rain had stopped. I locked the door and we walked hand-in-hand to the *Revenge*, the wind tugging at our clothes. The overhead light from the cockpit illuminated the gangplank and I could hear the burbling sound of the generator and the hum of the air conditioning unit. After crossing over the gangplank with Alex behind me, I jumped down to the deck, turned and lifted her lightly down beside me.

When I opened the hatch to the salon, I found that Jimmy, Art, and Tony were sitting around the settee, checking out the storm on the laptop. Jimmy was a computer whiz and had installed a wireless satellite system, so when I was far offshore, or when local cell phone towers were out, like now, I'd still have internet.

Looking up, Art said, "It's moving faster now, still in the same direction, but at 30 miles per hour. Your first mate here thinks it'll make landfall south of Fort Myers about 0500 hours."

"Jimmy's probably right," I said. "He's lived here all his life. Any beer left?"

"I'm going forward," Alex said. "Don't be long, *friend*."

She disappeared down the steps to the forward stateroom. I grinned and told her I'd be right there.

Art opened the cooler and handed me a cold Hatuey and two bottles of water. "What's with this *friend* thing?" he asked.

"Long story, Art. About two years," I replied. I was wondering about it myself. "If Jimmy's right, it should be fairly calm here by morning. There's gonna be a lot of work to do when we get up. Good night, guys."

I headed down the steps and opened the hatch to my stateroom. Alex's purse and bag were sitting on top of the little front-loading washer and dryer combo on the port side. The door to the private head was closed. After moving her things to the long shelf on the starboard side, I kicked off my Topsiders and put the beer and water bottles into a small cooler built into the step on the port side of the queen-sized island bunk. I made quick work of pulling off my T- shirt and shorts, tossed them both in the washer, then pulled down the covers and sheets and climbed in wearing only my skivvies. I turned the lights down to very low and waited, listening to the wind howl outside.

Finally, the door to the head opened, and Alex stepped out wearing a pale blue, very sheer nightgown. The light from inside the head silhouetted her firm body through the flimsy material. Then she flicked the switch off and moved slowly onto the bed beside me. The warmth of her body next to mine felt like a furnace.

"I'm so glad to be home," she whispered, and curled up into my embrace. Within minutes, I was glad there was a hurricane blowing outside, with the howling wind, driving rain, and rocking waves. Or was there?

CHAPTER
TEN

Sunlight was streaming in through the overhead hatch when I woke up. My skivvies were lying on the shelf to my right and a satin blue nightgown was pooled on the steps up to my side of the bunk. Alex was curled up next to me with her head on my shoulder. I wanted nothing more than to just lie there like that for the rest of the day.

Well, maybe wake her up for round three, I thought.

She stirred and opened her eyes. "Are we still alive?"

Chuckling softly, I kissed her cheek. "Yeah, the storm's passed. I'm guessing it's after 0900."

"Do you always do that?" she asked, laughing.

"Do what?"

"You're not in the Marines anymore. It's after nine o'clock, or even nineish." She jabbed me in the ribs and said, "We better get out there. There's probably a huge mess."

Rising from the bed, Alex grabbed her bag from on the shelf.

Dammit, Jesse, I thought, while admiring her body, *it sure took you long enough.*

When she turned around, pulling a denim work shirt on, she caught me looking at her backside and smiling. "Don't even think about it, mister," she said with a smile. "I'm already going to be walking bowlegged for a week."

"You know, I've really missed your laugh," I said, climbing off the bunk. I reached below the foot of it and pulled the release that allowed the bed to lift up on twin hydraulic arms. Then I grabbed a clean pair of skivvies, a T-shirt and a pair of denim shorts from the locker and started to close it back up.

"What's in that huge box under there?" she asked.

"Just some tools and things," I lied. Truth was, you could take the man out of the Marines, but you couldn't take the Marine out of the man. Inside that box was a small arsenal.

She was pulling on a pair of jeans, wiggling them up over her hips, when I grabbed her from behind and held her tight. "Where are you staying?" I asked.

"I hadn't even thought about it," she said. "I only got here yesterday morning and spent the day with Julie catching up on the Coconut Telegraph until she left to get you. Is there someplace you recommend?"

"I know of a little house, not too far away. It's sort of remote but the fishing is supposed to be pretty good."

"Of course, I'll have to inspect it, you know, just to make sure it's suitable." She turned inside my embrace, reached up, and kissed me. "Let's get some work done first."

She was out the hatch while I was still struggling to get dressed.

Stepping down from the salon to the cockpit, I looked around the anchorage. The lines were all secure and the water was calm. There was a lot of flotsam in the water near the barge and the palm trees on both sides of the basin were frayed. A large lignum vitae tree had been uprooted and fallen, narrowly missing the bar. Alex was walking in when I saw Tony and Art with a chain saw, about to start cutting the tree up to remove it.

"Tony," I yelled as I crossed the gangplank onto the barge, "hold up a second." I walked over to them. "That's a lignum vitae tree—it's super hard wood. There's no way that little chain saw will last through two cuts. Notice that none of the branches are broken?"

Art replied, "Yeah, we noticed that. Thought maybe it fell over softly in the wind."

"No, this wood is so hard, no wind on earth could ever break the larger branches. A ten-foot-long two-by-four made of this stuff would support all three of us. Rufus has the right kind of saw for this project. Have you seen him?"

"He's out back, cooking," Tony replied. I'd noticed something about these two sailors. Ask one of them a question and the other would answer.

"That guy sure can cook," Art added.

"Yeah," I said, "he was the head chef at a five-star resort in Jamaica for about 30 years. He retired and came here a few years back. If you go out to the shed next to his cabin, you'll find the big brother to this little thing. If you would, make the cuts at the ends of any straight branches and leave the trunk whole. Rusty can have it hauled to a mill up in Homestead. It's worth a lot of money to some people, namely me."

"Sure thing, Jesse," Tony said. "Doesn't seem to be any other damage here, except for some scattered debris. Jimmy got up at 0530 hours and checked the storm. Never got any closer than 80 miles, it looks like. But your wind gauge was showing gusts to 90. He said he had to go check on his mom and would be back later."

"We dodged the worst of it. Your first hurricane?" I asked.

"No, we've been through a couple," Tony replied, without further explanation. Looking around the property conspiratorially, he said, "The commander talked to you about our change of duty status?"

"All three of you?" I asked and both men nodded. "Well, from what he said, it sounds like it'll be a benefit to the country as a whole, but I can't help thinking it'll be a great loss to the Navy."

"Thank you, sir," Tony said and they both headed off to the back of the property where Rufus's cabin was located. Now my curiosity was piqued. An agency that didn't bind its men with ridiculous rules and was able to recruit from the best of the best? What would be the incentive? I headed into the bar to find Rusty and Deuce.

"'Bout time you rousted yourself, Devil Dog," Rusty said as I walked through the door. "Julie and me done cleaned up the whole damn island all by ourselves," he added, smiling at Alex.

"Sorry about your tree, Rusty," I said as I sat down next to Alex, who leaned over and kissed me on the cheek. "Tony and Art are gonna cut it up into board length. Where's Deuce?"

Julie looked up and replied, "He's just outside. He said he had to make some phone calls. Don't know how he's gonna make a call. All the phone lines are down and there's no cell service."

Deuce stepped inside and motioned for me. I followed him back outside. "Our training's been moved up. We have to leave at noon to make a flight out of Miami. I've been authorized to tell you a bit more." He was all business now.

"Deuce," I said, "I told you last night, I love it here and I love what I do. I doubt anything could tempt me away."

"That's just it, Jesse," he said. "Nothing much will change. If you accept what my boss is offering, you'll just keep doing what you've been doing. Occasionally, you might be called on to do something a little different, but you're free to say no at any time. My boss is meeting us at the plane, and he'll come back down here in the rental. He really wants to meet you in person and explain things in more detail. Just hear him out, that's all I ask. I think you'll like what he has to say. I'll have to wait a few weeks until I can get back down here to take care of Dad's ashes."

The roar of Rusty's big Stihl 8.5-horsepower chain saw suddenly split the air like an over-revving outboard engine.

"What the hell is that?" Deuce asked, astonished.

"I think Tony and Art found Rusty's big saw," I replied. "I'll listen to what he says, Deuce, but no promises. Let's go give your guys a hand."

Art was wrestling with the twenty-pound saw, his large arms taut as Tony was trying to manhandle the branches that he'd cut from the tree. I knew from experience they were more than the wiry man could handle. Hell, they'd be more than I could handle alone, but he was giving it all he had. Art shut the saw off as we approached and said, "You weren't kidding about the big brother or this wood, man."

I just laughed and said, "Yeah, we'll need to sharpen that blade at least twice before we get this done."

Struggling with a small branch, Tony asked, "Is this damn tree made of steel, or what?"

There was a small knot from one of the branches sitting on the ground. It wasn't useful for anything, so I picked it up and said, "Watch this."

I carried it over to the dock, with all three men following me. When I got to the edge, I tossed it out into the basin. It sank straight away to the bottom and never came back up.

"Damn," Deuce said. "A wood that doesn't float?"

"Lignum vitae is about the densest wood on the planet," I replied. "My house is made of this stuff."

"Someday I'd like to see that house," Deuce said.

"Be glad to show it to you. The island's small and surrounded by mangroves. I cleared part of the interior, a circle about 150 feet around, intending to plant some vegetables. Except the ground's too rocky and the water too salty. Now, there's just a single coconut palm in the middle of that huge clearing."

Deuce looked at me and said, "You know, if you cut down that tree, a clearing that big would make a great LZ."

A landing zone? To land what?

"I'll have to keep that in mind," I said, "if I ever decide to buy a chopper."

"Or if friends want to come and visit," Tony said with a grin.

"You too?" I said. "Already told Deuce I wasn't interested."

We went back to work and had the rest of the tree cut up in just over two hours, even stopping to sharpen the blade twice. Everything that was usable we stacked neatly behind the bar. The trunk we left where it had fallen, once it was cut away from the roots. Rusty would have to use the backhoe to load it on a flatbed. It would probably weigh a couple of tons. The small stuff we put in the back of Rusty's pickup and carried it out by the old boat ramp, where he had a fire ring and some chairs.

The ramp was supposed to be his next project. As it was, the concrete all cracked and broken, there was no way to launch anything but a kayak from there.

Alex came out just as we were finishing, carrying four tall glasses of sun tea. "We got everything cleaned up inside. Rufus has lunch ready."

It was already getting hot, so we drank down the tea, as Deuce apologized. "We'll have to eat and run, ma'am. I mean, Alex. We have a plane to catch up in Miami in a few hours."

Alex looked at her watch and said, "It's over 100 miles—you'll never get there in time to get through security."

"It's a private plane we're taking out of Miami," he told her.

Hmmm, a chopper and a company plane? Just what the hell kind of outfit were these men working for?

We headed inside and sat at the bar, eating jerked chicken and potatoes and talking about the storm. Afterwards, Deuce and Julie strolled outside, while Tony and Art returned to the *Revenge* to grab their sea bags. When they came back inside minutes later, Deuce said, "Thanks for the hospitality, Rusty. We really appreciate it."

"No, sir, thank you for all your help," Rusty said, shaking hands with all three men. "Y'all come on back down here anytime."

Tony made his way to the back to talk to Rufus for a minute. The old Rastafari wrote something on a notepad and handed it to Tony. After shaking his hand, Tony returned and announced, "I got a recipe."

Everyone laughed as we all walked with the three sailors out to their car. Tony and Art carried the sea bags to the trunk and Julie gave Deuce a bear hug, much like her dad had when they'd first met. She kissed him and told him he'd better be back soon. Then the three men climbed into the sedan and disappeared down the shell driveway.

"Think he knows Rule Six?" Rusty asked as we walked back toward the bar.

We both laughed and Alex asked, "Rule Six?"

"There are a bunch of dumb rules jarheads have for men who want to date their daughters," Julie replied, rolling her eyes.

"Really?" Alex asked. "Do you guys have rules for everything?"

Without missing a beat, Rusty and I said in unison, "Yep, Semper Fi."

"Rusty?" I asked, as we strolled back to the bar. "Mind if Alex and I borrow your skiff to go out to the house and get mine? I'll have it back tomorrow."

"No need to even ask," he replied. "Julie can trailer it down to *Dockside* while I finish up here."

"I'd also like to borrow your barge and loader. Jimmy said he knew how to operate one just like it and he's agreed to come up to the house later this week and help me enlarge the channel. My permit's still good until the end of the year and I'd really like to not have to pay *Dockside* to dock there forever."

"Sure. You wanna borrow my skivvies, too?" he joked.

"I'll get the skiff hooked up to the truck, Dad," Julie said. "Give me a hand, Alex?"

The two women headed around the side of the bar, where the skiff had been secured the night before. Rusty turned to me and asked, "What's your take on those three men?"

I knew exactly what he really wanted to know. Julie had never shown much interest in men, but she was interested in Deuce. I had some experience at being the guy who was always away, and it had cost me two marriages and a few relationships. It seemed those three men had chosen a similar path and Rusty didn't want his daughter to be hurt.

"I could be totally wrong, Rusty," I said. "But I think Deuce is a straight-up guy. I haven't seen either of my daughters in years, but if I could choose a man for them, I'd pick someone cut from Deuce's cloth."

My daughters from my first marriage lived in North Carolina with their mom. She'd filled their heads since childhood with stories about what a terrible person I was. Other than sending them cards on their birthdays with a check inside, I hadn't really had any contact with them in fifteen years. The checks were never cashed. Guess that said something, in and of itself.

"Truth is," I said to my old friend, "I look at Julie like she was my own kid. I don't think we have anything to worry about. Besides, how much of a romance can bloom in just two days?"

Just then, Rusty's pickup pulled up on the side of the bar, as if answering my own question, and Alex leaned out of the window. "Let's get a move on, Captain. I want to see that house."

"We'll be back tomorrow," I told Rusty.

"Yeah, right," he said. "I won't hold my breath."

I climbed in next to Alex and Julie drove down the long shell driveway and turned left onto the highway. A half mile later, she turned left at the light, onto Sombrero Boulevard, then made an immediate right, toward *Dockside*.

Julie leaned over and looked at me. "So, what do you think of Russell?"

"Who?"

"Russell. I'm not crazy about a nickname like Deuce."

"Um, Julie, Rusty is your dad's nickname. You don't have a problem with everyone calling him Rusty, do you?" She didn't answer. "Deuce, I mean Russell, is a good enough guy. What do you think, Alex?"

"He's the sort of guy I imagine you must have been like a lifetime ago." She hunched her shoulders and made a face. "Very serious."

"I like a guy who is serious about things."

"Look, Jules," I said, "I can see you like the guy and he's a decent person, that's for sure. But you're not likely to see a lot of him."

"I wouldn't be too sure," she said, smiling.

I just left it at that, hoping she was right. We pulled into *Dockside* and found a mess. Several of the boats that lay at anchor in the harbor had broken loose and were crashed against the shoreline all around the bay.

"Oh my," Alex said, pointing to where the *Revenge* had been docked the day before. A 30-foot catamaran had crashed into the docks and my finger pier was now halfway through the boat's cabin. "I'm so glad you moved your boat," she added.

We idled on down to the launch ramp, which was thankfully cleared. Dozens of people were busy everywhere, cleaning up what they could. That was the thing about a storm like that. It brought out the best in people.

CHAPTER ELEVEN

We backed the trailer down the ramp into the water and I told Julie we'd be back tomorrow with the skiff. Then Alex and I boarded Rusty's boat, which, I noticed, had already been loaded with Alex's overnight bag, a suitcase and two rod cases. I started the big Johnson outboard and it settled quickly into a low burbling. Backing away from the ramp, Alex said, "I sure hope nothing's sunk in the channel."

"Yeah, me too."

We idled along, following the channel along the docks, amazed at all the damage that had been done there. "You think your house is all right?" she asked.

"That's something I'm certain of. The island might be a mess, but the house will be fine."

I passed Sister Creek and turned right toward the bridge and open water. Once we were clear of the old bridge, I could see that the water outside was nearly as calm as usual and opened the big motor up as we crossed under the Seven Mile Bridge. I was anxious to show Alex the house, so I steered a rhumb line straight across the flats, toward Johnson Keys and the Spanish Banks.

When we were several miles out Alex leaned close. "Out here on the water, you'd never know a major hurricane had just passed through. You have no idea how much I've missed being here."

She stood up next to the helm then, and spread her arms wide above her head, her blond hair flying in the wind. She let out a loud yell. I admired her love for the open water; it was the one thing I knew we'd always have in common. Ten minutes later, we rounded Little Spanish Key and the small island just to its north and turned due west to cut between Big Spanish Key and Cutoe Key. The water there was usually very skinny, but the tide was high, so I knew we had at least eighteen inches under the outboard's skeg. More than enough for Rusty's skiff.

"What's that?" Alex said, pointing toward the small island on our left.

I looked and at first didn't see anything. Alex, being a flats guide, was much more attuned to reading the water. Then I saw what looked like a coconut just off the tip of the island. The coconut suddenly lifted from the water and splashed. *What the hell?*

Alex was already unhooking the pole from under the gunwale and said, "Turn that way, it's a dog!"

I turned toward the island and slowly backed down on the throttle. When I reached idle speed, Alex stepped back to the poling platform and I shut down and raised the engine. She poled us toward the island and sure enough, there was a dog in the water. It kept jumping and going under, as if it was in trouble. Then suddenly, it came up with a good-sized snapper firmly in its jaws. "Well, I'll be damned," I said. "A fishing dog?"

Alex poled closer. The dog hadn't noticed us yet. It was too wrapped up in catching the fish. It turned and headed back to the little island, which really wasn't anything more than a sandbar with a couple of very frayed palm trees on it.

About twenty yards from shore, we grounded. I stepped out as Alex put the pole on the deck and joined me. Together, we hauled the skiff a little higher onto the sandbar and followed in ankle-deep water after the dog. Our sloshing must have alerted it. It turned toward us, the snapper still in its mouth, flopping to get free. The dog's ears came up and it started wagging its thick tail.

"He's some kind of Labrador Retriever mix, I think," Alex said, walking toward the large dog. "How'd you get out here, boy?" She turned to look at me. "You think he was washed away from wherever he lived during the storm?" she asked me.

"Could be," I replied. "But there's not a house for several miles out here." The dog looked at me, as if it expected me to do something. "Here, boy," I said. The dog trotted straight to me, with the fish still in his mouth. He stopped directly in front of me and sat in the water, his large tail stirring the sandy bottom. I reached my hand out and the dog dropped the fish right in it.

"Unbelievable," was all I could say.

"I think you've made a new friend, Captain," she said, laughing.

The dog looked over at her, then back up to me. He wasn't wearing a collar or anything to identify him. He was large, probably over 60 pounds, with a face shaped like a Lab's. His salty black coat was coarse and stringy, and the hair on top of his head was matted and curling up, making him look like one of those gremlins from the movie.

"We can't leave him here, Jesse," Alex said.

"No, I don't suppose we can. Let's try to get him into the skiff. We can take him back to Marathon with us tomorrow. Maybe the vet there can scan him for a microchip or something. I don't think he's a wild stray. He seems pretty well trained."

Looking down at the dog, I said, "Want to go for a boat ride, boy?"

With that, he sprang up and went straight to the skiff in about four big leaps.

"Unbelievable," I said again.

He stood waiting by the side of the boat as Alex and I walked back.

When we reached the skiff, Alex said, "Get in, boy." The dog just glanced at her, then looked back up at me.

"Do what the lady says, dog," I told him. "Get in the boat."

The dog instantly leaped in, went straight up to the bow, and sat, looking forward.

"Unbelievable," I said for the third time.

"Well, he's certainly a man's dog, wherever he came from," Alex conceded with laugh.

We pushed the skiff back out a few feet to where it floated and turned it toward deeper water. Alex climbed in and I pushed it deeper, until the water reached the middle of my shin, and then climbed in. Meanwhile, Alex took her position on the poling platform and poled us out until the water was deep enough to lower the engine, then came forward and stored the pole in its place under the gunwale.

I lowered the engine and started it up. The dog remained in the bow of the skiff and only looked back once when I started the engine. I slowly idled out away from the island into deeper water and then gradually increased the throttle until the skiff lifted onto plane. Then I turned toward my island home and opened up the throttle once more. A few minutes later, we entered Harbor Channel, where I sometimes caught big snook. I turned into my channel and slowed the engine to idle speed. Just as I suspected, the island was a mess. The palm trees were frayed, and a lot of the scrub was completely washed away, including the several large piles I'd made. But the house looked to be completely unscathed.

"It's beautiful, Jesse. Just like I'd imagined it." Alex turned toward me, her face beaming. "It sits pretty high off the water, though."

"I built it with the intent of bringing the *Revenge* up here and docking her underneath," I said. "Jimmy and

I are going to use Rusty's barge and loader to dig the channel enough to get her through." I motored into the little turning basin and backed the skiff up under the house to the dock.

"Oh my God," Alex said, looking around worriedly. "Where's your Maverick?"

"Up there," I said, pointing to where the skiff had been lifted directly above the other side of the docks. "We'll lower her later. I want you to see the house."

She looked up, puzzled. Then, noting the boxed-in area with the corrugated steel on the underside and the two lifts at either end, she commented, "Very ingenious, Captain."

"One of the mottos of the Corps," I said. "Improvise, adapt, overcome."

I tied off the skiff and together we grabbed the bags and started toward the steps leading up to the house. The dog was still sitting patiently in the bow of the skiff.

"Come on," I said, and the dog jumped over the gunwale and onto the dock. He trotted past us and up the steps to the deck, where he barked once and sat down, looking out over the island.

"Hmm, what do you make of that?" I asked.

"Almost like he thinks this is his home, huh?" she said.

The dog sat there looking out at the clearing and then up at me. "You want to explore, don't you?" I said. "Go ahead, then."

He was off like a shot, leaping down the back stairs to the sand and off toward the underbrush. I experimented and yelled, "Stop!" The dog immediately stopped in the sand and looked back at me.

"Amazing," Alex said. "He's obviously very well-trained."

"Go ahead," I called out to the dog and he was off again, nose to the ground, running back and forth across the newly cleared patch of the island toward the brush on the far side.

"Unbelievable," I said under my breath for the fourth time.

I unlocked the door and opened it for Alex to step inside, leaving the bags on the deck by the door. She stepped into the large front room and looked all around as her eyes adjusted to the gloom. In the galley area, she ran her fingers along the smooth, polished mahogany countertop. Then she spotted the small radio on the shelf and switched it on. Smooth jazz resonated off the dense wood walls. She turned completely around in the middle of the living room, noting the heavy oak furnishings and comfortable-looking couch and recliner.

Slowly and seductively, she started toward me, then wrapped her arms around my neck. "I approve, Captain." She stepped up on her toes and kissed me, grinding her pelvis into my own. Then she let go and turned around again, saying, "But it's kind of dark in here for mid-afternoon."

"Tell ya what," I said. "If you'll put the bags away, I'll get the storm shutters off the windows. Then we can relax before supper."

"What's on the menu?" she asked.

Lifting the fish, the dog had caught, I said, "Fresh snapper, fried light."

She began to laugh heartily, holding her stomach. Finally, she got control and said, "Give me that. Where's the cleaning board?"

"Down by the docks, on the right," I replied. "But you don't have to do that." I should have known better with a woman like Alex.

"What?" she said, "You think I'm some kind of squeamish city woman who can't clean a fish?" She started laughing again and headed out the door. I grinned, reveling in her amusement.

It only took me a half hour to get the storm shutters off and stored away. I started with the kitchen window and worked my way around the house, stacking two or three together before carrying them down to the storage locker below. By the time I was finished, I could smell garlic and onions, mixed with the wonderful aroma of fresh snapper.

The sun was starting to get lower in the sky, painting the wispy cloud tops with pastel pink, orange and red hues as we sat down at the table on the deck to eat. She'd found her way around my little galley pretty well, it seemed. Along with the snapper, we had fried plantains, which grew wild all over the island, big hunks of roasted potatoes, and fresh biscuits, with a bottle of French Merlot.

Setting down her wineglass, she looked at me and smiled. "It's really beautiful out here. I've always loved the back country. I find the quiet and solitude is comforting. How'd you ever find this place to start with?"

"Well," I replied, "I was at the courthouse down in Key West, getting the *Revenge* registered."

"Before we met or after?

"A few years before," I said. "So, I'm waiting there and there's a bunch of flyers in a little display thing on the counter. *Own Your Own Island*, they said. I picked one up and was idly looking it over while I waited. The county was selling several of the smaller islands around here, with the idea that they'd be used for fishing camps. When the clerk finished with my title transfer and registration, she saw me looking at the brochure and asked me if I was thinking about buying an island. She said there hadn't been a lot of interest, due to the remoteness of the islands that were available for sale and the high price the county was selling them for. So, I asked about selling prices and she said it depended on the size and location. I showed her the map on the flyer, pointed to the Content Keys, and asked about one of the smaller islands here. She had me wait while she went to get the county clerk. He told me that there were several islands available here, about $15,000 an acre and asked if I was interested. Long story short, I went to his office and made a deal on this island for $25,000 and got the septic, construction, and channel permits thrown in, with a ten-year construction clause. I didn't do much the first few years, just cleared the brush in the interior and cleaned it up a little."

"Well, I love it here. Who did you get to build the house?"

"I did everything myself. Well, except the septic system and the concrete piers. That cost more than the island. The piers go down fifteen feet and the septic system is discharged into a deep well that goes way down below the limestone bubble."

"What do you do for water?"

I pointed up to the far corner of the back of the house. "A rainwater cistern on the roof. The gutters go into a sump and the water's pumped up to the tank. There's a cold-water shower right under it, plus a hot-water shower in the head. It only holds two thousand gallons, though, and the propane water heater's only fifteen gallons, so I have to be conservative, especially in the dry season. That's one of the main reasons I want to bring the *Revenge* up. It has a desalinization system on board. It'd be nothing to top the cistern off if it gets low."

Just then, we heard the clicking of the dog's claws on the steps as he came back from exploring the island. We both had a little left on our plates, so Alex went inside and got an old bowl from the cupboard and scraped everything into it.

"You're going to need to get some dog food," she said, placing the bowl on the deck. The dog sniffed it and looked up at me. "Go ahead," she said. "It's yours—you caught it." The dog glanced up at her, and then looked back at me. "Oh, good grief, tell him it's okay."

"Go ahead," I said to the dog, and he dug into the bowl of leftovers. "No, he's not staying long, so leftovers will be fine for a while. That dog belongs to someone and I'm sure they're missing him right now."

"Well, in the meantime, he needs a name," she said. You can't just keep calling him *dog*. How about Pescador?"

I laughed at the inference, *pescador* being the Spanish word for fisherman. "Yeah, fisherman it is," I said. "What do you think, Pescador?"

The dog had finished eating and looked up at me, barking once.

"If he's going to stay inside, he needs a bath," she said. "If you take care of that, I'll get the dishes. I imagine after that storm your cistern should be full."

I got up and said to the dog, "Heel, Pescador," and walked around the deck to the cold-water rinse, with the dog trotting right beside me.

"Unbelievable," I said yet again.

Alex gathered up the dishes and the empty bottle of Merlot and went inside. I got the dog under the shower and rinsed him down well. He stood perfectly still while I lathered him up with a bar of hand soap and rinsed him again. When I turned off the water, he shook himself vigorously, sending sheets of water all over the place, including me. I took the dog over to the other side of the deck and, experimenting again, ordered him to stay.

Since I needed a shower anyway, I went back over to the outdoor shower, stripped down, stepped under the cold shower until I was completely wet, then shut off the water and started lathering up.

"Starting without me, Captain?" Alex asked. I opened my eyes and saw her standing hipshot, leaning on the railing, looking at me. Without saying another word, she removed her shirt and jeans and stepped into my embrace. When I turned the water on, she shrieked at the sudden cold flow pouring over her. Then she melted into my arms again and we kissed, long and slow, as the sun slowly dropped down to the horizon.

We finished our shower, not without some discomfort and obvious arousal on my part and padded naked into the house.

I held the door as she walked inside, then turned to the dog and said, "You coming?"

"Not even breathing hard," Alex shot back as she disappeared into the bedroom, enjoying her own joke.

The dog followed us into the house. I pulled a musty old poncho liner off a shelf in the closet, folded it up in the corner for him, and said, "This is your place, okay?"

To my surprise, he stepped onto the liner, turned around twice, and then curled up in the middle of it.

"Goodnight, Pescador," I said, scratching him behind the left ear.

When I walked into the bedroom, Alex had a hurricane lamp lit on the dresser, turned down low. She was lying on her side in my bed, with her head propped up on one hand.

"Unbelievable," I breathed once more as I closed the door and joined her.

CHAPTER
TWELVE

I woke before sunrise. Alex was still asleep, her head resting on my shoulder. Slowly, I eased my arm out from under her and rose from the bed. Quietly, I opened the door and found Pescador still lying in the same spot I'd left him in the night before. He lifted his head and looked at me expectantly, so I eased the bedroom door closed, crossed the room to open the front door and then motioned to him with my finger. He trotted over to me and out the door, and once I told him to, "go ahead," he bounced happily down the steps and lifted his leg on the pier under the house. I stood at the railing and urinated into the water below.

Just two guys being guys, I thought. He came back up the steps and stood by the door waiting for me.

"No opposable thumbs, huh?" I asked, as I opened the door.

Alex was in the kitchen, wearing one of my long-sleeved denim shirts. Man, did she look sexy like that. I came up behind her and wrapped my arms around her narrow waist as she mixed eggs with some cheese and chives in a bowl.

"Is that the uniform of the day?" she asked, noting my nakedness without looking.

"It could be," I replied, kissing her neck and cupping a breast through the fabric of my shirt.

"Go get dressed while I make breakfast," she said. "We're going fishing as soon as it gets light."

"Aye aye, ma'am," I said and did as I was ordered.

I was looking forward to seeing how she earned a living. I was an open water angler, using heavy rods and reels. Her lightweight fly rods were foreign to me. This was going to be an experience.

We ate outside on the deck again, using a hurricane lantern for light as the eastern sky slowly changed from black to indigo. It was going to be a beautiful day.

As if reading my thoughts, Alex said, "I've always marveled at how crisp and clear the sky is after a storm. It's like the earth has scrubbed itself clean."

"Should be a good day on the cut. Will you show me how to cast one of your fly rods?" I asked.

"You've never used light tackle? That's hard to believe."

"Spinning reels, sure," I said. "Never had a chance to use a fly rod, though. I've always thought it looked cool, though. Very graceful and artistic."

"Okay, I'll teach you. Can't be any harder than when I taught my brother."

Her eyes went kind of cloudy for a second or two. I knew she must miss him terribly. Then she shook it off. "He turned out to be pretty good at it. But somehow, I don't think there's a lot of grace in that big, raw-boned body of yours." She laughed that laugh I'd fallen for over two years ago. "You need any help getting your Maverick down?"

"No, I can handle it easy enough," I replied.

"Get to it then, Captain. I'll get these dishes cleaned up and join you in a few minutes. Should we take Pescador?"

"Well, I don't think it'd be smart to leave him here. He might swim off again," I replied as I got up and started down the front steps to the docks. "Come on, Pescador. The admiral wants her launch in the water."

The dog rose from where he had lain after eating his breakfast and trotted along beside me. At the docks, I got the heavy plank down and laid it across the handrails to remove the nuts holding the corrugated metal in place under the skiff. Once I had the metal put away and the nuts threaded back on, I removed the plank and started lowering the skiff. First the bow, then the stern, working back and forth until she was riding in the water once more. I tied her off, pulled the straps clear and winched them back up to the underside of the floor.

Then I pulled one of my lightweight spinning rods out of the storage closet and stowed it aboard, just in case. I had just started the outboard when Alex came down the steps to the dock. She handed me her rod cases and a small box of flies and I held her hand as she stepped into the skiff.

Glancing at the dog still watching from the dock, I ordered, "Load up."

He jumped over the gunwale, went straight to the forward casting deck and sat down, looking forward.

"I'm starting to like this dog," I said with a smile.

"He certainly seems to know boats," she said. "I can't help wondering how he ended up way out here."

I cast off and put the skiff in forward, slowly idling down the channel to deeper water, then turned left. We headed northeast toward the cuts that opened into the deeper waters of the Gulf of Mexico. The natural channel we were in was about fifteen feet deep on the left and shallower on the right. I'd pulled quite a few lobsters out of there last season.

At the end of this channel were several cuts made by the changing tides moving water over the flats. As we moved quietly over the water at about ten knots, the dog turned his head to the left, stood up on the casting deck and started barking. Alex and I both looked over to see what he was barking at.

"Slow down, Jesse," Alex said.

I backed the skiff down to idle speed, still looking off to port as the dog continued to bark at something. I couldn't see anything other than the sandbar on the other side of the deep part of the channel and the undulating green water. The sun was just peeking above the horizon behind us.

"Right there," Alex said, pointing. "Turn into those flats and shut off the engine." I still didn't see anything, but the backwater was her habitat and I trusted her instinct. The dog stopped barking once we nudged the sand flats. He just stood there, staring intently at whatever it was that had caught his eye.

Alex opened one of her cases and took out a three-piece fly rod and reel. She had it assembled in seconds, tied one of the flies to the line, and was on the casting deck standing next to the dog before I even had the engine tilted up. Standing up, I turned to where they were both looking, but still didn't see a damn thing.

"What is it?" I asked.

"Right over there," she said, pointing with her rod. "There are three bonefish tailing the flats near that small coconut tree. You don't think the dog saw them, do you?"

"At this point, I don't think there's much about this animal that would surprise me. There! I see them now," I replied.

"Okay, here's your first lesson. Watch carefully," she said. Then she stripped 30 or 40 feet of line off the reel, dropping it at her feet. Lifting the rod tip so that ten feet of line fell from the end, she dropped the fly into the water. Then she whipped the rod back horizontally to her right before rolling it in a low arc forward. Some of the line came up off the deck and stretched out in front of her. Just before it fell to the water, she whipped the rod horizontally back and repeated the slight arc forward. More line came up off the deck as it stretched in a slow roll out to its full length again. Once more, just before it settled to the water, she repeated the whipping movement. Now the rest of the line came up off the deck and stretched forward. The fly at the end of the line slowly rolled out and very lightly touched the water. Her line still hung in the air, only the fly touching the water, very near where the three fish were moving, slightly in front of them. She whipped the rod once more, with the same arcing motion behind her, then snapping it forward. The fly touched the water again, right in front of the lead fish. This time, the fish exploded on the fly.

Alex's rod bent nearly double. She moved to the side, away from the direction the fish was going. It started stripping line from the reel at a dizzying pace, headed across the flats away from us. When the fish turned right, she brought the rod around and pulled to the left. It was really a beautiful thing to see.

"You never want to pull straight up," she said nonchalantly, as if nothing was going on. "Side pressure will tire the fish faster and with light tackle it's all about tiring the fish. Bonefish have a hard palate, which is how they get their name. A barbed hook is useless, so it's very important to always keep pressure on the rod, so the hook doesn't fall out of its mouth. If he turns and makes a run at you, you have microseconds to strip line back and keep the pressure on him."

As if the fish were following her instructions, it turned toward us and she quickly stripped back ten or fifteen feet of line, always keeping the rod tip bent. Then it turned back to the left and she brought the rod over her head and down to her right. She held the line with her fingertip now, and as the fish started to tire, she reeled the line up off the deck, still keeping the rod tip bent. Once the line was off the deck, she started reeling the fish in toward the boat.

The bonefish turned and made another run, stripping a few feet from the reel until it became exhausted. She quickly reeled the fish up close to the boat and dipped it up out of the water with a net that seemed to appear in her hand from nowhere. She reached in and easily removed the fly from the fish's mouth, lifted the fish out of the net and held it up to me. It was the first bonefish I'd ever seen up close. It was a beautiful fish, long and powerful-looking, with silvery flanks and darker gray stripes running the length of its body.

She bent over the side of the boat and lowered the fish back into the water. Holding it by the forked tail. With her other hand under its belly, she slowly moved it back and forth, forcing water through its mouth and across its gills. Suddenly, the fish shot out of her hands and disappeared.

"That was incredible," I said. "Lady, you are a true artist. Now, I see why you have such a reputation around here." I was dumbstruck and in complete awe of this fantastic woman. I suddenly saw her in a completely new light.

"Well, bonefish are fun and challenging," she said. "But they don't put food on the table. Let's go get some snook."

The dog barked, wagging its tail.

"Your wish is my command, Admiral Fish Slayer," I said.

She laughed and came back to sit next to me, planting a big wet one on my lips. We fished the cuts the rest of the morning, but I'm afraid the woman was right. I just couldn't get the hang of the magical way she used a fly rod. Eventually, I had to break out my spinning rod. We both caught two nice snook, which we put in the live well, and headed back to the house. Once there, I cleaned the fish and told Alex we really needed to get back to Marathon before sunset. I didn't want to risk hitting anything that might've blown up into Rusty's canal and could possibly tear the bottom out of the skiffs. Plus, I wanted to get the dog to a vet as soon as possible to see if he was microchipped.

After a quick lunch, we loaded our stuff into the two skiffs, and I locked up the house. Alex would take Rusty's and follow me in my Maverick. Since Pescador seemed more comfortable with me, he rode in the bow of my boat, and when I started the engine, he just looked back at me and barked once.

We returned the same way we'd come, across the flats. Crossing Spanish Banks, I happened to glance down at the console and noticed the light on my phone was flashing and the display showed Rusty's number. I backed the

Maverick down and Alex pulled up alongside. "What's wrong?" she asked.

"Rusty's calling," I replied. By the time I picked the phone up, he'd disconnected, so I called him back and he answered on the first ring.

"Someone's here looking for you, Jesse," he said, without even saying hello.

"Who is it?" I asked.

"Didn't say. Bro, he's on your boat."

"He's what?" I yelled, standing up.

"I told him not to, but he just said to mind my own business. I'm looking at him now, just sitting there in the fighting chair, like it's his own damn boat."

"We're on our way in, should be there in a half hour. Keep an eye on him, would ya?"

"Consider it done," Rusty said and clicked off.

"What's going on?" Alex asked.

"We'll figure that out when we get there, but let's haul ass." I was pissed. The number one rule of the sea was that you never boarded a man's boat without first asking permission. I opened the throttle and together we roared across the flats and motored into the canal to the *Rusty Anchor* about an hour before sunset.

We pulled up to the dock and tied off. I could see the guy sitting there on my boat. So did Alex. "Why's someone on the *Revenge*?" she asked. "Do you have a charter scheduled?"

"No, no charter," I replied. "Why don't you go on up ahead to the bar? I'm gonna see what this clown wants."

As she walked toward the bar, I took my time setting our bags up on the dock next to where Pescador sat waiting. The last one was my go bag, and before I set it up on the dock, I pulled my Sig out, stuck it behind my back under the waistband of my pants, and pulled my T-shirt down over it. I walked slowly toward the barge, watching the guy closely, the dog at my side. He was about average height and weight, neither tanned nor pale. He had dark hair graying a little at the temples. I couldn't see his eyes, as he was wearing a pair of expensive-looking dark sunglasses. He wasn't dressed like a local, but didn't look like a banker, either. As I stepped onto the gangplank, he stood and faced me.

CHAPTER
THIRTEEN

Sorry for boarding without permission, Captain McDermitt. But I knew it would be the easiest way to separate you from anyone that might be with you. Your wife?" he asked.

"Who the hell are you and what are you doing on my boat?" I asked, purposely ignoring his question. I'd removed my own sunglasses and I'm sure he could tell by the look in my eyes that I didn't like him being there.

"Deuce told me about you," he replied. "He also said he'd told you that I'd be visiting. I'm Jason Smith."

The name on the card Deuce gave me. His new boss. I quickly and lightly stepped down off the gangplank. The dog stayed at the end of the gangplank and sat down. Smith extended his hand, but I ignored it.

"I don't like anyone, especially people I don't know, coming aboard when I'm not here."

"Like I said, Captain, I needed to talk to you alone." He turned and opened a briefcase that was sitting on the stern fish box, pulling out a thick, plain file folder. "I've read your SRB, captain. Very impressive."

A Marine's Service Record Book contained everything a person did during their time in the military. Everything. In my case, there was quite a bit of confidential information in there. If he had my full SRB, he had connections.

"I told Deuce I wasn't interested in any job offer. Besides, at 44, I'm way too old to be of any help to you guys."

"Deuce wasn't able to tell you what I can. Please, just hear me out. If you're not interested, I'll buy you a beer and be on my way. However, I am going to give you a basic outline and tell you some things that are of a— shall we say— sensitive nature. Nothing we discuss can go further than this boat. May we go inside the salon?"

"After you," I replied and unlocked the cabin hatch. "Stay, Pescador," I said to the dog. He looked at me and raised his ears but remained where he was.

Smith picked up his briefcase and stepped through the hatch into the salon. "Make it quick," I said. "I have things to do."

"This will only take a few minutes, I assure you." He took a seat at the settee and opened the briefcase, sliding the file folder over to me. "Go ahead, see for yourself," he said.

I picked up the folder and opened it. It was my SRB, all right. The whole thing. No redactions. How could anyone outside of high-level personnel in the special operations community get their hands on this? Okay, so the dude was the real deal.

"Captain, I'm the head of one of four teams being created to form a new anti-terrorist organization," he said, as I leaned on the counter across from him. "Each of these teams will work totally independently of one another and each team leader will handpick and train their own personnel. I've been tasked with creating a team of highly trained operatives and have been given carte blanche access to our country's best-trained military and civilian personnel. Deuce, Art and Tony are part of my team, along with another twenty or so men and women from various military, law enforcement, and IT organizations. My team's focus will be on the Caribbean, primarily. There's a growing terrorist threat down here. A number of terrorist factions are at work throughout the Caribbean and Central and South America. Gaining access to our shores here is quite easy, as I'm sure you're aware. I've filled just about every position needed, except one. Deuce is my team leader and as I said, he contacted me after meeting you, suggesting that you might be a good candidate for our needs. I must say, after reading your jacket there and coming down here to see for myself, I tend to agree. The last position is that of a transporter. The ideal person would be someone in, or recently separated from, the spec-ops community, with a strong background in underwater work. He'd be well- established in the local community, with easy access to a boat large enough to move men and equipment to where we need them."

"Whoa there, Smith! No way would I take the *Revenge* out onto blue water with twenty people aboard. Even if I was inclined to accept your offer. Which I'm not."

"Please allow me to finish, Captain," he said. "Our team consists of twenty or so people, but only half of those will be field operatives and those will be broken down into three-to-five-man teams, as the need presents itself. They'll all train together to maintain unit cohesion, but when they go afield, they'll work mostly alone, but in constant contact with their other team members. Our missions, thankfully, should be rare, with most of our time spent training. Your services might be called upon once or twice a year. You'd continue doing what you do now, but you'd be supplied with some extra equipment to facilitate our needs. When called upon, you'd take a fire team and their equipment out for a *fishing* trip, so to speak. You'll be compensated with a generous monthly stipend, deposited into an account in the Caymans. Any specialized equipment will be at your disposal. Any *proceeds* picked up during a mission can be kept or disposed of, as you and the team you're working with see fit. You'd have to come up to Homestead to go through some training, perhaps a week. Mostly to familiarize yourself with new equipment and for the teams to get to know you."

I stood up and, from the large porthole at the rear of the salon, looked out across the cockpit to the *Anchor*, where Alex and my friends were. The dog gazed back at me from where I'd told him to stay. I pretty much liked my life just the way it was, and with Alex back in it, I damn sure didn't want to upset the apple cart. What he told me was intriguing, though. Deuce and his guys would be the pointy tip of the sharp end of the spear.

Rusty was the only person around here who knew anything at all about my time in the Corps and even he didn't know everything.

Would Alex stay if she knew about my past? Could I take this offer and risk losing her again? No, I decided. It just wasn't in the cards anymore. There was a time when I'd been a warrior. I'd done my duty and performed to the best of my ability. I was good at what I did. But those days were behind me now. A warrior had to have a warrior attitude. I'd lost that over the past few years down here and doubted it could be honed back into a person's psyche.

"The answer's still no," I said, without looking back. "You owe me a Red Stripe."

Then I opened the hatch and stepped down into the cockpit. Without looking back, I crossed the gangplank and headed across the yard to the *Anchor* to rejoin my life, the dog trotting by my side.

Smith followed. I walked into the bar, where Alex was sitting on a stool, talking to Julie and Rusty. When I walked in, all three of them went silent and turned to look at me.

"Who is that guy?" Alex asked.

"Just a prospective charter," I replied. That seemed to satisfy Alex and Julie, but Rusty looked skeptical.

"Oh my God," Julie said. "Where'd that Portuguese Water Dog come from?"

"What the hell's a Portuguese water dog?" I asked.

"That scraggly mutt you just came in with," she replied.

"We thought it was a Lab mix," Alex said. "We found him on a sandbar, up on Spanish Banks."

"I'm pretty sure he's a Portuguese Water Dog," Julie said.

Alex laughed. "Well, that would sure explain a lot of things."

Just then, Smith came through the door. I sat down next to Alex, turned to Smith, and said, "Just give me a call when you and your friends firm up the date you want to go fishing, okay?"

"Sure thing, Captain," he replied. He took a stool at the end of the bar and said to Julie, "Beer's on me, miss." Julie pulled two cold Red Stripes from the icebox and set them on the bar in front of Alex and me. Rusty still stood behind the bar, near where I knew he kept a short-barreled shotgun, closely watching Smith. I caught his eye and gave an almost imperceptible shake of my head, letting him know to stand down. He relaxed then. A little.

"The power's still out," Rusty said. "FPL guys are working on it, but it'll prolly be a few more days. I gotta run over to Dion's to get more gas for the generator. He's got a big diesel back-up going, so he can stay open. You guys want anything?"

"Sure," Alex replied. "Give Rufus the day off and get some of Dion's chicken."

"I can do that," Rusty said, smiling as he headed to the door. Just then, it opened, and two guys came in, one holding a gun.

"Let's see some hands, people!"

The guy who shouted it was skinny, with long, stringy hair. He was holding a nasty-looking snub-nosed .38 revolver, moving it back and forth over all of us. The other guy looked like he'd just crawled out from under a dumpster.

"Out from behind that bar, you two," second man shouted, motioning to Rusty and Julie.

The guy with the gun herded us all toward the back corner of the bar, while the other guy moved behind the bar to the register.

"Easy with that thing," I said. "No need to hurt anyone here."

The dog was standing beside me, obviously on full alert. I looked down at him and said, "Stay." He immediately sat down but kept his eyes and ears on the intruders.

"I'll give the orders, old man," Stringy said, taking a step closer.

Rusty's shotgun was in plain view behind the bar, but Dumpster had his back to it. In a few seconds, he was sure to turn around and see it. I needed Stringy to take one more step before then.

"Well, ain't you a pretty lady?" Stringy said to Alex, who was standing behind my right shoulder. "Two pretty ladies," he added, when he noticed Julie standing behind my other shoulder. Rusty was to her left and Smith was beside him. Stringy took another step forward and said, "Step aside, pops."

I made to step aside slightly, to his right, in front of Alex. Then my left hand shot out, grabbing his gun hand at the wrist. Yanking it straight up and away from him, while twisting his wrist unnaturally made the gun go off. It discharged harmlessly, straight up, but caused Dumpster to spin around.

Stepping forward with my right foot, I hooked it behind Stringy's knee, and in the same motion, brought my elbow straight into his face, smashing his nose and toppling him backwards. Blood sprayed in an arc as he went down, landing head first. The gun clattered across the floor. I instinctively reached to the small of my back and pulled the Sig out as Rusty rolled forward, coming up in a kneeling position with the revolver. He pointed it at the unconscious and bleeding gunman. Dumpster had finally noticed the shotgun and was reaching for it when I fired one round, striking the oak armrest at the edge of the bar, sending splinters into his face. I now had his complete and undivided attention. Smith was just starting to reach under his coat.

"Get out here and on the deck, next to your buddy," I hissed. "Or the next one goes through your thick skull."

He stepped slowly out from behind the bar and got on the floor next to Stringy. Rusty came up from his kneeling position, stepped over to me and handed me the .38.

"Gimme the Sig, Jesse," he said. Turning to the others, he asked, "You guys want that chicken spicy or regular?"

Alex stepped out from behind me and kicked Dumpster right between the legs, causing him to curl into a fetal position, moaning and holding his balls.

"You animals got a lot of nerve, looting defenseless people after a hurricane," she said. For a second, I felt sorry for the guy.

The dog stood over Stringy's head, a deep, menacing rumble seeming to come from his whole body. I handed Rusty my Sig and took the .38, keeping both men covered. Rusty headed out the door without another word. I knew that he knew my Sig was unregistered. He'd stash it in his pickup and be back from Dion's after the cops got here.

It was doubtful that the cops would notice the hole in the roof; instead, they would assume I'd disarmed one guy and simply missed shooting the other, hitting the bar. At least, that was the story I'd tell. Hopefully, they wouldn't do a ballistics analysis. But a 9mm bullet and a .38 are very close to the same size.

Julie went out the back door and came back with a length of nylon rope, talking to Marathon PD Dispatch on her cell. "Yeah, the *Rusty Anchor Bar and Grill*," she said into the phone. "Mile marker 50.1, oceanside. Both men are down and probably need an ambulance, as well as handcuffs. So, no need to hurry. I know you guys are busy."

She handed Alex one end of the rope as she closed her phone and shoved it into a hip pocket of her shorts. Together they bound Stringy and Dumpster with their hands behind their backs, tied to each other. I knew that with Julie and Alex's combined boating experience, those two guys weren't going anywhere. So, I walked over and laid the .38 on the bar, next to the splintered armrest.

Smith followed me to the bar and said, "Remind me to never fuck with you islanders."

"You can leave, Smith," I said, picking up my beer. "No need for you to be here when the locals arrive. Thanks for the beer." I knew he didn't want to be around to answer any questions.

"I'll call you next week," he said as he headed toward the door Rusty had just left through. Walking by me, he said under his breath, "Very nice work, Gunny."

I heard his engine start up in the parking lot and the crunch of tires on the shell driveway.

Three cops arrived after about ten minutes. Before they got there, I'd told Alex and Julie the story they were to give. I was sitting at the bar while two cops were questioning the women when Rusty came back in carrying three large bags from Dion's.

"What the hell's goin' on here?" he asked.

One cop, who was pushing the two thugs toward the door, stopped and asked, "Are you the owner?"

"Yeah, Rusty Thurman," he replied, putting on a stellar performance as a surprised man. "What the hell's goin' on?"

"These two dirt bags tried to rob your place at gunpoint, Mister Thurman. You can thank Captain McDermitt over there for keeping that from happening. He stopped them." The cop then marched the thugs out to a waiting patrol car.

Rusty came over to where one of the cops was questioning Julie behind the bar. Setting the bags down, he said for the benefit of the cop, "What happened, sweetie?"

"Those two guys were going to rob us, Dad. Maybe worse. Jesse stopped them."

"That right, Officer?" he asked.

"Seems that way," the cop said. "Lucky for Captain McDermitt, he missed shooting one guy. He'd have a lot of questions to answer if he hadn't. He did hit your bar, though. I think we're all done here. Those guys will probably be held over until their trial, down at the Department of Corrections in Key West. Your daughter already swore out the complaint."

"Damn," said Rusty. "Step out for some chicken and miss all the fun."

The cops drove slowly down the crushed shell driveway, taking the looters away as we stood in the yard at the *Anchor*. "Your Sig's in the glove box of the pickup, Jesse," Rusty said.

"Why were you carrying a gun?" Alex asked.

"I almost always have one nearby. Especially when someone's on my boat uninvited." Turning to Rusty, I said, "Thanks, *amigo*."

"No problem. Hey, you gonna take that barge north and dig out your channel tomorrow?"

"I promised Deuce I'd go up to Fort Pierce and box up Russ's stuff for him. How about Friday?"

"Yeah," Rusty said, "Friday should be good. FPL's saying that power should be back by Saturday morning. I was thinking of doing a reopening thing on Sunday. Wait a minute. You gonna drive *The Beast* all the way to Fort Pierce? It'll never make it."

"Don't tell me you still have that ugly old thing," Alex interjected.

"Form follows function, lady," I said.

"As I remember, the function part was suspect," Alex said. "We could take my Jeep."

I looked at her and smiled. "I was hoping you'd offer. Didn't really have a plan B."

"Hey, guys," Jimmy said, coming around the barge at the end of the canal. "What's shakin'? Whose dog?"

"Hiya, Jimmy, where've you been?" I asked. "Alex and I found him stranded on an island up near my house."

"He's a cool-lookin' dog. I kinda been with my girlfriend on her houseboat, man. She's cooled off since her close encounter with the storm. Just dropped by to grab my stuff off the *Revenge*."

He hopped down onto the barge and headed toward the gangplank but stopped and turned around halfway across the deck. "Oh yeah, there's some guys over at *Dockside* looking for a fishing charter. Robin at the bar told me to tell you. And to remind you that the dock fee is due next week."

"My dock's destroyed," I said. "It'll be longer than a week before that mess is cleaned up."

"Leave her here," Rusty told me. "Once we get that channel dredged, you can move her up to your house. Ha! Maybe then you can pay your bar tab." Rusty laughed at his own joke.

"Are you going over to *Dockside*?" Alex asked. Robin was a constant flirt who had been a thorn in Alex's side last year. "You know, to see about that charter?" she added.

"No, not right now," I replied. "I think I got enough coin to cover my tab for a week or so longer." Jimmy was stepping down off the gangplank into the cockpit of the *Revenge* as I yelled out to him, "Hey, Jimmy. Rusty's got some chicken from Dion's inside. You interested?"

"Thanks for the invite, man. But Angie's cooking."

The three of us turned toward the bar and the dog trotted along beside me. "Jimmy turning down Dion's chicken?" Rusty said. "Angie's good for him. Keeps him away from the ganja. Hope they can work it out."

Julie had a table set for us inside and Rusty had picked up some food for the dog, too. Until the power came back on, they were keeping the closed sign up. So, we had a nice meal with no interruptions, just good friends and good, cold beer. Afterward, Alex and I retired to the *Revenge* to watch the sunset from the bridge.

"You don't have a tuna tower like most of those big fishing boats," she remarked, while pouring two glasses of wine.

"I would've had to build the house another ten feet higher and I'm scared of heights."

The dog had found a spot in the corner of the salon's L-shaped couch and after making two turns, he'd settled down for a nap.

"I saw you in action a little while ago, Captain. I don't think you're scared of anything."

"Not true," I said. "You scare me."

"*Moi?* How could you be afraid of little old me?"

"I'm afraid you might try to domesticate me," I said, grinning.

She elbowed me in the ribs. Hard.

"Hey, what was that French you and Deuce were talking yesterday?"

"He just said he was pleased to meet me, and I said the pleasure was all mine," she replied. We watched the sunset, finished our wine, and went below.

CHAPTER FOURTEEN

I woke up about an hour before dawn, with Alex once more by my side, curled up and softly snoring. I'd set the coffee maker in the salon to start at o6oo and I could hear it gurgling while the aroma of coffee was wafting up through the hatch. I got up without disturbing her, pulled on my skivvies and a T-shirt and climbed the steps to the galley, where I poured a cup of joe into my big black Force Recon mug before continuing through the salon. The dog looked up at me and whined.

"Come on," I said, and he was through the hatch ahead of me, leaping onto the gangplank. While he crossed the barge and hiked his leg on a gumbo-limbo tree. I kicked back in the fighting chair, put my feet up on the fish box and enjoyed my coffee as I kept an eye on him.

I had always liked the time just before dawn. It was the best time for me to think. Still dark enough to see the stars if it was clear, and it was. The temperature was down in the low 60's and the air was dry, with a slight wind blowing out of the east-southeast, which gave promise for a beautiful morning. If you closed your eyes, you could almost smell the scents of Africa, carrying all the way across the Atlantic.

My thoughts turned to Russ and his new, muscle-bound diving partner named Lester. Deuce had been right; Russ always dove with at least one knife, usually two. One strapped to the inside of his calf and another on the strap of his BC. And just how the hell did an anchor line tangle someone to the point that they couldn't unbuckle and ditch their gear?

I figured if the wind or current were strong, the boat pulling tight on the line might prevent a person from untangling whatever it was fouled on. But cutting the anchor loose would always be an option. Things just didn't add up. Maybe something would turn up when I went up to Fort Pierce.

After about a half hour, the sky to the east was starting to turn purple, and the dog had curled up in the corner of the cockpit. I heard Alex's bare feet in the salon, and the clinking of the coffee pot on a porcelain mug. Then she stepped through the hatch and down into the cockpit. Leaning on the back of my chair, she said, "Looks like it's going to be a beautiful day. Been up long?"

"A little while. Yeah, it's gonna be one of those great south Florida fall days, crisp and clear." I tipped my head back and she leaned forward and kissed me. She was wearing another one of my work shirts and apparently nothing more.

"When do you want to drive up to Fort Pierce?" she asked, sipping her coffee.

"Couple hours. I want to go by *Dockside* when Aaron gets there and settle my account. I've been thinking. Most of my charters are walk-ups and referrals. Without the exposure *Dockside* offers, I might have to advertise or something."

"All you need is a website and some brochures, maybe. Oh, and you need to answer your cell phone occasionally."

"Very funny. But, yeah, I think a website and brochures might do the trick. I'll get Jimmy to start on it."

"That guy on your boat yesterday? The charter? How'd he find you?" she asked, turning to go back into the salon. "More coffee?"

"No, thanks," I replied. "He was a referral. Told him my price, but I doubt I'll hear from him again." Sometimes, lies were necessary.

"Let's go for a run," she said.

"Great idea. If Aaron's at *Dockside*, we can stop in for a minute and kill two birds."

We got dressed and put on our running shoes, then spent ten minutes on the barge, stretching. Since the dog sat watching us, I asked him, "Want to join us?" He jumped to his feet with his tail wagging.

"We need to stop at a vet and see if he's been microchipped," Alex said. "Before you and he get too close."

We started at a good seven-minute-per-mile pace and the dog ran along effortlessly right beside me. I always enjoyed running with Alex. Her form and stride were flawless, and she kept pace with me very easily. We ran along the western dock, then cut through the woods on a trail to Sombrero Beach Road and turned north, up to Sombrero Boulevard. Running west past *Dockside*, in the near darkness, I could see that Aaron's pickup wasn't there yet.

Damage from the storm seemed to be limited to broken branches and downed trees. We continued all the way around the loop and when we got back to *Dockside*, we saw him getting out of his pickup, so we stopped.

"Alex! When'd you get back?" he asked.

"Couple days ago. How've you been?" she asked.

"There've been better days. Nice-looking dog y'all got there. We had quite a bit of damage here. More than a dozen boats went down and another ten or so broke loose. You're lucky you took the *Revenge* out, Jesse. You see that catamaran crashed into your dock?"

"Yeah," I said. "That's what we came by for. I'm moving the *Revenge* up to the house. Wanted to settle up."

"Sure, come on in."

"I'm going to head back and get a shower, Jesse," Alex said. "Good to see you again, Aaron."

"Pescador, go with her," I said to the dog.

She took off at a good pace, with the dog trotting along beside her. Watching her run, I couldn't help thinking that I was slowing her down.

As I walked into the back office with Aaron, a rental car came around the corner and pulled up on the far side of Aaron's pickup. Aaron rolled his eyes and mumbled,

"Them again. Wish you'd take those wharf rats out and drown 'em, man."

"What do you mean?" I asked.

"Those guys keep coming around, asking where you are," he replied. "They said you're taking 'em fishing. You don't know 'em?"

"Nope," I replied. "And when they come in, I'm not me, okay. I got a lot of other things to do besides taking out a charter."

"Yeah, no problem," Aaron said, going through a file cabinet. "Here we are. Your lease is up the end of this month and you're current. Nothing to settle."

Just then, the office door opened and the strangest-looking guy I'd ever seen walked in, followed by another one that looked like a cover model for Steroid Monthly. The first guy was short and had no hair. Not just bald—the dude didn't even have eyebrows. As I was standing by the door when they walked in, they didn't see me.

"Hey, man," Baldy said. "We're still looking for our buddy, Jesse McDermitt. Has he checked in yet? We're really anxious to go fishing."

"McDermitt?" asked Aaron. "No, he's still not back in port."

Stepping out from behind the door, I said, "I got a fishing boat. When you wanna go out?"

Roid Boy was startled, but said, "Nobody's talkin' to you, mister."

"Shut up, Lester," said Baldy. He turned to face me. The guy had very pale blue eyes and almost translucent skin. Very disconcerting. "Thanks, mister. But we're going out with our friend, Jesse McDermitt. That is, if he ever gets back."

Lester? Russ's muscle-bound dive partner? I didn't believe in coincidence. What the hell was Russ's dive partner doing down here? Why was he looking for me? And he apparently didn't even know what I looked like.

"No worries," I said. "I overheard Jesse on the phone the day before the storm. Sounded like he was talking to a client. Something about an offshore charter this week and because of the storm, told the guy he'd take *Gaspar's Revenge* up north and meet him at the Rickenbacker Pier, up in Miami. After the call, he told me he'd be back by the weekend, though. It's not like Jesse to double-book. Are you sure I can't take ya out? I can guarantee a dozen dolphin."

"Well, we, um, didn't exactly set a date with him," Baldy said. "Just kind of a 'when you're in town' sorta thing. Thanks, but we'll just wait till our friend gets back. Or maybe meet him up in Miami." He and Roid Boy smiled when he said that. The guy had a creepy-looking smile. They left the office then and I waited until I heard their car start and drive away.

"Okay," said Aaron. "What just happened?"

"You got me," I said. "But thanks for playing along. If you see those guys again, I had a charter in Bimini for the next two weeks, okay?"

"You got it. Hey, how the hell you gonna get the *Revenge* up to your house?"

"Rusty's got a barge with a backhoe on it," I said. "We're going up there Friday to enlarge my channel."

"Good luck, man."

"Thanks, Aaron. I'll stop by and get my gear and signage off the dock early next week."

I walked slowly back to the *Anchor*, thinking.

CHAPTER FIFTEEN

Lester drove away toward US-1 as Walt dialed his cell phone. When it connected, he said, "No good, Boss. We just found out the guy is out on a charter. Picked his clients up in Miami after the storm and won't be back until the weekend." He listened for a second then said, "At the docks on the Rickenbacker." He listened for a few more seconds, and then said, "Okay, Boss, we can be there by noon. How we gonna find him, though?" Walt listened for a few more minutes, and then said, "When you think he'll be back?" The connection ended. Walt looked over at Lester and said, "Sometimes, I could kill that dweeb. Head to the motel. We gotta be in Miami by noon."

Lester drove the rental to the motel they'd been holed up in for two days to pick up Tomas and Benny. Benny was in the kitchenette cooking jerked chicken, frying a bunch of plantains, and setting off the smoke alarms. Tomas had created a Santeria shrine between two parked trucks and was calling on Chango to better endow him for the ladies.

"Let's go, you idiots," Walt shouted. "Get packed up. Boss says we gotta be in Miami by noon. He's gonna meet us at the docks in a boat."

These two clowns are worthless, Walt thought. *Why the Boss keeps 'em on is anybody's guess. At least the new guy has half a brain.*

Ten minutes later, they were on A1A headed north out of Marathon. The whole way up to Key Largo, they were slowed by power crews working on the lines and construction crews cutting up downed trees. By the time they reached the Rickenbacker Causeway, it was almost noon.

Sonny was waiting at the entrance to the marina when Lester turned in.

"About damn time you guys got here," Sonny said, as Walt climbed out.

"Sorry, Boss," Walt offered, "There was all kinds of road blocks down there from the storm."

"Whatever," Sonny said. "I got my boat docked down at the end. It's the *One-Eyed Jack*. You guys get out there. I want one of you at the helm at all times. If that guy picked his clients up here, he'll have to drop them off here, too. That's when we'll grab him. Remember, the name of the boat we're looking for is *Gaspar's Revenge*. It's a big boat. Try to take him down, get him on my boat and haul ass. If not, take my boat and follow him. It's plenty fast enough to keep up with any fishing boat. Tomas, you can drive a boat, right?"

"*Sí, Jefe,*" Tomas replied. "I worked on boats in Cuba. Is outboard or inboard?"

"It's a thirty-two-foot Carver with twin inboards," Walt replied.

"*Es no problemo, Jefe,*" Tomas said.

"Get to it, then," Sonny said. "Work in six-hour shifts. The *Jack* has two bedrooms. Remember, I want one guy on the bridge at all times. When that guy comes off, I want him alert in the cabin during the next shift as backup. Call me at every shift change. Got it?"

"Whatever you say, Boss," Lester said. "Does your boat have a stove or should one of us go out for some food?"

"Yeah, it's got a stove," Sonny replied. "But don't use it, you'll just fuck it up. Breakfast, lunch, and dinner from now until this McDermitt gets here, one of you make a run. Got it?"

"Will do, Boss," said Walt. "Tomas, take the car and go get some lunch. None of that beaner shit, either. Make it simple— Mickey D's burgers and fries. Come on, you two. I'll take evening watch—this sun kills me. Benny, you're up first. I'll come up and take over at six o'clock. Tomas will take watch from midnight to six in the morning, then Lester from six to noon. We'll keep that schedule until the guy shows up. Whoever's ending the standby watch in the cabin will make a food run."

Sonny nodded to Walt. "Good. Stay on it," he said before turning and walking to his car.

CHAPTER SIXTEEN

I got back to the *Revenge* a few minutes later. The dog was dozing under the same gumbo-limbo tree he'd peed on earlier. I crossed the gangplank and could hear the shower running in the forward head. Walking through the salon, I stripped down and joined Alex as she was rinsing off. The shower stall wasn't exactly built for two people, so it was very cozy.

"Is this your idea of *taking it slow*?" she asked.

"No, just trying to conserve water, is all," I replied, holding her close and kissing her as the water poured down over us.

She broke away and said, "Get cleaned up. We have a lot to do today."

Then she stepped out of the shower. I did as I was ordered and when we were both dressed, we walked to her Jeep, the dog following beside me.

"First stop, the vet," I said. "I called ahead and they're open. They have a lot of animals that were displaced by the storm and said they'd do the check for a microchip, but they wouldn't be able to board him. So, we'll have to take him with us up to Fort Pierce. That okay?"

"Of course," she replied. "I don't think I've ever seen a better-behaved dog in my life. You know, when he and I got back to the boat, he followed me aboard, but when I started to undress in the cabin, he turned and walked out. Very gallant."

"Yeah, he's a real gentleman, that one," I said. "Is there such a thing as a gay dog?"

Alex jabbed me in the ribs with her elbow as we walked to the Jeep.

When we got to the vet's office, one of the assistants checked the dog over top to bottom, stem to stern with an electronic gizmo that was supposed to detect any imbedded microchip. She didn't find one.

"That doesn't mean he doesn't have one," the assistant said. "They only have a lifespan of three or four years. But he looks to be only about two or three years old, at the most. My guess is that he's never been chipped."

"Well, thanks, anyway," I said. "Guess we can run an ad in the local papers. Maybe his owner will respond."

"If you don't find the owner," the woman said, "he'd make a great boat dog, Captain McDermitt. You know he's a Portuguese Water Dog, right? I'd bet he's a pure-bred, too."

We left the vet's office and climbed into the Jeep for the long drive up through the Keys to the mainland and on up the coast to Fort Pierce.

"Let's take Card Sound Road," Alex suggested as we drove through Key Largo. "We can stop for lunch at Alabama Jack's. I haven't been in there in a while."

The trip up through the Middle and Upper Keys took a while, due to all the work on the power lines and downed trees. We made it to the Card Sound Bridge about 1100. After eating an early lunch on the deck overlooking the water, we got back on the road. I truly hated driving through Miami at any time of the day. The interstate was always crowded with drivers going to or from the Keys or the beach, and surface streets were always packed with locals going to and from work. There was really no way to dodge it, but the Sawgrass Expressway at least thinned the herd some because it was a toll road. We took it to avoid traffic. A couple of hours later, we got off the interstate at Highway 70 and headed into Fort Pierce.

CHAPTER
SEVENTEEN

My first order of business was at the Saint Lucie County Sheriff's Office, to pick up Russ's boat and dive gear. I'd looked it up online before we left, so I had a good idea where it was. We took the Midway Road exit off the interstate and found it just a couple of miles toward town. Alex parked the Jeep and we went inside.

Deuce had called ahead to both the sheriff and the apartment manager to clear the way for us. I introduced myself to the desk sergeant, who said he'd been expecting us. He picked up his phone and a few minutes later, a young deputy wearing a name badge that said "Andrews" arrived and took us to the impound lot in back of the building. It was mostly full of cars and pickups, but there were a number of boats, too.

"Should be right down this row," the deputy said, leading us down the second row of cars. "I have the inventory sheet and once you check out the boat, I'll take you to where we stored everything that was on board, and you can put it back in the boat to tow home. Were you a relative?"

"We served together," I replied. "His son's not able to pick his stuff up, so he asked me to."

"Army?" he asked.

"Marines," I replied.

"Here it is," Deputy Andrews said, pointing out a dirty twenty-foot Grady White center-console with a Bimini top, sitting on an aluminum trailer. I walked around to the stern, looking it over. It had a 250-horse Yamaha four-stroke hanging on the back that looked to be only a year or two old. The boat itself was probably five years old but would clean up nice. The smoked-glass cabinet door that housed the electronics was open and empty.

"He kept his boat at a marina," I said. "Where'd the trailer come from?"

"Fort Pierce Inlet Marina," he replied. "When the Marine Patrol towed it in, that's where they docked. The manager there recognized the boat and said he'd stored the trailer with them too, because they didn't allow trailers at Mr. Livingston's apartment complex."

"Okay, everything looks all right," I said. "Let's get the gear."

Andrews took us in through a back door and down a hall to a door marked *Evidence Locker*. Inside was a cage with a door and another deputy sitting just inside the enclosure, working on a computer. There was a counter along the wall, outside the cage.

"Halston," the deputy said, "these are the folks come for Russell Livingston's property."

Halston got up from his desk and said, "Gimme just a minute."

He disappeared down one of the rows of metal shelves, then returned pushing a wheeled cart. He unlocked the cage door and wheeled it out.

Andrews handed me a clipboard and said, "Check over the inventory, then sign on the bottom."

I went over the list of items on the clipboard, matching everything on it to what was on the cart. "Where's the GPS? And car keys?" I asked.

Andrews took the clipboard and looked over the inventory list, then said, "No GPS on the list, Mr. McDermitt. Only keys found were in the boat's ignition."

"I can see that, Deputy," I said. "But there was one on the boat—I saw the wiring and mount for it. And he lived a good seven miles from the marina. Doubtful he walked there."

"Hang on," he said. "The deputy that inventoried the boat is a buddy of mine. I'll give him a call."

Andrews moved near the door and talked on his cell phone for a few minutes, while I finished checking everything on the inventory list.

He walked back over to us and said, "Avery, my buddy that did the inventory, said there was no GPS on the boat, and no car keys found anywhere on the boat or body when he inventoried it. Said it struck him as unusual, so he checked the report and pictures that were taken at the scene, when the Marine Patrol found the body, still tangled in the anchor line. He said the pictures showed the cabinet open and no GPS inside. He checked with the marina manager, who told him the victim's vehicle, an older model Ford pickup, was not in the lot. Might've been stolen, but without anyone to file a complaint, he didn't pursue it further."

I signed the inventory list and handed the clipboard back to Andrews. He took the bottom copy and handed it back to me. "We can wheel this out to the boat, while your wife pulls your car around back to hook up to the trailer."

Both Alex and I ignored his assumption.

Fifteen minutes later, with everything loaded on the boat and the boat hitched to the Jeep, we left the sheriff's office. Alex turned to me as we made our way east on Midway toward US-1, and said, "Any chance your friend forgot his GPS?"

"Not a chance," I replied. "Besides, it wasn't a hand-held—it was mounted and hardwired to a through-hull transducer. He'd have had to intentionally remove it."

I'd been to Russ's place a few times several years ago, but it had been a while. We finally found the apartment complex just off US 1 and found the manager's office. I explained who I was, and the manager told us that Deuce had called ahead to let them know I was coming. After giving me a key to the apartment and directing us to it, she also told us they had a good assortment of boxes for sale to offer tenants who were moving, and she'd be happy to provide whatever we needed. I doubted it'd be very much. She also gave me a list of the furnishings that had been provided by the apartment complex and cautioned me not to take anything on the list.

"We're in a Jeep, ma'am," I said. "If anything, there may be a piece of furniture or two we'll leave behind. All the family wants are his personal affects. Is his pickup in the lot, by any chance?"

"No," she replied. "It hasn't been since the police came, the day he drowned."

We left the office and located the apartment where Russ had lived by himself for the last ten years. I unlocked and opened the door and was immediately shocked at what I saw. I cautioned Alex to back away from the door and slowly pushed it open further. The living room was trashed. Everything was knocked over and strewn all about the place.

"Stay here," I said and slowly entered the apartment, drawing my Sig from the holster at the small of my back.

I went through the living room, stepping around overturned furniture and following the sights of the Sig. I looked across the countertop into the kitchen, and then carefully made my way down the hall. There were only two doors, and both were open. The one on the right was the bathroom. Everything in the medicine cabinet had been knocked to the floor and the shower curtain was open. I crossed the hall and peeked into the bedroom. It too had been thoroughly tossed, but nobody was there. I went back to tell Alex she could come in, and she came through the door with the dog following behind her.

"What happened here?" she asked.

"Someone's been here before us," I replied. "It looks like they were looking for something. I have no idea what, though."

"Should we call the police?" she asked, standing in the middle of the living room.

"No," I said. "Not yet, anyway. Let's look around and see if we can find out what they were looking for. Thieves usually go straight for the bedroom. That's where most people keep their valuables. Whoever did this, it looks like they started in here. Just don't touch anything."

All the cushions were off the couch and the small cocktail table was flipped over. In the kitchen, all the cabinets were open and what little was in them now lay on the floor.

"What we're looking for is where this mess ends," I said. "Once they found whatever they were looking for, they would have stopped tossing things around."

Since the living room and kitchen showed signs of every nook and cranny having been emptied, we went back to the bedroom. Both nightstands were open and everything in them lay on the floor. Same with the dresser. The closet, however, was only partially trashed.

"Here," I said. "This is where whoever searched this place found what they were looking for."

"What do you suppose it was?" she asked.

"Treasure would be my guess. Russ was a treasure hunter and had found quite a bit of it over the years. Not enough to get rich, by any stretch. But enough that he didn't have to work very often. He did some security consulting for a few companies on the side, but he spent most of his time underwater. He was kind of obsessed with it. I know he kept meticulous records in a journal and probably had a few pieces that he hung onto. My guess is that anything of value was stored on the closet shelf up there, along with his journal, which I haven't seen anywhere. Notice how the clothes are still hanging and everything in the bottom of the closet is untouched?"

"Okay," she said. "So, somebody came in and robbed him after he drowned. What good would the journal be, though?"

"It had dates and GPS locations of places he'd searched," I replied. "I'd helped him a few times and he'd written my name on those entries. Had anything turned up from any clues we found, he wanted me to get a part of it."

Lester, the muscle head, I thought.

He obviously had the strength to kill with his bare hands. But could he take out a Recon Marine, trained in hand-to-hand and underwater fighting? Maybe, I thought. If said Marine was older and slower and trusted him. I wanted to have a talk with this Lester. But how to find him? I'd just sent him and Baldy on a wild goose chase to Miami. One thing was certain, he and Baldy were looking for me. Maybe I'd just have to let them find me.

"Okay," I said. "Let's call the cops and report this. Once they get here and take a report, we can clean up this mess and box up Russ's belongings."

The cops arrived about thirty minutes later. I'd told them there was no hurry, that whoever had robbed my friend's apartment was long gone. Fort Pierce, being a small town, did its best to look professional. A crime scene unit arrived a few minutes after the first two patrol cars and they took dozens of pictures and fingerprints. I doubted they'd be able to find who it was, though.

The lead investigator asked, "Did either of you touch anything?"

"Only the doorknob," I replied. "When we first walked in, we had no idea there'd been a break-in."

"I wouldn't exactly call it a break-in," he said. "There's no sign anywhere of forced entry. My guess is whoever did this had a key. A disgruntled ex-wife, maybe?"

"No," I replied. "His ex lives in Philly and hadn't had any contact with him for several years. I really don't know if he'd been involved with anyone else."

"Been?" he asked.

"Yeah," I replied. "Russell Livingston, the guy who lived here, drowned in West Palm a couple weeks ago. You didn't know that?"

"News to me," he replied. "So, what are you two doing here, then?"

"His son's in the service. He contacted me, knowing that Russ and I were friends, and asked me to come up and box up his belongings to send to him."

One of the forensics guys interrupted, saying, "Judging from the mold on the leftovers that were tossed out of the fridge, I'd guess this happened at least ten to twelve days ago, Sergeant."

"Where were you ten to twelve days ago, Mr. McDermitt?" the sergeant asked.

"At home, probably," I replied angrily. "On an island about 270 miles south of here."

"You live in Cuba?" he asked.

"The Content Keys," I replied. "North of Big Pine Key. That's in Florida. And before you ask, she was in Oregon. You're the lead investigator?"

The sergeant looked around and said, "Okay, wrap it up, guys. Looks like this was just a random break-in. Probably left the door unlocked."

"Are you for real?" I said.

"Mr. McDermitt," the sergeant said, "we have pictures and prints. It happened more than a week ago. Not much chance of the perp being anywhere close by. We're done here."

The forensic team packed up their gear and followed the sergeant out the door. They loaded their gear in their vehicles and left.

"You do have a way with people," Alex said, watching them drive away.

"Those guys were imbeciles," I said. "That sergeant couldn't pour water out of a boot, with the directions printed on the sole. Let's go get a few boxes from that manager and get this mess cleaned up."

It took us the whole afternoon and evening to get everything boxed up and the furniture set back to right. We decided to get a room and drive back to Marathon in the morning. After we ate at a nearby restaurant, we checked in at a pet-friendly Holiday Inn near the interstate, just a half mile from Russ's apartment. Sitting at the table in the room, I was wondering how I could find Lester and Baldy. More to the point, I was wondering how I could let them find me and at the same time keep Alex at a safe distance.

I still had the channel to dig this weekend and I'd called Deuce while we were waiting for the cops to let him know what had happened. He told me there were only two things of value that he knew about. One was a Spanish doubloon on a gold chain that Russ usually wore. The other was a gold cross with three imbedded emeralds and a spot where a fourth had been. He said he'd be able to come back down this weekend and asked if I'd be available to go out to Conrad Reef.

"We need to find out who did this," Alex said. "And I'm going with you."

How does she keep reading my mind like that?

I knew it was futile to argue with her, but I wanted her to know everything. So, I told her about Russ having told Deuce about his new muscle-bound dive partner,

Lester, then about my meeting him and his buddy at *Dockside,* when they were looking for me, of all people, and how I'd sent them on a wild goose chase up to Miami.

"So, you think that this guy Lester killed Deuce's father?" she asked. Her intuitive powers had always scared me.

Maybe that's why she's such a great fishing guide, I thought. She knows what the fish are going to do before they do it.

"Yeah, I do," I replied. "Just don't know why."

She was sitting on the edge of the bed, watching me. "You're going to set yourself up as bait, aren't you?"

"Dammit, Alex, stop doing that." I smiled.

Playing innocent, she said, "Stop doing what?"

"Reading my damn mind. How do you do that?"

"Men are easy to read, that's all. Not much different from fish, really."

"You're doing it again," I said, as I walked over and lifted her to her feet. "You really scare me sometimes, lady. Let's get a shower. Pescador, watch the car." The dog actually walked over to the window and nosed the curtain open so he could look outside.

"Unbelievable," Alex said.

CHAPTER EIGHTEEN

We got up early and started back. A thought had come to me when I got up before sunrise and started the coffeemaker in the hotel room. It seemed that Lester and Baldy were very intent on finding me and had mentioned going to Miami in order to do so. Since I'd pointed them toward the Rickenbacker docks, they'd probably be holed up near there, waiting for my return. Would they stay until I did return?

The docks on the Rickenbacker Causeway were only a couple of miles out of the way if we took Interstate 95 through the city, instead of the Sawgrass Expressway around it. Since they'd seen me, I'd have to be careful looking around for them. Odds were, they wouldn't be sitting in a car—too hard to see the end of the docks. My guess, they'd be on a boat at one of the docks, so they could spot the *Revenge* coming in.

Alex was driving, and we were nearing Pompano Beach, where we'd get on the Sawgrass Expressway. "You know," she said, "from what you told me, those guys might very well be waiting at the docks over on the causeway. If we were to stay on Interstate 95, we could swing by there and have a look."

I rolled my eyes and looked over at her. She just smiled and said, "I told you, Jesse, you're easy to read."

"Okay, so let's swing by there and I'll take a little stroll on the docks."

"If they see you, they'll know something's up."

"Then I'll just have to make sure they don't see me."

"Or, I could take a stroll by myself. What do they look like?"

"No way," I said. "These guys could be dangerous."

"Only if they suspect something," she said. "Otherwise, I'll just be a girl checking out the pretty boats."

I considered her plan. It was broad daylight and there was little risk of them doing anything to a random woman walking along the dock.

"It might work. But if you see them, you gotta promise me that you'll *di di mau* out of there."

"*Di di mau?*" she asked.

"It's Vietnamese," I said. "Means *move quickly*. Marines picked up a lot of the lingo there and still use it in everyday speak."

"I promise I won't get anywhere near them," she said.

"Okay, but I want you to call me as soon as you get out of the car and pretend to be talking to a girlfriend or something and tell me what you're seeing. They were driving a rental car. It's a dark blue Chevy Impala. Both guys will be easy to recognize. Lester's the muscle guy. He's young, mid-twenties probably. Looks Italian, dark curly hair, under six feet tall, probably 220 to 230 pounds. He looks like a weightlifter, big arms and chest, but skinny at the waist. The other guy is really strange-looking. Very pale skin, light blue eyes, short and wiry. He's completely bald. I mean, no hair anywhere that I could see, not even eyebrows. It seemed to me that he was the boss, not Lester."

We arrived at the docks a few minutes later. Alex parked the car in a spot near the boat ramp and got out. "Be careful, babe," I said.

"Don't worry, I'm just a girl looking at pretty boats."

She turned and walked away. A few seconds later, my cell rang. Alex was doing what she'd been told. She chatted away, like she was talking to a friend, describing the boats as she walked toward the docks. After a couple of minutes, I could hear the sound of her footsteps change as she walked out onto the wooden dock. She whispered, "I'm going to check the north dock first. It'd be the best place to watch from."

"Alex, please be careful," I said.

She continued chatting away as she walked along the dock. Then her voice changed, but she continued speaking. From the sound of the wind over the phone, I could tell that she'd turned around. After a minute she said, "I saw him. The muscle guy. He's on a boat called *One-Eyed Jack*, near the end of the southern dock, but on the north side of it. Just the one guy, though."

"Okay, get back here," I said.

"*Di di mau?*"

I laughed out loud. "Yeah, most *riki tik*, lady. Did he see you?"

"Yeah, he made a rude suggestion that I'm too much of a lady to repeat. Slime ball."

Within minutes, she was back in the car. "I didn't see the car, though," she said. "It's nowhere in the parking lot."

"Maybe Baldy is on a beer run," I said.

Just then, the car pulled into the parking lot and passed by us. But it wasn't Baldy driving. Some Hispanic-looking guy. He parked a few spots down, got out and headed toward the docks. He was carrying two bags from McDonalds and a drink tray with four cups on it.

"Well, that changes things a little," Alex said. "Four drinks means four guys. What now?"

"Now, it's time to get my channel widened," I said.

We pulled out of the parking lot and headed south on US 1 toward the Keys. I was trying to formulate a plan that would get Lester to come to me without the other three guys, and at the same time keep Alex out of harm's way. I needed to get back up to Miami in the *Revenge* to lure them back down to Marathon. That was the only way. The city was their turf. The Keys and the water were mine.

But I'd need an accomplice. Someone to stand in as my client, who I could put off at the docks on the Rickenbacker, then pull out immediately, and head back south. Alex was out of the question. I thought I might ask Deuce to do it. Maybe Alex could pick him up, though.

She could be parked near the launch ramp. Deuce could step off, get in the car and drive away before Lester and his buddies even got near them.

They were at the far end of a 500-foot-long dock. They'd have to go to the other end of that, cross over the connecting dock to shore, and walk around the parking lot to the launch ramp. Deuce and Alex would be long gone, and I'd be halfway back to open water. Odds were, they would forget Deuce and go back to the boat to follow me, which is exactly what I wanted them to do.

"You've been quiet," Alex said when we were driving through Key Largo. "You're planning something, aren't you?" I hadn't even kept track of where we were going.

"Yeah, I'm gonna have to ask you to help me out again," I said. "You and Deuce. He's coming back down Saturday."

We drove on through the Upper and Middle Keys as I explained my plan, finally arriving back at the *Rusty Anchor* at 1600. We parked, and I noticed that Rusty had moved the *Revenge* from the middle of the turning basin and tied her off to the east dock. Just then he came out of the bar. "Julie told me what happened up there in Fort Pierce," he said, walking toward us.

"How'd she know?" Alex asked.

"Deuce told her," Rusty replied. "They've been talking on the phone all week. When you wanna go up to the house with the barge?"

"I have to take the *Revenge* up to Miami Saturday morning. So, let's get it moved up there tomorrow and I can work on the channel after I take care of something up there. They get the power back on here?"

"Yeah, just a few minutes ago, in fact. Why you gotta go to Miami?" he asked.

"Deuce told me that a few weeks ago Russ had mentioned that he had a new dive partner, a muscle guy named Lester. Turns out the prospective charter Jimmy was talking about the day after the storm was a muscle guy named Lester, too."

"Too much of a co-inky-dink, man," Rusty said. "So, you're thinking this Lester guy had something to do with the break-in at Russ's and somehow got your name and is now looking for you?"

"Not only that," I replied, "I think he killed Russ. Ran into him and another guy at *Dockside* yesterday morning, but they didn't know who I was. I sent them on a wild goose chase to the Rickenbacker, saying I was picking up a charter there. Alex and I stopped by there on the way back and they were on a boat, apparently waiting for my return."

"But," Alex said, "there were four of them on the boat, not two."

"Four guys looking for you?" Rusty asked, concerned.

"Looks that way," I replied. "And I don't have any idea why. Russ kept a journal of all his dives, looking for treasure. I know, because I've seen it and am pretty sure my name's in it. Couldn't find it anywhere in the apartment. My guess is, Lester killed Russ when they were on a dive, and then broke into his apartment and found the journal and some treasure pieces Russ was hanging onto. Lester must have seen my name in the journal and is looking for me, for whatever reason. What doesn't add up is that the other guy with Lester at *Dockside* seemed like he was the leader, not Lester."

"So, what ya gonna do?" he asked.

"That's why I'm taking the *Revenge* up to Miami. Since they don't know me, they must know my boat. Don't know how unless they somehow checked boat registrations. If I can get them to follow me back down here, I can cut this Lester guy from the herd and have a little talk with him."

"It goes without saying, bro, if there's anything I can do to help, you just say the word."

"Thanks, Rusty," I said. "Right now, I think I got everything worked out in my head. You still having that party Sunday?"

"Yeah, just the locals. Told everyone to bring some seafood and Rufus will put on a big spread."

"Looking forward to it," I said. "Did Julie say when Deuce's gonna get here?"

"Flying in Saturday morning, arriving at 0400," he replied.

"He must be flying out of Virginia about midnight, then," Alex said.

"No, he's coming on a company plane, is what Julie said."

"Company jet? Sounds like true love to me," Alex said. "I'm going aboard to get dinner started. See you, Rusty." She turned and started toward the *Revenge*.

"Bye, Alex," Rusty said. Then he leaned in close to me. "You be careful, Jesse."

"I'm not too worried about four goons— at least not down here."

"Wasn't talking about the bad guys," he said as he looked toward the *Revenge*, then smiled and walked away.

CHAPTER NINETEEN

Earlier That Day

Lester had been kicked back at the helm of Sonny's boat after Tomas had left to get lunch. Boring didn't begin to describe it. Bunch of old farts, sitting around on fancy boats, or hired help sanding and polishing the old farts' boats. Maybe he shouldn't have told Sonny about the gold and treasure he'd found. Maybe he could get to this Jesse dude on his own and ditch the old loan shark and his posse.

When he'd heard footsteps and a woman's voice coming toward the boat, he'd swiveled around in the captain's chair to see.

Hot damn, Lester thought, *that's more better.*

There was a tall, good-looking blonde coming along the dock, talking on her cell phone. She had long, shapely legs, and wore tight jeans and a tank top. Her shoulders were kind of mannish.

But with tits like that, she probably needed them shoulders to hold them up, he thought.

The tank top she wore was straining to hold them in, but then flattened out to a narrow middle.

"Oh, you should see this one. It's really big and looks like it can go really fast," she said into the phone, describing the go-fast boat next to Sonny's, one of those offshore racing types.

"Hey, baby," Lester said. "I got something big I think you'd really like to see. You can drive it as fast as ya want, too."

She looked up at Lester and stopped. Then slowly, as she turned around and walked back up the dock, she lifted her middle finger back over her shoulder.

"Fuckin' bitch," Lester mumbled as Walt poked his head up out of the cabin.

"Who you talkin' to, Lester?" he asked.

"Just some stuck-up bitch headed down the dock there." He tilted his chin in the direction the blond babe had left. Both men eyed her hungrily as she walked along the dock, her tight jeans barely hiding anything.

"I could really do some damage to that," Walt said. "Hey, when's Tomas s'posed to be back? I'm hungry."

"Should be any minute," Lester said, glancing down at his watch. "He's been gone twenty minutes already. Hey, Walt, how long do you suppose Sonny's gonna have us sit out here on this boat?"

"Ya got me, man. I ain't even got any idea why he wants to get this guy."

"Yeah, me neither," Lester lied.

Walt went back down the hatch into the boat's salon. They'd been playing poker at the table down below, switching lookouts every six hours. Lester was anxious to get off the deck and back down there, not just to win his money back from Walt, but because Tomas had found the controls for the generator and had the a/c cranking. But if the blonde came back, he'd just as soon stay up here. He could still see her, crossing the parking lot by the boat ramp and getting into a yellow Jeep Cherokee, towing a boat that kinda looked familiar. Then he saw Tomas pull into the parking lot, and Lester's stomach growled. Tomas got out and start heading toward the docks.

About time, Lester thought. He was getting hungry, too.

CHAPTER TWENTY

Alex was up before me. I'm a very light sleeper, so I was surprised when I opened my eyes at 0430 and she wasn't there. But then again, she'd pretty much worn me out last night. I could smell coffee wafting through the open hatch to the salon and heard bacon grease sputtering in a pan as I was looking around for my skivvies. I found them where Alex had tossed them on the deck last night and now, I could also smell the bacon, mixing with the coffee aroma.

Man, I thought, *a guy could get used to this.*

"Rise and shine, Sleepyhead," she called down from the galley. "Or I'll give this to the dog." So much for breakfast in bed.

Together, we ate a big meal in the salon. "Funny, that cop thinking we were married," she said, buttering a slice of toast.

"Natural assumption," I said. "He'll have to hone his observation skills if he wants to make detective, though. No rings."

"Have you ever thought about getting married again? They say the third time's the charm."

"Why, *Mademoiselle* DuBois, are you proposing?"

"I've been thinking about it. What would your answer be, if I did?"

That right there floored me. We'd spent a year as friends and workout partners. Then she'd come back after being gone longer than that and it turned out we both wanted more. But how much more? Marriage? While the thought of a long relationship with Alex was appealing to me, what could I offer her?

"Cat got your tongue?" she asked. "Relax, Jesse. I didn't mean to frighten you."

"It's not that," I said. "I've only recently realized that I am, in fact, in love with you. Just can't fathom what you'd want with a run-down boat bum like me."

She smiled and her eyes sparkled. "I've recently realized the same thing," she said, leaning over the settee to kiss me. "And you're a long way from being *run-down*. That was you last night, wasn't it?"

Through the porthole, I could see lights on in the house just past the bar. While we were eating, I noticed the lights in the bar come on, too. The dog was in the cockpit, but I saw him jump up onto the dock. He trotted toward the bar and nudged the door open, disappearing inside. Julie had bought a large bag of dog food for him.

I looked back at Alex and smiled. "Rusty and I are taking the barge up to the house in about half an hour," I said, changing the subject. "He wants to catch the incoming tide to help move it across the flats. What are your plans?"

"I have a noon appointment at Skeeter's, over on Big Pine," she replied, smiling excitedly. "To look at a Maverick that he's had there for over three years. Somebody had apparently abandoned it. When I called him the day of the storm, he said it was in rough shape, but he had a clear title and would fix it up really nice and hang a brand-new motor on it, just for me."

"I bet a lot of fishermen will be glad to hear you'll be back in business," I said. "And probably quite a few guides will be equally frustrated. We should have the barge up there before noon. If you buy it, come on up and let me have a look. We're towing the barge up there with both my and Rusty's skiffs."

Through the porthole, I glimpsed Rusty crossing the backyard, heading to the dock where his skiff was tied up. He had a bag over his shoulder and a cooler in his hand.

"He's early," I said.

"Go. I'll clean up. I'm going up island to get some tackle."

Grabbing my go bag from the far side of the settee, I leaned in and kissed her. "Good luck with the skiff. Don't let Skeeter take advantage of you."

"Yeah, that's likely to happen," she scoffed.

I kissed her goodbye again and stepped up to the dock. The dog had returned from his breakfast with Julie, and together, we hiked over to where Rusty had already started up his skiff.

"Where you going?" I asked.

"Help you move the barge," Rusty replied. "Jimmy called late last night. He can't make it."

That's just the way Rusty was. If something needed doing, he just stepped in and did it. I dropped my bag on the casting deck of my own skiff. "Just how wide is that barge?" I asked. "Gotta be twenty feet, at least."

"Twenty-four. We'll have to tow it out front and rear. Once we're clear of the canal, we can tie off to either side and take it the rest of the way up. Try that in the canal here and a gust of wind could shove us against a bank and crush one of the skiffs. Got some coffee here in the Thermos—want a refill?"

I extended my mug and he topped it off. Then I climbed down and cranked up my own skiff. The sound of the two engines burbling in the predawn echoed off the concrete piers as we walked over to the barge together and started to untie it. We could make out Alex through the portholes of the *Revenge*, cleaning up.

"I topped off your tank already and took the liberty of adding another twenty-gallon tank for reserve," Rusty said. "I'll tow from the front and we'll tie you off to both corners on the stern with about twenty feet of line. That way you can move it left or right easier. Alex not going with us?" Rusty asked.

"I didn't think she'd enjoy it much. Besides, she's going over to Skeeter's. He's put together a Maverick for her."

"I overheard her talking to him," he said, "while we were waiting for Julie to fetch you the other day. Didn't think he'd have it ready this quick. Gonna be some pissed-off guides around here when they find out. What's Deuce gonna do with that Grady?"

"He told me to sell it along with all of Russ's gear," I replied. "Thought I might make him an offer myself."

"That'd be a good idea," he said. "Adding a smaller deep-water boat along with your and Alex's flats skiffs to your charter stable could be pretty profitable."

"Alex's skiff? She's an independent. But the Grady's the perfect boat for fishing the reefs."

"Listen, you old salt. That woman's got her hook in you and she's just about ready to set it. Trust me, I know these things. Besides, the two of you would be great for each other and as a charter business, you'd be unmatched."

"Let's just move this barge, okay?"

Damn, had Rusty been listening in on our conversation? Had Alex talked to Julie and she, in turn, had talked to him?

Once we had the barge free from the end of the dock, Rusty secured the two bowlines from the barge to the stern cleats on his skiff and started pulling the heavy barge away from the dock. I secured the stern lines from the barge to my bow cleats and motioned to Rusty that

I was ready. Once we had the barge lined up between us, we wouldn't be able to see one another, so keeping the damn thing in the middle of the canal would be all on me. For the most part, I planned to let the Maverick just idle in reverse and let Rusty tow us both. The extra drag of my skiff should keep it straight and if a wind did come up, I could turn and increase throttle to keep it off the banks. Fortunately, we had no wind, and within fifteen minutes, we were beyond the canal entrance and moving through the channel.

Once clear of the channel, I heard Rusty's engine drop to an idle and he shouted out, "You take the starboard side, I'll take port!" I untied the two bow cleats and tossed the port line up onto the deck of the barge, as far forward as I could, then tied the starboard line to the stern cleat on the port side of my skiff with what I hoped was enough slack to put me close to the center of the barge. I idled around the starboard side. Rusty had tied off several large bumpers near the center of the barge and my stern line became taut just about where I wanted it. I noticed that Rusty had also tossed the bowline back far enough, so I reached up, grabbed it and had it secured to my bow cleat in just a few seconds. Looking across the deck of the barge, I saw that Rusty was also ready.

"Steering's gonna be tricky," he said. "More throttle control than wheel. Tide's with us, so that'll give us a little more speed. Should be high tide up in the Content Keys about 1100."

"That's about what time I figure we'll get there," I said."

"Once we clear the Seven Mile Bridge, we'll keep her at 280 degrees and make for the southern tip of Little Pine, then turn northwest and run Big Spanish Channel and across Cutoe Banks."

"Sounds good," I said. "Doesn't look like it draws much more than the skiffs. Should be easy going until we get to Cutoe Banks. Even at high tide, it's only a couple feet deep there."

"That'll be more than enough," he said. "With the backhoe centered, it only draws sixteen inches." He laughed and added, "If it does get stuck, the backhoe can push it off the sandbar."

"Saw a Seabee use one to paddle a barge once," I said. "If we're lucky, I think we can make four knots."

"Yep, that'll put us crossing the flats just about the time the tide goes slack. I put four deep-cycle batteries on board to power the lights and hooked them to the backhoe's battery, so they'll charge when the engine's running. We can anchor it right at the mouth of your little channel. I sure hope Jimmy's as good at operatin' a backhoe as he says. That barge ain't got a motor, so the only way to maneuver it is with the bucket."

"Never known him to exaggerate before," I said. "Let's rock and roll."

With that, we dropped both engines into forward and, working together, turned the barge until it was headed nearly due west. Using hand signals, we synchronized our engines to 2000 rpm and before long, we were moving along at a good four knots. It'd be an hour before we got to the main ship channel under the Seven Mile Bridge, so Rusty tied a lanyard to his wheel and crossed over the barge, carrying his big Thermos. After stepping down lightly onto my casting deck— which always surprised me, as big as he is—he sat next to me, leaned against one of the fenders and topped off my mug again.

"Gonna be a nice day," he said. "I brought some sandwiches Julie made us. But I also brought my rod and tackle box. Thought we might troll for snapper and cook that up instead."

"Good idea. Brought mine too."

"You and Alex seem to have stepped over that line, brother. Hope you know what it is you're doing."

Rusty and I had known each other since I was just seventeen and he was eighteen. We were always open and honest with each other— no subject was off limits, and nothing was kept secret. Truth was, we regarded each other as brothers.

"Yeah, that line's astern," I said. "We're still taking it slow, just seeing what happens. Turns out we'd both been thinking of crossing that line the whole time she was here before."

"All I'm saying, bro," he went on, "is you don't have exactly the best track record with the women. But I think with her it might stick. She ain't no yuppie type. Good solid woman there."

"Yeah, I mentioned that to her. Know what she said?"

"What?"

"Both my exes were weak."

He laughed at that. "Yeah, well there's some truth to that, for certain. Why you married the second one, I can't even fathom. But Alex, she ain't weak. She's about the toughest woman I've ever known. But that could bring problems all its own, man."

We rode on for several minutes, looking out over the water to the bridge. The Seven Mile Bridge is quite a feat of architecture and really beautiful in its own way. Henry Flagler had first built the railroad bridges from island to island all the way to Key West in the early 1900s, but much of the system had been destroyed by the Labor Day hurricane of 1935, which killed thousands of people on the Keys. The original bridge now only went two miles out to Pigeon Key, which remained a kind of a museum of how life was for the workers building the bridges and rail lines a century ago. The new Seven Mile Bridge had been completed in the early '80s, replacing the one built in 1938, part of which still stood, running almost parallel to the new one. It had a high arch over Moser Channel, the main shipping channel, that was 135 feet across and soared 65 feet above the water. We could cross under it between any of the spans, but the current flowed fastest in Moser Channel, so our plan was to take advantage of that extra push. As it was now, the slight current across the flats east of the channel was slowly pushing us closer to the bridge. So, I bumped the throttle up slightly and about a minute later the barge responded, turning us slightly away from the bridge. I dropped the throttle down to 2000 rpm again.

Rusty broke the silence and asked, "She gonna move in with you, up there at the stilt house?"

I thought about it for a minute. I had actually built the place with her in mind. Not consciously, I don't think, as I didn't even know if she'd come back, but always with her preferences shaping my plans.

"We haven't really talked about it. She's only been back for five days. But if she wants to, I think I could live with that." To change the subject I asked, "What's going on between Deuce and Julie?"

"I don't think they've slept together, if that's what ya mean. Deuce doesn't strike me as the kinda guy that would sleep with a man's daughter under his own roof. I do think there's a spark there, though." Then he laughed heartily and said, "About damn time."

"I'm gonna ask him to ride with me to Miami tomorrow," I said, "after we scatter Russ's ashes on Conrad. Lester and his crew are expecting to see me show up there to drop off my charter. Alex said she'd drive up and be waiting to pick him up at the boat ramp."

"A charter of one? You think they'll buy that, and then follow you back down here? Maybe I should come along, you know, to sell the ruse a little better."

"Can you cut loose like that, the day before your grand reopening?" I asked.

"Cut loose?" he laughed. "Damn, bro, Julie runs things around the *Anchor* now. Pretty much has since she finished high school. She'll be glad to get me outta her hair. Tell me about the boat they're on."

"Alex said it's an older 32-foot Carver aft cabin. Probably has twin Mercruisers for power. They might be able to squeeze 25 knots out of her. Staying ahead of them won't be a problem."

"Okay, so you drop me and Deuce off at the ramp, we ride back with Alex and you play cat and mouse and get them back down here, right?"

"Yeah, that Carver probably has enough range to make Marathon, but not much further. I was thinking I'd cruise along and let them follow, until I make Alligator Reef. Then open the *Revenge* to full speed and be way out of sight when I make it back to the *Anchor*. If I wear a hat with a flap and sunglasses and play it right up in Miami, they won't get a good enough look at me to recognize me as the guy that sent them up there. They'll naturally go to *Dockside* for fuel and I'll let Aaron know that just about everyone will be at your party. They'll probably need to rent a car, 'cause they'll be stuck walking from there. At the party, they'll recognize me as the guy that told them the *Revenge* had gone up to Miami and ask where Jesse is."

"How you gonna get that Lester guy alone?"

"Haven't quite worked that out yet," I replied. "If they rent a car and split up, that'll be two on the boat and two on land. I have the advantage of knowing what three of them look like and they don't know what I look like, except as the guy that told them I'd gone to Miami."

We'd reached the turn into Moser Channel and no boats were coming from either direction. About 100 yards from the edge of the channel, I dropped the engine to idle speed, but the barge didn't seem to be responding. So, I dropped the Maverick into reverse and brought the engine up to 1200 rpm and that did the trick. The big barge turned into the channel and I kicked the engine into forward and brought it back up to 2000 rpm. With the current running at about five knots in the channel, we crossed under the bridge pretty quickly. Directly under the bridge, the dog started barking over the side of the skiff.

"Quick," I said, "grab a rod and put a line out."

"What kind of lure?" he asked.

I noticed the dog was looking straight down into the channel. "Put that Rapala deep-running shad on the leader. Hurry!"

While putting the lure on the swivel, he asked, "What the hell is that dog yapping at?"

"Get that lure in the water and you'll see," I replied.

Rusty threw the line out and a few minutes later reeled in a nice red snapper, which he put in the fish box.

"Don't tell me that dog saw that snapper," he said.

"That's the third time I've seen him do it. Crazy, huh?"

"I'd say so. Never heard of a fish pointer. Well, that's lunch," he said. "Time for a snack." He opened the cooler, got a sandwich out, and offered it to me. When I declined, he wolfed it down in just a few bites, tossing the last bite up on the casting deck to the dog.

The dog looked at it, and then gazed expectantly at me. "Go ahead," I said, and he gobbled it down.

Once we were about a mile past the bridge, Rusty had to cross over to his skiff and do the same trick that got us into the channel to get us out. After he'd gotten the barge set on the right course, slightly north of west, he crossed back over again and joined me.

"Think Deuce will mind if I go along to spread Russ's ashes?" he asked.

"No, I don't think he'll have a problem with that," I replied.

"Been thinking on how to separate Lester from the others," he said. "Like you said, they'll likely rent a car and split up once they make *Dockside*. When they split up, ya got two scenarios. First, they split into twos. But more likely, since they're landlubbers, they'll leave one guy to watch the boat, trusting that people can only be found on land. That'll put three in a rental car. A bit harder to separate, but if we're lucky, Lester'll be the one on the boat."

"Don't tell me you started counting on luck, man," I said.

He laughed hard at that one. "No, but like the man said, 'Fortune favors the prepared mind.' It could happen."

"Yeah, it could," I said. "And I do favor being prepared."

Then at the same time we both said, "The Seven *Ps*," and started laughing.

"Yeah," Rusty finally said. "Sergeant Livingston was a good teacher."

After a moment, I said, "Deuce told me the only things of value that we should have found at Russ's apartment were a two-escudo gold coin, mounted and hanging on a gold chain that Russ usually wore, and a gold cross with three emeralds. Alex and I didn't find either of those. If Lester did kill Russ and break into his apartment, he's got them, along with Russ's journal."

"I know the doubloon necklace Russ had. I got one exactly like it. Never wear it anymore, too touristy. What if I was to loan it to Aaron? Think Lester would take an interest? Compare 'em? He might even hang back with the boat, while the others go off to get a car, so he could maybe talk to Aaron about it?"

"Good idea," I said. "The thing that's been nagging at me, though, is when Lester and the bald guy were in Aaron's office, it seemed like the bald guy was the boss, not Lester."

"If that's the case, this Lester guy would be sure to take an interest in my doubloon and hang back, if he really was the one who stole Russ's. The other guy might not even know about it."

I gave it some more thought. Why were these guys after me, anyway? How dangerous were they? I damn sure didn't like Baldy's looks. He just had an evil aspect about him. And I was pretty sure that Lester had had something to do with Russ's death. So, they were dangerous enough.

"Yeah," I said. "Let's get Aaron to wear that doubloon. I'm certain they'll come directly to *Dockside* first, once I run off and leave them, since that's where I dock my boat. If Aaron's wearing a doubloon necklace exactly like the one Lester stole from Russ, Lester's bound to be interested. And he'll suggest that he be the one to stay back with the boat."

"Be nice if you knew a little more about 'em."

"No doubt there," I said. "If we go early, we can anchor up just off the Intracoastal and watch their boat at the docks. Likely, they're watching for incoming boats and not knowing when I'll arrive, they'll have to set up some kind of shift."

"Slow is smooth," Rusty said.

"And smooth is fast," I responded.

Part of our advanced infantry training under Russ Livingston had been urban warfare—house-to-house fighting, and the clearing of buildings to attain an objective. Each house had to be methodically swept and cleared, which took time. Go too fast, and something could be missed, causing the mission to not go smoothly. Doing something twice was very time consuming. Russ had moved through each house with us. We went in tactically and he moved around us, acting as an invisible director, giving direction to the fire team and pointing out hidden dangers that had to be checked.

"If we wait to come in," I said, "until the end of Lester's shift, he'll be tired. After sitting in the sun for several hours, then chasing me for three or four more hours, he'll be really tired."

"I like it when the enemy's really tired," Rusty said, grinning. "People make mistakes when they're really tired. So, you're gonna want to leave before daylight, to be able to anchor in the Intracoastal early in the day. It's gonna take you a good three hours to get there and you're gonna need to stop for fuel to be able to get back here running wide open non-stop. You could put in at Key Biscayne Yacht Club and top off. That'll give you just enough fuel to get to Rickenbacker and back here without stopping."

We continued bouncing ideas off each other the rest of the morning, as we slowly motored up to my house. As predicted, we got there just before noon and made it across the flats with no problems. The barge had legs at each corner that rose and lowered with a hand crank system of gears, so that it could be held in place. We positioned it on the flats, to the left of the channel to my house, and dropped the legs to the bottom. Since it was high tide, we only needed to crank them enough to raise the whole barge a few inches to make it secure. It wasn't going to drift off before we got back, as the tide rose and fell.

We idled our skiffs up under the house and went up for lunch. As Rusty was cleaning the fish, I threw a can of beans in a pot and put them on a low simmer. When

I went back outside, I could hear an outboard approaching, so I reached back inside, grabbed my binoculars off the hook by the door and trained them to the south.

I immediately recognized the skiff flying over the water as a Maverick Mirage, just like my own. It had a red upper hull, was white below the waterline and had a poling platform over the engine. Man, that boat was moving fast. As I focused on the driver, the familiar light blue, long-sleeved denim shirt and long-billed fishing cap stood out only slightly more than the blond hair flying behind and the excellent form that the wind created in the shirt. Alex was back on the water in her own boat.

I hustled down to the dock and Rusty asked, "Who's that boat I heard coming?"

"It's Alex in her new Maverick," I replied.

The sound of the outboard slowed as she dropped off plane to come up the channel to the house. After a minute, she appeared through the overhanging mangroves.

"Dayum!" Rusty said. "Now that's a fine watercraft."

Alex was beaming as she tossed Rusty a line and he tied her off to the dock.

"You like?" she asked.

I walked along the dock and admired the work that Skeeter had done. He'd gone above and beyond to please Alex, it seemed.

"Is that for real?" I asked, nodding toward the Mercury outboard with a big "300" on the side.

"Sure is," she said, grinning. "A brand-new aluminum-block, 300-horsepower, four-stroke Merc. Weighs only 100 pounds more than your Yamaha."

"Skeeter did a fine job," I said. "That's a damn beautiful boat. I'm really happy for you."

"It sure is," Rusty said, admiring the work done. "Skeeter did a great job. Hope he didn't charge you too much."

"I think I got a pretty good deal, guys. Cost me less than a brand-new boat and motor and it looks brand new. The only thing original is the hull and he reglassed the stringers with carbon fiber, just in case. Even used Kevlar along the keel and chines."

"Congratulations," I said. "I know you're happy to be back on the water. We were about to eat. Come on up."

"Hang on," she said, then reached in the icebox and pulled out a nice-sized red snapper.

"Gimme that," Rusty said. "Y'all go on up. I'll be just a minute."

Alex handed the fish to Rusty. "Caught him under the Seven Mile Bridge."

"Yeah?" Rusty said, grinning. "That's where that dog pointed out the snapper we caught."

Rusty turned back to the cleaning board and started in on the fish while Alex and I headed up the steps to the house. I wanted to go over the plans that Rusty and I had put together while running the barge up to the house.

Inside two minutes, Rusty joined us and while I went over everything with Alex, he started cooking the fish filets on the small outdoor grill. After I wrapped up, we sat outside and had lunch with a few cold Red Stripes. The dog even got his own snapper filet.

"Rusty," Alex said, "Julie said to let you know that she's got everything set for Sunday, except for a couple of things she has to wait till Sunday morning to do. She also said she'd be going with me up to Miami, to pick you and Deuce up."

"Wait a minute," Rusty said. "Me and Jesse only decided I was going while on the way up here. How'd Julie know?"

"My bet would be Alex told her," I said.

"And you'd be right, Jess," she said.

"So, how'd you know?" Rusty asked, a bit confused.

"We men are as predictable as fish to her," I answered.

"So you are," she said. "I'm guessing you'll want to leave as soon as Deuce arrives?"

"Yeah," I said. "Guess I better call him and get him up to speed."

I hustled down to the dock to get my phone and then returned to the deck, the only place I could get a signal. Then I hit the number my call history listed for Deuce.

"Hey, Jesse," Deuce said when the connection was made. "I was just about to call you. I'm going to be arriving there earlier than I originally figured. Just getting on the plane now. Should be there in three hours."

"That change in schedule wouldn't have anything to do with a certain bar wench, would it?"

I could almost hear the color change in his cheeks. "Yeah, that has something to do with it. What's up?"

I told him the suspicions we had and the update on what we'd learned at Rickenbacker Marina. Then I went over the plans Rusty and I had put together.

"Really?" he asked. "Rusty has an identical necklace? That could work. I'm warning you, though. If we get the guy alone and he confesses, the police won't be involved. I'll personally use the guy for shark chum."

I believed him.

"Look," I said, "we're up at the house right now. We'll leave here in a few minutes and should be back at the *Anchor* by 1400. Want me to pick you up at the airport?"

"Julie's already said she'd pick me up. Might not see you until morning, though. She said she had plans and they involved room service at the Hyatt on Sugarloaf Key. What time do you want to leave?"

"I want to be down there by sunrise, so we need to leave the *Anchor* by no later than 0430. Make sure you get at least a few hours' sleep, okay?"

"Will do, Jesse. See you in the morning."

I disconnected and closed the phone, wondering how I was going to explain this to Rusty. When I crossed the deck, Alex was heading through the door with the dishes.

"We need to get moving, bro. Alex told me that Julie's gonna pick Deuce up and they'll meet us in the morning. We gotta top your tanks and get together with Aaron, then turn in early for a 0300 reveille."

So, Julie told Alex about her plans with Deuce and Alex broke it to Rusty. It didn't seem to bother him too much.

"Yeah, Deuce told me. You okay with that?"

"Hey, *amigo*," he said, "She's 24 years old. For all of those 24 years, she's been the perfect daughter. Never got stellar grades, but she's worked hard to get everything she's got. What kind of dad would I be if I got pissed that she's actually turned out to be a woman? She reminds me so much of her mom. Poor Deuce never had any more of a chance than I did."

Alex came out onto the deck and said, "Everything's squared away inside so let's *di di mau* out of here."

Rusty almost doubled over, he was laughing so hard. Finally, he was able to add, "Yeah, most *riki tik*, Alex. I think you been hanging around old jarheads too much."

We walked down to the docks, started the three skiffs, and one by one we pushed off into the little turning basin, headed out to Harbor Channel. The tide was still high enough that a nearly straight-line course could be run back to Marathon.

We spread out and accelerated up onto plane as we crossed the channel, with Alex in the center and Rusty to her left. My skiff was probably a little faster than Rusty's, so I backed off a little until my speed matched his, as did Alex. The water was clear with barely a ripple across its surface. It seemed almost as though we were three fighter planes zooming across a barren desert as we steered almost due east toward the narrow, shallow cut between Big Spanish and Little Spanish Keys. As we neared it, Alex increased speed slightly and took the lead through the cut toward Horseshoe Key six miles in the distance. Although it was high tide, the water across the flats there was only ankle deep, except for that cut. Later in the day, at low tide, the shallows became a sandbar. The cut was not marked on any charts because it was less than a foot deep at low tide. Only locals knew that you could go this way. Right then, it was at least two feet deep, but only a few feet wide. Once we cleared the shallowest water, we spread out again into a V. I called ahead to Alex, "Show us what she's got!"

She looked over her right shoulder at me and smiled. Then she pushed her throttle to the stops and that little red Mirage shot away from us, as though out of a cannon. The big Mercury made hardly a sound. In less than a minute, she was nearly a half mile ahead, skimming across the water with only the last foot of hull in contact with the surface.

She turned sharply and came flying back toward us, passing between our boats in a blur. The closure speed had to be well above 100 knots. She made another sharp turn and came roaring back up between us, leaping across the V created by our converging wakes, then slowing at the last minute to match our turtle pace.

"Mother of God," Rusty said. "That thing must've reached 70 knots!"

"Sixty-four," Alex said, grinning from ear to ear. "That's over 70 miles per hour, which is what Skeeter promised me. That's gonna come in handy for tournament clients."

"Yeah," I said, "if you can find a client with big enough *cojones* to let you do it."

CHAPTER TWENTY-ONE

It was Lester's watch again. If anything, today was duller than the day before. Even the rich old farts weren't around.

This is really starting to get mega-boring, he thought.

They'd been cooped up on the boat for over 24 hours now, and the only excitement since they'd gotten on it had been yesterday morning, when the hot blonde had walked down the dock. They were still taking turns in six-hour shifts on the bridge. It was already getting hot, and it wasn't even noon yet. He'd played cards most of the night and lost even more money to Walt.

He knew the guy was cheating; he just couldn't figure out how. Now he wished he'd just gone to bed instead. If they could catch this McDermitt guy, there'd be a good chance that he'd have more of the treasure or could tell them where it was. Better still if they could force him to bring it up. It'd seemed so easy that day when he and the old man had found that gold bar. How hard could it be to find more? Lester was certain this McDermitt guy had a stash of it somewhere, stuff he and Russ had found on other dives. Russ hadn't kept much in his apartment, though, and Lester couldn't figure out where else he might have stashed the rest of the treasure.

Benny poked his shiny black head out of the cabin. "Yo, mon. I got di watch now. Tomas say he know a place wid good jerk fowl. Walt be sleepin'. Weh yuh tink 'bout dat, 'stead of dem greasy burgas we been eatin'?"

Damn, Lester thought, *I can't hardly understand a word that Bahamian guy says. Fowl? Chicken, maybe?*

"Yeah, I could go for some chicken. Way better for you than those greasy hamburgers."

"Dat wah I and I jest say, mon."

"Yeah, whatever. I'll be in the cabin, watchin' TV," Lester said as he went below.

Tomas went out, right behind Benny, with the keys to the rental car. It was a pretty nice boat, at least. Too bad the boss didn't let them cook, though. It'd save a ton of money. But then again, who gave a shit? The boss was buying.

Lester and Walt were sharing the rear bedroom, so when Walt got up in six more hours, he'd get a chance to get some sleep. The bedrooms were kinda small, but each one had two beds, at least. He guessed they were okay for boat bedrooms. The bathrooms were really small, and he couldn't fit his shoulders inside without leaving the door open. He flipped through the channels on the TV until he found one that was showing an infomercial about diet and exercise, then turned it up to drown out Walt's snoring.

After ten minutes of watching, he heard Tomas up on the deck, talking to Benny. A minute later, the Bahamian came into the cabin where Lester was, carrying bags from a place called Caribbean Delight.

"Lestah, mon," Benny said. "I tink yuh guh lacka dis." He started pulling out square Styrofoam boxes and round containers. "Got some goid Caribbean eats, mon. Got mhanish wata, rude bwoy joik fowl, oxtail, curray goit an fi mi own favrit, brahn fish stew."

It smelled good, but then Benny opened the one he said was his favorite, whatever he called it, and Lester saw a whole fish looking up at him with one big, glassy eye.

"You eat that shit?" Lester asked. "It's looking at you."

"Ya mon," Benny replied. "Yuh not be knowin' dis be goid food."

"Lemme try the chicken," Lester said. *No way to fuck up chicken.*

He opened the Styrofoam tray Benny handed him. Didn't look half bad and smelled pretty good. It was a seasoned, baked chicken breast, white rice, and vegetables. He sat down and dug right in. But almost immediately, he bolted for the kitchen, grabbed a bottle of water out of the fridge, and guzzled it.

"Oh ya, mon, fogot to woin yuh. Bahamian fowl be hot, mon."

"Hot?" Lester said. "That shit's volcanic."

Once back at the table with a second bottle of water, he decided to get to work on the chicken, "Maybe if I scrape all that hot stuff off, I can eat it," he told Benny. After cleaning it up, he tried another bite. "Yeah, that ain't quite so hot," he said.

"Git a boil, mon. Trah some a di mhanish wata. It a soip sposed ta mek yuh lass fah a loing tahm wit di ladies."

"An aphrodisiac soup?" Lester asked. "Sure, I'll try it."

He grabbed a bowl from the cabinet and Benny poured some into it. Lester thought it tasted pretty good. He went back to the vegetables, wolfing them down, and then ate more of the soup before going back to the chicken and rice.

"That soup's good," he said. "What's in it?"

"Goit meat, goit head, an' goit haht," Benny answered.

"Goat head? Goat heart? You're shittin' me, right?"

"No mon, goits are di most verile ah anmals."

Lester ran to the bathroom, leaving the door open, and puked in the toilet.

CHAPTER TWENTY-TWO

I woke up at 0300 and again eased out of the bed so as not to disturb Alex. I'd set the coffee maker for 0250, and the smell of fresh coffee motivated me. I'd wake Alex after I had a cup.

When we'd returned from the stilt house, Julie was already gone. Rusty had chased off a couple of local shrimpers, closed up early, and had Rufus make an early supper. While he was cooking, Rusty and I had stocked the *Revenge* with enough provisions for three days and topped off the tanks. Rusty always counted on the worst.

Alex had shown me all the special features Skeeter had included in her new boat. It had hydraulic power steering and trim tabs. The casting deck also had a platform that could be raised and lowered by a small, electrically-operated hydraulic motor. The poling platform was also Kevlar-reinforced. The console had all digital gauges, with a built-in GPS and VHF radio. It was really nice, and I could tell she was proud of it. Rusty had driven over to *Dockside*, given Aaron his doubloon necklace, and filled him in on what we wanted him to say when Lester stopped by. After Alex and I had eaten, we'd retired to the *Revenge* to get plenty of sleep. Well, some sleep anyway.

When I went into the galley, I poured two mugs of coffee, then returned to the forward stateroom and sat down on the edge of the bed. Alex opened her eyes and smiled as she reached for the mug.

"Mmmm, thanks," she said, sitting up and taking a sip.

"Afraid I'm gonna have to make you walk the plank, wench," I said.

"Julie and Deuce get here yet?" she asked.

I stood and looked through the long, narrow porthole above the shelf. "Just pulling in now," I replied.

"She and I are going to the Wooden Spoon for breakfast at five o'clock before we leave. We should get to the marina by seven."

"Make sure you park as close to the boat ramp as you can, okay?" I said. "I want Deuce and Rusty to be able to get in and y'all to be gone in minutes."

"Don't worry, Jesse," she said. "They're not going to try anything stupid at a public boat ramp in broad daylight."

"I know. I just don't want them to see you. Remember, Lester already saw you once. If he sees you picking up my 'charter,' he'll get suspicious."

We heard steps on the deck outside and then Deuce's voice. "Permission to come aboard?"

"Come aboard, Deuce," I said.

"Go," Alex said. "Let me get dressed."

I stepped up to the salon as Deuce and Julie came up the steps from the cockpit. "Good to see you again, Jesse," Deuce said.

"You too," I said. "Y'all want coffee?"

"None for me," Julie said.

"I'll have a cup," Deuce said.

I poured a mug and handed it to him as Alex came up the steps from the stateroom.

"Have a seat," I said to Deuce.

"Come up to the house with me, Alex?" Julie asked. "I want to make sure Dad's up."

"Sure," Alex replied. She kissed me on the cheek and went out the hatch with Julie.

Deuce took a seat on the settee and I sat down next to him. He was deep in thought and I could tell he wanted to talk about it. I just sipped my coffee and let him sort it out in his mind.

Finally, he said, "Do I strike you as crazy, Jesse?"

"No," I replied. "You strike me as a pretty levelheaded man. Besides, BUDS would have found out any crazy side and washed you out." The Basic Underwater Demolition/SEALs training is one of the toughest training courses in any military in the world. They weeded out at least half of the entrants.

He laughed and said, "You were married, right? Is it fair to a woman to marry men like us?"

"Whoa," I said. "What's all this marriage stuff?" But I knew exactly what he meant. "Look," I said, "someone way smarter than me once said that it takes a strong woman to be in a relationship with a warrior. Weak women can't handle it. Dude, Julie is definitely not a weak woman. But marriage? Y'all haven't even known each other a week."

"No, she's not weak," he replied. "But I guess what I'm getting at here is this: is it reasonable to even get involved with someone, knowing there might be long absences and I'd be causing worry? My new job will often entail grabbing a bag in the middle of the night and leaving without a word. I could be gone for weeks or months, without even a phone call. I don't know, it just doesn't seem fair."

"Take it from me, Deuce," I said. "I was married twice. And there were a few times I had to do the *go-bag-drag* in the middle of the night. It pissed them off. Mostly because they weren't prepared for it. Be straight up, tell her all you can and prepare her for those nights. Her dad knows how it goes and he can help. That is, if you two get serious."

"It's serious," he said. "I've known a few women, Jesse. I'm thirty years old. But I've never met anyone like her in my life. That girl literally takes my breath away."

"Well, like I said, be straight up with her. She's only 24, but she has an old soul. She's never been serious with anyone before. Me and Rusty figured she'd know when it was time. If it is, she'll let you know."

We heard footsteps on the dock and Rusty's voice called out, "Reveille, reveille, reveille. On your feet, maggot! It's reveille in the boondocks and time's a-was-tin'."

"Come aboard, Rusty," I said.

Rusty stepped through the hatch and said, "The girls are getting things ready up at the house. They said to tell you they'd see us at the docks. We ready to cast off?"

"Just waiting on Jimmy," I said. "He should be here any minute."

"If you're waiting on me, dude," Jimmy said from the dock, "you're backing up." He dropped his bag in the cockpit and said, "I'll get the bow line, Captain."

Rusty set a cooler on the deck under the settee and dropped his go bag next to it. Deuce went up on the dock to cast off the stern line while Rusty and I climbed to the bridge to start the engines. Each engine fired instantly and settled into a low rumble. The *Revenge* was facing open water and seemed to be anxious to get there. I checked the gauges, and everything looked fine.

"Cast off!" I called down to the dock.

Both men released the lines, and Jimmy shoved the bow away from the dock, then hurried aft, where he and Deuce stepped down into the cockpit. Deuce then started to climb the ladder to the bridge.

"I'll double-check the engine room, Skipper," Jimmy said, and Deuce stopped halfway up the ladder.

"Mind if I have a look?" he asked.

"Sure," I said. "Have at it."

I nudged the port engine into forward and turned the wheel slightly toward the dock. The *Revenge* moved forward and slightly sideways away from the docks. Once clear, I nudged the starboard engine into forward and brought the helm back to center.

As we idled slowly down the canal, Deuce and Jimmy climbed back up to the bridge. Deuce took the seat next to Rusty on the big bench to port while Jimmy took his usual seat to my right.

"Everything below decks looks good, Jesse," Jimmy said.

"Better than good," Deuce said. "I could eat off deck in that engine room."

I nodded to my right and said, "Jimmy takes his work very seriously."

As we passed the last light pole on shore, I flipped on the forward spotlight, as well as the navigation and stern lights, then switched the overhead light to red. I nudged the throttles a bit higher as we cleared the end of the canal and started into the channel. Jimmy reached up, turned on the Furuno radar system, and adjusted it to a two-mile radius.

"Everything looks clear ahead," Jimmy said. "Checking further out." He adjusted the radar to a ten-mile radius and said, "Looks like a big tanker out on the Stream to the southwest, heading east. Nothing else." He switched it to its maximum range and said, "A couple of shrimpers further southwest heading toward Key West, and several pleasure craft out at the edge of the reef, to the east about fifteen miles. Nothing else, Jesse."

"Okay," I said. "Let's get out ahead of that tanker."

I slowly pushed the throttles up to 1600 rpm and the bow lifted for a few seconds; then we planed out and it came back down. I increased speed to 25 knots, which is where I got the best fuel economy. In just a few minutes, we'd cleared the reef and I turned northeast.

Jimmy pulled up a saved waypoint for Conrad Reef and turned on the Furuno autopilot. It would keep us off the reef all the way there.

Jimmy checked the radar again and said, "The pleasure craft to the east seem to be stationary, Jesse. Should be able to see them in ten or twelve minutes. Probably a couple of early-morning anglers. Alert's set for four miles."

Since Jimmy didn't know everything we were going to be doing, I told Deuce, "Jimmy here's a squid like you, Deuce. I've found him to be completely reliable in every situation."

Jimmy said, "Dude, I was a machinist's mate, first class. But that was a past life."

Deuce understood my subtle indication that Jimmy could be trusted and nodded his assent. Jimmy already knew we were going to Conrad, but I'd told him to keep the rest of the day clear as well.

Rusty leaned over and looked down in the cockpit. "Hey, where'd your dog go?"

"He's not my dog," I replied. I turned around and didn't see him below either, and I knew the hatch to the salon was closed, so I stood up and looked forward.

"I'll be damned," I said.

The others stood up and also looked forward, to where the dog sat on the expansive foredeck, ears cocked and alert, with his nose in the wind. I cupped my hands and yelled, "You okay up there, Pescador?" He turned his head, looked at the four of us and barked once, then turned his head back into the wind. He seemed to be studying the far horizon, even though it was still completely dark.

Rusty laughed and said, "You could probably turn that radar off and he'd let you know if anything was ahead of us."

We all sat back down, and I gave Jimmy the whole scoop on what we'd planned to do that day. He listened, nodding when needed, and didn't ask a single question. When I was finished, he said simply, "So, what you're saying is, I've been shanghaied, man?"

"Yeah, I guess you could say that. You okay with it?"

"No worries, man," he replied. "Party on."

It only took us about ten minutes before the alert signaled that we were coming up on Conrad Reef. I disengaged the autopilot and slowed to ten knots while I studied the GPS and turned on the Furuno sonar. The waypoint I had set for Conrad was about a half mile due south of the reef. Conrad was a patch reef, about 1500 feet inside the reef line. There was a natural cut in the reef, just 100 feet north of the waypoint. I adjusted the sonar, so it read the bottom in front of us and dropped down to idle speed as we neared the waypoint. Then I turned the wheel, so that we were moving due north as we passed the waypoint. The sonar started to show the gap in the reef just ahead.

The gap was plenty wide enough for the *Revenge,* and the reef head was at least fifteen feet from the surface, but it was always best to play it safe. I'd heard of many boats crashing on debris that had been snagged by the reefs.

We cleared the gap with the sonar showing 21 feet under the keel, and the southern edge of the little patch reef just a few hundred feet ahead.

The bottom got deeper to 25 feet and the reef came to within ten feet of the surface. The tide was slack and what little wind was blowing was coming out of the east. When we were 90 feet from the reef, I told Jimmy to release the anchor and it dropped into the water with a splash from the bow. I took the engines out of gear and shut them down, then adjusted the sonar so it showed the bottom directly below us. The anchor dropped onto the sandy bottom and I told Jimmy to pay out 90 feet of rode. Slowly, the *Revenge* drifted forward, then began to swing slightly as the boat pulled on the 50-foot chain anchor rode. I readjusted the sonar toward the stern; it showed the southern edge of the little reef getting closer. As the anchor took hold and the slight wind straightened us, the sonar showed the southern edge of the reef to be directly below the boat. If it had been daylight, we could have looked down from the bridge and seen it, the water was so clear in this area. I turned on the underwater lights at the stern and sure enough, the top of the reef lay just below the swim platform. Though it was ten feet down, it looked close enough to touch.

"This is Conrad Reef," I told Deuce solemnly.

"Thanks, Jesse." He reached under the bench seat and pulled his bag out, unzipping it and pulling out a small, square, sealed box. Taking a knife from his belt, he slit the seal on the top, and opened it. Inside, he withdrew a brass urn in the shape of an old hardhat diver's helmet.

"I think Dad would have wanted you and Rusty to join me," he said.

The three of us climbed down to the cockpit and Rusty and I stood on either side of Deuce at the stern. Out of the corner of my eye, I saw Jimmy standing on the bridge, where he lowered the colors to half-mast. I flew both the American flag and the Marine Corps flag. Then Jimmy reached into his pocket, pulled his MP3 player out, and plugged it into the stereo on the console.

Deuce opened the diver's helmet and placed it on the stern. Then he looked at Rusty and me in turn and said, "Dad was gone a lot when I was a kid. I used to resent him for it. But as I grew older, I realized why he did what he did. Guess the apple doesn't fall far, does it? Now I'm the one leaving and staying away for weeks and months. I'm going to miss the old war horse."

I cleared my throat and recited the last verse of a poem I'd recently read.

> *"His face is rough*
> *his shirt is torn*

he is tired of fighting
in this war of the sea
He lost his ship of gold and
diamonds in battle
now he floats alone
The warrior of the sea."

Rusty then added, *"Vaya con Dios, mi hermano."*

As Deuce lifted the helmet and stepped out onto the swim platform, the doleful sound of a bugle split the air. Jimmy, up on the bridge, was playing a recording of "Taps." His way of honoring a fellow vet he never knew.

Deuce slowly poured the ashes and small bits of bone into the water. It spread on the surface behind us, drifting down onto the reef that Russ and I had first dived so long ago. The four of us stood rigidly at attention as the last notes of "Taps" blew mournfully out across the water. As Deuce placed the now-empty urn on the stern railing, I heard him whisper, "If it was by the hand of another, I'll avenge you, Dad."

"Hoist anchor, Jimmy," I called up to the bridge.

The rattling of the anchor windlass interrupted the quiet and pulled the *Revenge* slowly south, away from the reef, as Jimmy fired up the engines. The three of us climbed up to the bridge in silence and took our places. When I heard the windlass starting to strain with the weight of the anchor chain, I tapped the engines into forward, and adjusted the sonar ahead to pick up the gap in the reef.

"Thanks for that, Jimmy," Deuce said as he replaced the hard-hat in his bag.

"*De nada, hermano,*" Jimmy said. "Seemed like the thing to do."

We passed through the gap in the reef, each of us silent in our own thoughts. Deuce was right. If Russ had been killed by someone, that person would pay, and pay dearly.

Once clear of the reef, I pushed the throttles, brought the *Revenge* up on plane, and continued south for a few minutes to deeper water. Once we passed 50 feet, I turned northeast and reengaged the autopilot, entering the Key Biscayne Yacht Club for the destination. I knew that Rusty felt the same way I did, but Jimmy was the wild card. I decided now was the time to say what needed to be said.

"Jimmy," I said, "I don't want you to feel like you were roped into this and I don't want you to be a part of what might happen if things turn out like I think they might, if you don't want to."

"Skipper," Jimmy said, "you always been a straight shooter, man. I know you like a brother. You and Rusty, both. I only met Deuce here a couple times and never met his dad. I can add pretty good, though. I'm guessing all y'all think these hombres had something to do with Deuce's dad dying, right?" I nodded, and he continued. "You know I was a machinist's mate, but I don't think I ever told you what ship I served on, though."

"No," I said, "I don't recall you ever did."

"I served on the USS *Wasp*, out of Norfolk," he said, "from '93 to '97, Somalia and Kuwait." The *Wasp* was one of the first amphibious landing crafts built for the navy, kind of a mini aircraft carrier designed to move Marines into areas where they'd be needed.

"Actually, met Colin Powell," he said. "When he landed on the *Wasp*, off Mogadishu. He was still chairman of the joint chiefs then. We had about a thousand sailors aboard, officers and enlisted, and more than 2000 Marines. Always liked you jarheads for some reason, man. My guess is that if these guys had anything to do with Deuce's dad's death, they won't ever be seen again. The way I look at it, you step on one Marine's toe, they all go *ouch*, man. Goes for sailors, too."

Jimmy turned to check the radar, switching it to a five-mile radius, and said, "The lights of those two pleasure-craft should be visible now, just off the port bow." Then he laughed and added, "That is, unless they're fishing for square grouper." That settled that. Jimmy was in.

"Square grouper?" Deuce asked.

"Bales of marijuana," I explained. "Lots of drug trafficking goes on around these waters, especially at night." I glanced at the radar, then looked out to the horizon and spotted the anchor lights of the two boats. "Just fishermen," I said.

"Sunrise will be in about three hours," I said. "We should make Biscayne Bay about then."

CHAPTER TWENTY-THREE

Sonny Beech was behind his desk in his downtown office at eight o'clock in the morning, an unusual time for him. Actually, his office was in a strip mall in Lake Worth, about a block from the interstate, but he preferred to call it his *Palm Beach office*. Across from him sat a man wearing a fine silk suit named Hafez al Madani. He was a Miami businessman of Pakistani descent who'd come up to Palm Beach to meet with Sonny, mostly because of Sonny's reputation for taking on any kind of job without asking too many questions, and also, because Sonny owned a boat large enough for his needs.

"Let me get this straight, Mr. Madani," Sonny said. "You want me to have one of my guys take my boat to Brown's Cay, pick up four people and bring them into Miami?"

"For your trouble, Mr. Beech, I will pay you $20,000," al Madani replied.

"And you want me to take the chance of not going through U.S. Customs with these four people, right?"

"That is correct," al Madani answered. "There can be no interaction with American authorities."

"That's a big risk you're asking me to take. Bigger than twenty grand."

"I'll pay you $20,000 up front and another $20,000 once they're ashore without incident."

"Yeah, I can do that," Sonny said after a moment's thought. "But your people will have to bring 100 gallons of gas to Brown's Cay to refuel the boat. That's about the limit of its range."

Easiest money I'll make all year, Sonny thought. Couldn't be any harder than his monthly cocaine run for a local dealer, and it paid nearly double.

The two men rose and shook hands, and then al Madani added, "Yes, they can bring the petrol. I'd like to see the boat this morning, if I could. To be sure that it is suitable."

"That can be arranged. It's in Miami right now. When did you want this pickup made? My boat's currently on assignment."

"It will have to be early this Tuesday morning. I would expect delivery no later than seven o'clock that evening."

Sonny thought it over. He'd hoped his guys would have this McDermitt character at the junkyard by now. Hopefully, he'd arrive today or tomorrow. If not, he'd just have to pull them off and do this job, then start looking all over again. Finding McDermitt was becoming a more difficult task than he'd figured, and there was no guarantee that he had, or knew, the location of any other treasure. But sometimes you had to gamble.

"The job the boat is on should easily be wrapped up by Sunday," Sonny said. "I can have Captain Rodriguez leave Monday morning and be on Brown's Cay before sunset. If your people are ready, they can board before sunrise and be in Miami by four o'clock."

"When could you arrange to let me inspect your boat?" al Madani asked.

"I don't have anything pressing right now, as a matter of fact," Sonny replied. "Like I said, it's in Miami. If you can meet me at Rickenbacker Marina in about ninety minutes, we can make sure it fits your needs."

Outside, parked on the far side of the parking lot, sat a nondescript Chevy van with dark windows. Four men were inside the van, one in the driver's seat and the other three seated in back at a console where a lot of sophisticated video and listening equipment was mounted. Two of the men, one black and one white, were younger than the driver and the fourth man in the back.

The three men at the console were all wearing head-phones and listening intently. The older man, Jim Franklin, turned to the two younger ones and said, "We've had this guy under surveillance for two months. He's suspected of funneling money through several of his business dealings to al Qaeda in Afghanistan. Sounds like he's trying to bring in some other cell members. You two are lucky to be in on this. It was only supposed to be a routine surveillance training exercise. Find anything on this Sonny Beech?"

Art Newman looked up from the laptop and replied, "Real name's Elijah Beech. He's a local loan shark and is suspected of drug smuggling and other crimes. Been arrested a number of times, mostly small stuff, but never did any time. He has a boat registered in his name, a 32-foot Carver named *One-Eyed Jack*."

Tony Jacobs said, "We should call Deuce. He's down in the Keys. He can get up here in just a few hours. He's not going to want to miss this."

Franklin said, "Not just yet. He told Associate Deputy Director Smith he'd only be a couple days down there."

"Yeah," Art said, "he's probably scattering his dad's ashes right about now. I know he'd like to be in on this, though."

"He will be," the senior agent said. "The whole Caribbean will be our assignment. Right now, I'm just supposed to be showing you boys the finer points of surveillance without being seen. This's gotta be boring for a couple SEALs like yourselves, though. Don't worry, there'll be more than enough action to keep your skills honed with this new team. Mr. Smith tells me a lot of our team will come from your ranks, since we have a lot of water to cover."

"They're coming out," said the driver, watching the office in his side mirror while pretending to read a newspaper.

"Okay," Franklin said. "We know where they're going. It's only an hour's drive and we have ninety minutes to get there and get set up. Wait until they both leave the parking lot, then head to the Rickenbacker. Mr. Jacobs, if you'd like to call Mr. Livingston and bring him up to speed, that'll be all right. I need to email A.D.D Smith the recordings and let him know we'll continue the surveillance in Miami."

CHAPTER TWENTY-FOUR

We'd been anchored about 400 yards northwest of the docks since before the sun had risen. There were a couple of sailboats between us and the docks, but we could easily see over their decks from the bridge.

Before we'd arrived, I'd gone down to my stateroom, lifted the bunk, opened the large chest, and retrieved my Night Spirit XT-3 night-vision monocular. It was a really nice three-power spotting scope that also has infrared capability. We'd been lucky. Lester had been on the bridge of the Carver, on watch.

Deuce had been impressed. "A gunny, huh?" he'd asked.

"Hey, even retired jarheads have to have their toys," I'd replied.

Now it was late morning and Lester was still on the bridge. I'd called Alex and told her it might be a while—we wanted to wait until Lester finished his watch. She said they were fine. They'd go into the marina for breakfast but could be at the boat ramp within a few minutes of my call.

The Hispanic guy had arrived with food bags and coffee about 0630 and had gone below, leaving something for Lester to eat.

We'd eaten sandwiches and some really good chowder that Jimmy had whipped up in the galley. Deuce's phone chirped, and he answered it.

"Hey, Tony, how's the training going?" After listening for a couple of minutes, Deuce said, "You're kidding. Actually, I can be there faster than you can. We're sitting just a few hundred meters from the docks now." He listened another couple of seconds and said, "Yeah, the docks at Rickenbacker Marina." After a few more seconds he said, "Okay, keep me posted."

Rusty and Jimmy were down in the galley. Deuce looked puzzled as he placed his phone on the bench beside him. "That was Tony. He and Art were doing some surveillance training up near Palm Beach for our new employer. Their target is coming here. What are the odds of that?"

"Pretty slim," I said, watching through the binoculars as two new men boarded the boat. One was a slim, older man, dressed in golf shirt and brown slacks. The other looked Middle Eastern and was wearing a nice suit. Earlier, I'd noticed a white van pull in and roll slowly through the parking lot, finally parking near the end. I'd only noticed it because it was in my line of sight while I was watching the Carver. It had struck me as odd that nobody got out of it.

"Call Tony back," I said. "Ask him if he's in a white van."

"What's up?" Deuce asked.

"Here, take a look," I replied. "Two more guys just joined Lester on the Carver. Look just beyond the Carver, in the parking lot. See that white Chevy van? It pulled in before those two guys arrived. Nobody got out of the van."

Deuce lifted his phone and called Tony back. "Tony are you in a white Chevrolet van with dark windows?" he asked. I could hear the response but couldn't make out what he said.

"I'm looking right at you, Tony. Which of the two guys that just boarded is the target?" After a few seconds, Deuce said, "Okay, let me talk to Franklin."

Deuce looked at me and nodded while he waited. Then he said, "Franklin, yeah, I'm on the fishing boat, just beyond the two sailboats." After another moment he replied, "Yeah, he's the one Smith told you about. He's good. Never mind why we're here. Email me the recording." Then he hung up.

Turning to me, he said, "Tony and Art are on a surveillance training exercise and their target is a suspected al Qaeda sympathizer. He's sending me the recording of the meeting between him and the older guy."

Deuce's phone chirped again, and he opened it. After punching a few buttons, he glanced down toward the cockpit and said, "This goes no further than this bridge."

I touched the intercom button. "Rusty, you guys stay in the salon for a few minutes, okay?"

"No problem," came the reply over the speaker.

When Deuce pressed a button on his cell phone, we could hear the fuzzy recording of the conversation that Tony had sent. After it ended, I looked at Deuce and said, "Sounds like this Beech guy is Lester and Baldy's boss and he's going to smuggle some terrorists into the country for the Arab guy. I thought Baldy was the boss."

"This puts a different light on things, Jesse."

"Yeah, it sure does. How do you want to play it?"

"I need to call my new boss. He's already on board with you getting some information about what we're doing. I'll need to tell him about what you and I intend to do and our suspicions about Lester and let him decide if we can continue what we have planned. I want Lester, but this has national security implications now. Rusty and Jimmy can't know about this."

He made another call and gave Jason Smith the whole story. It took a good ten minutes of back and forth conversation. Finally, he ended the call and said, "Like it or not, Jesse, you're a part of the team for the time being. Mr. Smith is going to set up an account in your name at the Bank of America in Marathon and deposit $20,000 into it." He grinned and added, "You've been shanghaied."

"Whoa, slow down, Deuce. I never said I was going to hire on. In fact, I said just the opposite. Twice!"

"You're being compensated as a private contractor for this one job. You've been on the payroll retroactively since 0400 hours. Your contract ends when I say, and you'll need to sign a federal non-disclosure contract. I have some in my briefcase below. You can't say no at this point, Jesse." Then he chuckled and added, "Or I'll have to kill you."

I rolled my eyes and he continued, "I've been instructed to use my own discretion in bringing Jimmy and Rusty on board. Like I told you when we first met, I'm a crazy good judge of men, so I'm going to give them most of the details. You're to split the $20,000 with them, half to you and a quarter to each of them."

"Just when I was having fun," I said. "Back under Uncle Sam's thumb."

"We really don't have any choice, man," Deuce said. "Mr. Smith said to go ahead with our idea and get them down to Marathon. He's working on a plan to round up the whole bunch of them when they return from Brown's Cay Tuesday night. Until then, we'll try to find out what we can about Dad's death."

"Can you at least tell me which bunch of alphabets I've been shanghaied into?" I asked.

"All I can say is that our team is a division of Homeland Security and Jason Smith is an associate deputy director of that agency."

"Unbelievable," I said. Then it occurred to me that I'd been using that word a lot about another member of our "team."

"What about the dog? He getting paid, too?"

Deuce laughed and said, "Go ahead and get the guys up here so we can read them in. Have Jimmy bring my briefcase, too."

I called them up and when we were all together on the bridge, Deuce opened his briefcase, took out three sheets of paper, and passed them to each of us. He said, "Sign these."

"What is it?" Jimmy asked, reading it over.

"Never mind, Jimmy," I said. "Just sign it. You've been shanghaied again."

"DHS?" Rusty asked when he saw the letterhead. "What the hell?"

"Just sign it, Rusty," Deuce said. "I'll give you all the details once you do. It'll be simple and worth your while."

After they'd signed the contracts, Deuce outlined what was going on, withholding only a few details. He changed the plan slightly, saying that Jimmy and Rusty would go ashore and ride back with Alex and Julie. He'd need to personally make sure the boat followed us back to Marathon and didn't want them in any danger. Both men argued that point, but it was Deuce's call to make.

"Besides," he said, "I think I'm qualified to be the mate."

Jimmy was watching the boat through the binoculars and reported, "The older guy and the Arab are leaving."

We looked through the windscreen and saw them walking along the dock. We'd been on station since 0700 and it was nearly noon now. Jimmy handed me the binoculars and said, "There's activity on the Carver, man."

I trained the binoculars on the boat and saw that a new guy I hadn't seen before was on the bridge and Lester was walking down the dock, behind the older man and the Arab. Lester got in the blue sedan and drove off. I was hoping it was just a food run.

The new guy sitting at the helm had a shaved head and ebony skin. He took a seat at the helm and relaxed, surveying the marina. He looked more at home there than Lester did. He was dressed in boating attire, unlike the others.

Moving the binos to the two older men, I saw them shake hands. The Middle Eastern man handed Beech an envelope, which immediately disappeared into his pocket.

"Looks like the boat meets al Madani's approval," I said, watching the two men get into separate cars and drive away. "Deuce, give Tony a call and see if he heard what they said."

Deuce made a one-minute call. "Yeah, they struck a deal," he confirmed. "It's on."

"Call your boss," I said. "Since this is now your show, maybe it'd be a good idea to have Tony and Art join us after Rusty and Jimmy depart. Make out as if we're dropping one charter and picking up another. If he gives the okay, call Tony back and have them walk out to the pier at the boat ramp and wait there for us. Maybe they can kill some time by walking out to the end of the dock."

Deuce caught on instantly, "Do a little recon, huh? Great idea." He called Smith and suggested our updated plan. Without saying anything more, he disconnected and made another call.

"Tony how are you guys dressed?" he asked. After a few seconds, he responded, "That's perfect. You're our next charter. In a few minutes, we'll be at the pier by the boat ramp. Rusty and Jimmy will get off there. We've already arranged a ride back for them. Walk out to the end of the dock where the Carver is. Stop there, see what you can, and talk about your plans for the fishing trip. Drop Jesse's name and the boat's name, if you can. See how they respond. When you see us coming, head back to the pier and come aboard. We want to drop them and pick you up in a matter of seconds, and then head back out. It'll happen just after the blue Ford that the Italian-looking guy left in returns." He listened for another few seconds and closed the phone.

Minutes later Lester pulled back into the parking lot, got out and headed toward the Carver. Tony and Art were just behind him, talking animatedly as they neared the pier. Lester stopped in his tracks and turned around. He talked with them for a minute, then started toward the Carver at an increased pace, juggling the bag from McDonald's in his hands as he fumbled with his cell phone.

"Hoist anchor, Jimmy," I directed. "All three of you, head down to the cockpit. Deuce don't forget to shake hands and thank them for the charter. Whoop it up as we move along the docks."

When I heard the windlass start to strain, I started the engines and let them idle until I heard the anchor seat itself. Then I nudged both throttles into gear and idled around the sailboats, headed toward the docks. I could see Lester boarding the Carver and pointing our way. Then he disappeared below deck.

I called Alex and said, "There's been a change of plans, babe. Rusty and Jimmy will be riding back with you. Can't explain right now, but we're heading for the docks. Get over there to pick them up, okay?"

"Okay," Alex whispered. "We're on our way. I love you."

"I love you, too," I said and disconnected.

Although I hadn't said those words in a lot of years, it felt right.

Deuce was just climbing down the ladder and overheard me. "Really?" he asked.

"Yeah," I said. "Really. Now get your ass down there, mate."

As we idled along the south side of the southern dock, Rusty and Jimmy were talking loudly about the fish they'd caught and promising Deuce they'd charter us again. Jimmy had brought up the big cooler and pretended to struggle with it, as if it were full of their catch.

Normally, I like to back into a dock, but it was a long pier, open on the port side. I wanted a quick turnaround, so I nosed in forward. Tony and Art were at the end of the pier and boarded just after Rusty and Jimmy climbed up. Alex's Jeep was parked at the foot of the pier and my friends hurried over toward it.

My long-billed fishing cap with its side and back flaps to block the sun was a perfect disguise. I was wearing wraparound sunglasses and had even put sunblock on my nose to better hide my identity. At this distance, I doubted that Lester and Baldy could recognize me.

Glancing over at the end of the pier, I could see all four men climbing out of the Carver, moving our way at a pretty quick pace. Before they were even halfway, I was backing away from the pier. When I pushed the throttles into forward and turned back toward the southern canal, all four men turned around and ran back to the Carver. Idling along the southern pier, I watched three of them clumsily untie the Carver while the black guy went to the bridge and started the engines. Blue smoke belched from the exhausts; gas engine. This was going to be easier than I thought.

Deuce invited our new 'clients' to join me on the bridge and all three men came up. "Welcome aboard, guys," I said as we cleared the end of the docks.

"Good to see you again, Jesse," Tony said and gripped my hand firmly.

"Nice to be back aboard this fine vessel," Art said.

They sat on the bench seat to port and Deuce sat down in the second seat, to my right. He dutifully checked the gauges and turned on the sonar and radar. Having watched Jimmy earlier, he was familiar with them.

"Bottom is fourteen feet below the keel," he said. "Only those two anchored sailboats showing on the radar. Traffic a mile out on the ICW, headed south."

Looking back, he added, "Carver's leaving the slip with all four aboard."

"Saturday night, rock and roll!" I shouted.

"Huh?" Art said.

"Flashback," I replied.

Once, during a training exercise, we were just about to jump from a chopper into a small bay. Deuce's dad gave the order, "Line of departure, lock and load." But, somehow, I heard, "Saturday night, rock and roll."

Reaching up, I turned on the stereo loud enough for the men on the Carver to hear. Jimmy always had a classic rock CD in the player and sure enough, "Born to be Wild" came out of the speakers.

I pushed both throttles to 1800 rpm and the *Revenge* shot forward, the twin 22-inch, five-bladed propellers displacing a huge amount of water. In seconds, we were up on plane and accelerating.

"Don't show 'em too much, Jesse," Deuce said. "We don't want them to know we can outrun them until it's too late for them to turn back."

I dropped the throttles to 1600 rpm and we were cruising along at a sedate 25 knots.

"I researched that Carver," Art said. "Twin Mercruiser 5.7's, pushing 300 horsepower each. Cruising speed is sixteen knots, with a max of 26."

"Good," I said, "she'll be pushing her maximum speed all the way to Alligator Reef. That's where I'm going to hammer the throttles and pull away from them."

"How fast will that be?" Tony asked.

"Not quite double," I replied. "But close."

"Dayum," Tony and Art said in unison.

"What the hell you got down there?" Tony asked.

"Go have a look," I replied.

Both men scampered down the ladder to see the engine room. When they came back up, Art asked, "You ever think of running drugs?"

All four of us laughed. Tony stole a look back and said, "The Carver's just coming up on plane now, about half a mile astern. She's smoking a bit, though. Think she'll hold together for three hours?"

"I hope so," I replied.

CHAPTER
TWENTY-FIVE

When Lester had gotten out of the car and headed toward the docks, two guys dressed like fishermen were walking behind him and he'd overheard one say, "I've heard a lot about the captain of *Gaspar's Revenge*. He's supposed to be one of the top skippers in the Keys."

The other guy said, "Yeah, it'll be fun hitching a ride down there to meet the other guys. Glad you called McDermitt this morning. Boy, are they gonna be pissed."

Lester's ears had perked up. He needed to talk to those guys. "Couldn't help overhearing—you talking about Jesse McDermitt?"

"Yeah," the black guy said, "You know him?"

"We're old friends," Lester replied.

"He's coming here right now, to drop off a charter," the white guy said, then nodded to his friend. "My pal here called him this morning, just before we got in the car to drive down to Marathon."

"Yeah," Lester said. "I heard that's where he's been. So, you guys are riding down there with him?"

The black guy nodded. "Yeah, that's where we're meeting two other guys to go fishing on *Gaspar's Revenge*. We're gonna ride down there with Captain McDermitt instead of driving and then come back here with our buddies, after our fishing trip. Hey, there he comes now."

Lester turned and saw a big fishing boat headed in from the west. He started to walk quickly to the Carver, while trying to get his phone out and not drop his and Tomas's lunch. Once he got close, he called to Benny, "He's coming in!"

Just then, Sonny answered the phone. "Hey, Boss," he said. "McDermitt's heading in now."

"Are you back to the boat yet?" Sonny asked. "I'm just a few miles away."

"Yeah, Boss. I'm here."

"Good," Sonny said. You can grab him when he docks his boat. If his clients give you any shit, just push 'em in the water."

"Right, Boss," Lester said and hung up the phone.

Benny had already rousted Walt. He and Tomas joined them and together they started down the dock toward where *Gaspar's Revenge* was already tied up.

"I already called the Boss," Lester said. "He's headed back here."

They weren't even halfway to McDermitt's boat when the big boat started backing away from the dock. They picked up their pace, but McDermitt was already turning and heading back out.

"Back to the boat!" Walt shouted.

They ran back to the boat where Benny and Lester quickly untied it from the dock as Tomas started the engines. Walt pulled out his cell phone and called Sonny when he got back to the bridge.

"Boss, they headed back out before we even got close."

"Get to the boat and head after him," Sonny said.

"Untying the lines now," Walt said. "Want us to wait here for ya?"

"No, dumbass!" Sonny yelled. "They'll be long gone before I can get back there through this traffic. Get going and keep me posted. The tanks are full."

Walt closed the phone and mumbled, "One a these days, assbite." Then he turned to Tomas and said, "Get after him!"

Tomas pulled away from the dock and turned the boat toward open water. Once clear of the slip, he pushed the throttles to the stops and the boat lurched forward, belching blue and gray smoke from behind.

Tomas said, "Jefe say his boat *muy rapido*. Ha! It lucky to catch a dugout canoe."

Once they were away from land and heading south in Biscayne Bay, Tomas pushed the boat up to 23 knots—wide open on both throttles. He knew there was no way the engines would hold together for a long time at this speed and they were barely going as fast as the big fishing boat. Tomas throttled down to twenty knots and the engines sounded better.

"What the hell you slowing down for?" Walt yelled. "They're gonna get away."

"I blow up El Jefe's engines, he keel me dead," Tomas replied. "Don' worry, they slowin' down."

Sure enough, the big boat about a half mile ahead did seem to be slowing. Tomas turned on the radar and adjusted it to a one-mile radius. "Look," he said. "Da big boat is going da same speed. He jest showing out, with hees big engines and loud rock-and-roll."

"Okay," Walt said. "Just stay with him, but don't make it look obvious."

They stayed about a half mile behind the big boat for two hours, with Tomas complaining the whole way. He was tired; he'd been up since midnight and it was already three in the afternoon. Plus, the engines weren't sounding all that good.

"What the hell!" Lester said, looking ahead. "He's speeding up."

Tomas checked the radar and sure enough, the big boat was quickly pulling away. Within a few minutes he had to expand the radar range to five miles. The big boat was a mile ahead, still pulling away. Half an hour later, all four men watching intently, it went off the radar screen.

"Damn," Walt said. "Wonder if they're headed to Marathon or out fishing."

"They're headed to Marathon," Lester said. "I talked to those two guys that went out with him. They're meeting two others down there."

CHAPTER TWENTY-SIX

T he Carver was no match for the *Revenge*. I had to cut the speed down to just 23 knots to keep from running off from them. Finally, after two hours, the big black-and-white light tower marking Alligator Reef was coming up. I pushed the throttles to the stops. The wind had come around and was now blowing out of the east, giving us a good ten-knot tailwind, and the seas were nearly flat. I had the *Revenge* running flat out—2500 rpm. The knot-meter read just over 45 knots.

Tony was out of his seat, reveling in the speed. We were running on autopilot near the 100-fathom line, staying well clear of the Florida Keys National Marine Sanctuary. After twenty minutes, the Carver disappeared off the radar, which was set at fifteen miles. We'd lost sight of them well before that. I switched the radar to its maximum of 24 miles and found her again. Sombrero Key light was coming up, so I'd have to slow to cross the reef just before Delta Shoal.

Trusting that we were out of sight of the other boat, I slowed to the *Revenge's* most economical speed of 25 knots. We were still slowly pulling away, and I was counting on back scatter and other boat traffic to disappear from their radar.

Most of Delta Shoal was ten to twelve feet below the surface and it was low tide now. Turning the sonar to forward, I watched for anything that might have grounded on the shoals but saw nothing. Once clear, I pushed the throttles back up to 1800 rpm and headed north-northwest, toward the big microwave tower near Rusty's canal. The Carver had closed a little, but she wouldn't get close enough to see us until we were well inside the canal. I'd noticed she had a dome radar antenna, but it was a cheaper unit and probably couldn't pick us out of the background clutter at this range, and that was only if they knew how to operate it. At this point, I had my doubts.

I lined up the markers going into the canal and brought the speed down to idle as we passed the first one. Checking the radar one last time as we entered the canal, I saw that the Carver was still just over ten miles away. No chance they saw us.

I brought the Revenge into the little turning basin and swung her around, then gently nudged her up to the dock on the east side of the canal, next to the bar, but in front of Alex's and my Mavericks. Rusty and Jimmy were waiting there to tie us off.

"Took ya long enough," Rusty said.

"We had to run slower than I figured," I said. "That Carver's a real pig. She might not even make it to *Dockside*. Where're the girls?"

"They're inside, decorating the place," Rusty replied.

"Decorating?" I asked.

"Don't even get him started, Jesse," Jimmy said. "He bitched about their plans all the way from Miami. Personally, I think they have a good idea. Angie's inside, helpin' out, too."

The six of us walked over and sat down at a long, wooden table next to the bar. "Aaron's gonna tell those guys you're likely gonna be here tomorrow for the party," Rusty said.

"You need a cover ID," Deuce said. "Nothing deep, but a different name. How many people will be here? Can you trust them?"

"In any matter where an outsider and a local is concerned," Rusty answered, "the locals around here can be completely trusted. We're a small town, on a small island, in a group of small islands. Everyone's tight, especially where outsiders are concerned. Everyone that comes tomorrow will be a local, except you three and those four."

"Yeah," Art said, "we already got a sense of that last week when we were looking for Jesse. Y'all are a bunch of tight-lipped people."

"I got an idea," Jimmy said. "How about I be out at the end of the driveway, to kinda direct folks where to park, man? As the locals come in, I can tell 'em that Jesse is

Joe Smith, or whatever, if anyone asks them and that Jesse isn't here. I can also tell 'em that you three cats are Jesse's fishing clients. Locals treat clients a whole lot different than outsiders."

"No, not Joe Smith," Tony said. "Our trainer was just telling us yesterday that there are surprisingly few Joe Smiths and Bill Joneses in the world. When creating an alias, it's better to use uncommon names or nicknames."

"Stretch Buchannan," Art said with a grin and a snap of his fingers.

"That'll work," Deuce added. "Stretch is a member of our old SEAL team. Big, lanky guy like yourself, Jesse."

"Jesse?" I asked. "Name's Stretch."

Everyone laughed, and then Rusty said, "A lot of folks will be coming by boat. I can do the same down at the docks."

"Okay," I said. "But where's Jesse? His boat's here, his clients are here, where'd he go?"

"I don't know," Deuce replied. "But maybe Stretch can take one of them to where he is, in his little boat over there. Would it be safe to say that it's too small for you and four people?"

I grinned at the way he was thinking. "Stretch is a bit of a cutthroat," I said. "Why, just the other day, he tried to snake Jesse's clients away from him. Right there in front of Aaron. And yeah, my skiff's not big enough for three men, especially if two of them are over 200 pounds, which both Lester and I are."

"If this works," Deuce said, "you need to be able to bring him somewhere secluded. Somewhere I could be waiting."

"Jesse's house," Rusty said. "Up in the Content Keys. You could fire a cannon up there and nobody could hear it. Take my skiff. The GPS will take you right to it."

We continued to discuss options and alternatives for half an hour. Russ used to tell us that just as soon as any operation started, you could pretty much throw the initial plan out the window, and you should always have redundancies for redundancies. Rusty's phone rang; he looked at it and said, "It's Aaron."

"Put it on speaker," I said.

Rusty punched a button and said, "Hey, Aaron. I'm sitting here with Jesse. You're on speaker."

"Hey, guys," came the voice through the phone. "Your buddies just left. The same two came in as before, Jesse. They arranged for dock space and fuel, then took off. The one guy, the body builder, came back a second later. He did just as you said he would, Rusty. Asked about your doubloon necklace. And guess what? He was wearing one exactly like it. Pulled it out and compared it to yours. Only difference was an 'RL' inscribed on the top of the mount, on the back."

"That ties it," I said, looking at Deuce. "Aaron be real careful around those guys. The one with the necklace is a killer. That necklace belonged to a friend of mine who drowned up in Palm Beach. I'm going to have someone come over to babysit those guys. His name's

Art. Should be there in fifteen minutes. Where'd you dock the Carver?"

"Right now, she's at the fuel dock. I put her in slip ten, two down from your old one. They were pissed you weren't here. Asked a bunch of questions and made up some lame story about having to rent their own boat to go fishing. I said I didn't know where you were mooring the *Revenge*, but you'd probably be at the *Rusty Anchor* tomorrow for the party."

"Jesse," Jimmy said, "that's right next to Angie's slip. I'll go talk to her, man. Art can use her houseboat."

"Tell her she's welcome to stay in the guest room, Jimmy," Rusty said. "You and her both."

"Thanks, amigo," Jimmy said as he and Art got up and headed toward the bar.

"You did good, Aaron. Thanks a lot. See you tomorrow. Oh, yeah—until further notice, my name's Stretch Buchannan. Keep it on the down low but pass the word to any locals and warn them to steer clear of those guys. One more thing. Can you be here early tomorrow? I'd like to borrow Rusty's necklace."

"No problem, Jesse, er, I mean Stretch. See ya tomorrow." The line clicked off and Rusty closed the phone.

I turned to Art and Jimmy, who were headed across the yard, and said, "Art, see me before you go over there." Then I asked Deuce, "How are you guys armed?"

"I'm carrying," he replied. "But Tony and Art aren't."

"Follow me," I said to Tony and Deuce.

"You sure, Jesse?" Rusty asked, knowing what I was about to do.

"Dead sure," I replied.

The three of us walked over to the dock and boarded the *Revenge*, with the dog trotting along beside me.

"Stay and watch," I said to the dog. He promptly turned around and sat down on the dock. I unlocked the hatch to the salon and took them forward to my stateroom. I punched in the code on the keypad under the foot of the bunk and then pulled the release. The bunk rose with a hiss. I spun the combination lock on the large storage box beneath it, and when I opened it, both men exhaled sharply.

"Seriously," I said, "Us old jarheads just have to have our toys." Inside the storage box, which I called my war chest, was my arsenal. "I've always believed a man would be a fool to go out on open water in the Caribbean with no means of defending his vessel from pirates. Your dad did too, Deuce. Pirates still exist, but not the swash-buckling type from the old Errol Flynn movies. Today's Caribbean pirates are mostly drug runners and slavers and they've replaced their cutlasses with Uzis. Hundreds of boats have disappeared, and their owners have never been seen again. They'll use the boat to haul drugs and take care of the owners either by murdering them and tossing them overboard or selling them as slaves in the sex trade."

Art called out from the dock, "Permission to board?"

"Come forward," I called back. I took out two holstered Beretta M9s, four matching magazines and a box of 9mm ammo and handed them to Art and Tony. The M9 had been the standard issue for both the navy and Marine Corps for twenty years, so I knew they'd be very familiar with them. The holsters could be worn inside or outside the pants, clipped onto the belt. I also removed my Night Spirit monocular and handed it to Art, who put it in a cargo pocket of his shorts. I then pulled out one of many long, narrow fly rod cases and handed it to Deuce.

He hefted it, noting that it was probably too heavy to hold a fly rod and reel. When he opened it and removed my M-40A3 sniper rifle, he let out a low whistle. A U.S. Optics MST-100 scope designed by John Unertl lay next to it. Deuce picked it up and snapped it onto place on the rail. It was obvious from the way he inspected the weapon that he'd handled an M-40 before. I also handed him a small box of .308 Lapua ammo.

"What's it zeroed at?" he asked.

"Two hundred meters, and I've fired it accurately over 900," I replied. "The case is actually an old Sage fly rod case I gutted to install form-fitting foam pads for the rifle and scope. It won't look a bit out of place on Rusty's skiff or anywhere else in the Keys, for that matter. Ammo is match grade Lapua. If I can get Lester to go with me to the house, you can set out just ahead of us. Rusty's skiff will cross any skinny water between here and there, and I'll make a few turns to give you time to get up there and get set up."

Deuce's eyes came up and met mine. "Killing him is no longer an option, Jesse."

"When faced with overwhelming odds, most people will give up," I said. "When you get to my house, the deck will give you a clear view all around for nearly a mile. When I get about 200 yards from the house, I'm going to stop and let Lester know who I am and that he's covered, just in case he has any ideas to take the boat and come up to the house alone. To prove the point, I'll raise an oar up in the air. Think you can put a nice round hole in it, center mass, at that distance?"

"He can," Tony said. "Even at twice that distance."

"Let's keep it at 200," I said. "The skiff might be rocking some and that's the distance where you can first start to make out the house."

I closed and locked the storage box, then lowered the bunk. Tony smiled and said, "What else you got in there, Gunny?"

"Just toys, like I said," I replied.

Tony and Art had loaded the mags, holstered the Berettas and stuck them under their shirts at the small of their backs. Deuce put the rifle back in the case and we climbed back up to the dock, where Rusty and Jimmy were waiting. Rusty noted the case Deuce was carrying and said, "That'll fit in the fish box up on the front of my skiff. It's airtight and has a lock." He handed Deuce the key ring and Deuce walked down the dock and locked the case where Rusty had directed him.

When he came back, he said, "Never heard of a locking fish box before."

"That's the only place to store an expensive fly rod," Rusty responded with a knowing grin.

Deuce turned to me. "I need to contact Director Smith to update him and see if he has any more intel on Beech and al Madani. I'd rather do a face-to-face, but emails will have to do."

"Use my laptop, dude," Jimmy said. "There's a secure server on the *Revenge* and I built my own encryption into the laptop. It'll match any encryption sent or received."

"And you were a machinist's mate?" Deuce asked skeptically.

"First class, bro," Jimmy replied. "Angie said *no problemo* for using her houseboat. Here's the keys."

He handed a key ring to Art, who said, "I'm going to go ahead over there. I'll stop in the office and let your friend know who I am and where I'll be. I'll check in every half hour, till 2200, or sooner, if anything develops." Then he made his way around the end of the turning basin and disappeared down the trail through the woods.

"Tony," Rusty said, "you can bunk on Jesse's boat tonight." But to Deuce, he said, "Son, you're welcome in my house, or you can join Tony if you like." Then he turned and headed over to the house. The implication was obvious. Rusty accepted the relationship.

The sun was getting low in the sky and it looked to be another beautiful sunset in paradise. What the next day was going to bring was anyone's guess, though.

"We should all turn in and get some rest," I said as I saw Alex and Angie come out of the bar. "Tomorrow could be a long day."

Deuce climbed aboard the *Revenge* to make his video call and I went over to talk to Alex. Jimmy intercepted Angie and they headed into the bar so she could show him the decorations.

"Is Deuce planning to do some fly fishing?" Alex asked. "He has about the same build as you and could probably use a few pointers."

"Fly fishing?" I asked.

"I saw the fly rod case he stowed on Rusty's skiff. But something tells me there's no rod and reel in that case. What's going on?"

The lady was sharp as a tack, no denying that. Rather than try to lie about it, I knew the best idea was to give her most of the truth, so I told her about our plans for tomorrow. Then I surprised her with, "I think we should get married."

For the first time since I'd met her, she was speechless. She looked deeply into my eyes, then wrapped her arms around my neck and held me so tightly I thought I couldn't breathe.

"If that's a proposal, the answer is yes," she said.

"It was," I said, feeling more secure. "If you want, we can go down and get the license first thing in the morning."

"Can Rusty officiate on board the *Revenge*?" she asked.

"I know he's a notary," I replied, "so he can do it aboard the *Revenge* or anywhere else. You in a big hurry?"

"No, nothing like that," she said. "I'm not one of those women who started looking at bridal magazines at fifteen, planning every detail of my dream wedding. All our friends will already be here tomorrow, that's all."

"Okay," I said, getting that shanghaied feeling again. "Tomorrow it is, then." I saw Deuce coming out of the salon and added, "Why don't you go ask Rusty if his notary license is up to date?"

She'd seen Deuce coming too and said, "Okay, I'll get out of the way."

"Good news, Jesse," Deuce began, after Alex was out of earshot. "The Director has given approval for our plans. If it comes down to it, taking Lester out is sanctioned, but only as a last resort. He wants to know if he's involved in any way with the terrorist smuggling. What's up with you? You look pale."

"Pale?" I asked. "Yeah, well, I think I just got shanghaied again. I asked Alex to marry me."

"Hey, man, congratulations!" he said. "Why would you feel shanghaied if you asked her, though?"

"The wedding is tomorrow."

Rusty and Alex came out of the house, and she ran toward the bar as Rusty casually walked out to us on the dock.

"I told ya she was about ready to set the hook, brother," Rusty said, with a wink.

"It's not like that, Rusty," I said. "I asked her, and she said yes. Plain and simple."

"Bet you didn't ask her to marry you tomorrow, though," he said.

To save face, I lied and said, "Actually, I did. We'll go get the license in the morning and you can marry us before the shindig gets started at noon."

"Sure, ya did," he said as he turned and walked back to the house, laughing. Then he yelled back over his shoulder, "Congrats, bro. Y'all are right for each other."

CHAPTER TWENTY-SEVEN

The Carver had pulled into Boot Key Harbor after completely losing sight of the big fishing boat. Walt had expected to see it at the dock, but it wasn't there.

"Damn," said Walt. "The boss ain't gonna be pleased about this. Tomas, you shoulda put the hammer down and kept up with him like I told ya."

"*No es posible*, Walt," Tomas argued. "That big boat *es muy rapido*. It took off at over 40 miles an hour. *El barco, One-Eyed Jack*, not do that even if she was new."

"What we gonna do now, Walt?" Lester had asked.

"Head for the fuel dock, Tomas," Walt said. "This tub's runnin' on fumes. Lester, me and you gonna go see that manager and get a place to dock this piece of shit and see what we can find out."

Tomas pulled up to the fuel dock, and Walt and Lester headed off to the manager's office to pay for the fuel and get a docking space. "He must be picking up the rest of his fishing party somewhere else. Les, you shoulda got more information from those two fishermen."

"I was in a hurry to get to the boat," Lester said.

"Yeah, I guess you did right," Walt said as the entered the marina office.

When Walt and Lester walked in, Lester immediately noticed that the manager was wearing a necklace exactly like the one he'd taken from the old man. It surprised him, at first.

Walt said, "We never did find our buddy, Jesse, up in Miami like that guy said. We ended up renting our own boat, as you can see. Need some gas and a place to park it, if you got room. We figured he'd come back here."

Lester stared at the doubloon hanging on a gold chain around the man's neck.

"Actually, he did a couple days ago," Aaron said. "Closed out his account and said he'd come back next week to remove his signage and gear from the dock. Sorry to see him go. He brought a lot of business to the marina."

"Well, that sucks," Walt said. "Did you tell him we were looking to charter with him?"

"I wasn't here," Aaron lied. "That's what my assistant told me later. I can put you in slip ten, down near the end. They're numbered on the pilings."

"Any idea where he's staying now?" Lester asked as he handed over a credit card that the boss had given him for expenses.

"No, he didn't say," Aaron replied, running the card through the machine. "I asked Robin that, specifically.

But you can probably catch him at the big party tomorrow at the *Rusty Anchor*. All the locals'll be there."

"A party, huh?" Walt said. "Yeah, where is this *Rusty Anchor*?"

"Go out to the highway," Aaron said, "turn right and go about half a mile. It's the crushed-shell driveway on the right. No signs or anything. Just a weathered mailbox on a crooked post."

"Hey, thanks," Walt said. "Maybe we'll get lucky and catch up to him there, before we, um, head out on our fishing trip. Let's go, Lester."

The two men left the office. Once outside Lester said, "I'll be right back, Walt. Forgot something."

"Be quick about it," Walt said.

Lester walked back in to the office just as Aaron was just about to dial the phone on his desk. "Hey, I just wanted to ask ya where ya got that necklace," Lester said. Reaching down the front of his shirt, he pulled his own necklace out and said, "I got one looks just like it."

"Oh, this," Aaron said, lifting the necklace Rusty had given him. "My wife gave it to me for my birthday a few years ago. It's from the Atocha."

"The *Atocha*?" Lester asked. "That a store, or something?"

"No," Aaron said laughing. "The *Atocha* was a Spanish shipwreck that Mel Fischer found some years back. Had a huge fortune of treasure on board. They made a lot of the coins into necklaces. Can I have a closer look?"

Lester held it up so Aaron could look at it. Aaron turned it over and noticed the initials RL neatly engraved in the top of the mount. Thinking quickly and counting on the man not knowing anything about treasure ships since he'd never heard of the *Atocha*, Aaron said, "No, yours must be from the *Rio Lagos*. They put that 'RL' on the back of some of them. That, and the chains are a little different."

"Know how much your wife paid for yours?" Lester asked.

"No, not married to her anymore," Aaron lied. In fact, he'd never been married. "But I had it appraised after we split up. It's worth about three grand." He knew this because he'd seen them for sale at the Mel Fischer museum.

"Three grand!" Lester said. "Son of a bitch!"

"Don't tell me you got ripped off," Aaron said, nervously.

"Um, yeah," Lester said. "I paid over four for it, three years ago."

"That's too bad," Aaron said. "It might be worth that today—been a while since I had mine appraised."

"Thanks, man," Lester said, walking out of the office.

Damn, he thought, *if Sonny lied about what this is worth, he probably lied about all of it. Son of a bitch ripped me off.*

Lester walked back to the boat, dejected. Sonny had given him $70,000 for everything, saying it was only gonna bring a hundred grand. *If he was off by a third on the necklace that means he ripped me off by about a hundred grand. That damn weasel.*

When he got back to the boat, Walt was on the phone with Sonny. He ended the call and told him, "Boss wants us to rent a car and split up. If we can't find out where the dude parks his boat by tomorrow afternoon, we snatch him at the party. But, either way, Tomas has to have the boat over to Brown's Cay by early Tuesday morning, preferably Monday night, and it's an all-day trip there."

"How the hell we s'posed to split up if we only rent one car?" Lester asked.

"One of us stays here with the boat on the off chance the guy shows up here. The rest of us go in the car, find him, and grab him. Then we come back here and beat it back to Miami."

"I'll stay here," Tomas said. "I been up since midnight."

"No," Lester said, thinking quickly. "You need to go. Might need your Spanish at some of these backwater marinas. I'll stay here. If he does show back up here, I'm probably the only one that can take him one-on-one without shooting him. Boss said he's pretty big, six-three and 230."

The other three men looked at one another. Then Walt decided, "Yeah, you stay with the boat, Lester. Stay sharp. I got a cab coming to take us to the airport to rent a car. I'll go out front and wait for it. You guys dock the boat over in slip ten, then Tomas, you and Benny get out front."

Walt stalked around the bar, which was now in full swing on a Saturday night. The other three men finished gassing up the boat, which took twenty minutes— the fill was almost 200 gallons. Tomas put the bill on the card the boss had given him for just that purpose, they backed the boat away from the fuel dock and motored over to slip ten. As Tomas backed the boat into the slip, Lester noticed a man boarding a houseboat two docks down.

"Must be nice to live on a houseboat like that," he said.

"Livin' 'pon a boat sucks, mon," Benny said.

<hr />

Art boarded the houseboat, unlocked the door and turned on the aft deck light. He found an empty beer can in the trash, rinsed it and filled it with bottled water from the fridge. Then he went up to the sundeck to watch the men who had just docked in slip ten.

They sure didn't look or act like any boat people he'd known, and growing up in a coastal town, he'd known a lot. He texted Deuce to check in and tell him that the boat had just tied up in the adjacent slip, just as Aaron had said. After he disconnected, he watched as two of the men, one Hispanic and one black, walked around the bar, where the pale bald guy had gone, leaving the body builder alone on the bridge of the boat.

Art's phone chirped. He had an email from Deuce, forwarded from Mr. Smith. It was a list of known associates of one Elijah Beech, who'd met earlier with the suspected al Qaeda sympathizer. The list was complete with pictures and a short history of arrests on each man. Three of the four men he saw matched three on the list, but the body builder wasn't on it. He emailed Deuce back and said that the three men on the boat were indeed Walter O'Hara, who appeared to be in charge, Tomas Rodriguez, who was the only one aboard that seemed to know anything about boats, and Benjamin Simms, from whom he'd caught a few words, and who was obviously from a Caribbean island. At the front of the bar, he noticed a taxi pull up. The three men from the boat got in and left, and he texted that info to Deuce.

CHAPTER TWENTY-EIGHT

The County Clerk's office was usually closed on Sundays. But in a small town like Marathon, on a small island, all it took was a quick phone call if you were a local. The clerk, who was a client of both Alex's and Jesse's, was beside himself to get to the office and issue them a marriage license.

"I knew I'd see you two in here one day," he said. "Welcome home, Alex. When will you be back to guiding?"

"Thanks, Felix," Alex said, smiling. "I just got a new boat and should be ready to go back to work in just a few days. I've heard the tarpon are really hitting hard this month. Want to give it a try?"

"I've never caught anything that big on a fly rod. That'd be a lot of fun," he replied. "So, you two are gonna combine forces, huh?"

"Yes, we are," I agreed, smiling at Alex.

Felix was a real busybody and I knew that within an hour or two, every angler and boater on the island would know. "In fact, Rusty's gonna do the ceremony in about an hour. That is, if we can get the license."

"Well," Felix said, drawing the word out. "Normally, there's a three-day wait, just like buying a handgun. Unless you've both attended a state-sanctioned marriage prep class. I'm licensed by the state to give that course. I can postdate it to show that you took it three days ago. That would allow you to go through with the ceremony this morning."

"Thanks, Felix," I said. "You won't get into trouble doing that, will you?"

"Oh, Lord no. I do it all the time for people I know should be together, and you two should have been together a long time ago."

"That's so sweet," Alex said. "Please come early to the party at *Rusty Anchor* today. We're going to do the ceremony at ten o'clock and the party starts at noon."

"Wouldn't miss it for the world. Can I bring Kevin?"

"We'd love to have you both, wouldn't we, Jesse?"

"Absolutely," I agreed.

With that, Felix went to work on his computer and within minutes handed us a form to sign for the preparatory class. We both signed and returned it, then he presented us with the marriage license, which we also signed and handed back. He peeled off the top copy of both, handed them to me and said, "You're all set, you two. Best of luck, and Kevin and I will see you in a few hours. We both just love weddings."

After leaving the County Clerk's office, Alex asked, "Is it okay with you that I invited them? They're both very good clients and always tip me well."

"Of course," I said. "They're nice guys."

We drove back to the *Anchor* with our marriage license signed and sealed. When we got there, Jimmy was already positioned at the front of the driveway.

Alex rolled down her window. "You're out here a little early, aren't you, Jimmy?"

He just grinned and said, "Seemed like the thing to do, considering."

"Considering what?" I asked suspiciously.

"Well, dude, you know how the Coconut Telegraph works. The parking lot's half full already. Everyone's waiting for y'all. I got a chain here that I'm gonna put up about ten o'clock. That be all right?"

"Shit," I mumbled. "Sorry, Alex. Looks like you're gonna have a big wedding, whether you want it or not. Yeah, Jimmy, put the chain up a little before that, so you can be there with me."

Jimmy nodded, and Alex drove on, smiling at me. "It's all good, as long as you're here."

When we turned into the parking lot, we discovered Jimmy wasn't kidding. Though I recognized many of the cars and pickups, there were a number that I didn't. Nothing looked like a rental.

There were tables set up outside, with chairs arranged on both sides, even a makeshift altar at the far end of the yard, with all the tables lined up toward it. But there weren't any people in the yard.

We got out of the Jeep and walked into the bar, which erupted in cheers. Julie and Angie rushed over and took Alex away, with Julie saying, "Time to get you ready." They disappeared out the door behind the bar, headed toward the house.

I walked over to the bar and gave Rusty the license. He looked it over quickly. "Guess you're all set. You have rings and a best man?"

"No," I replied. "This came up pretty sudden."

Deuce was standing at the bar, drinking a cup of coffee. "Deuce, if I'd had time to plan this better and your dad was still around, he would have been the one to stand up with me, since Rusty is officiating. Would you take his place?"

"Jesse," he said, "I'd be honored."

Rusty reached under the bar and pulled out a small box, saying, "That just leaves the matter of the rings. These were Juliet's and mine. I'd be proud if you and Alex would accept them as my wedding gift."

"You gotta be kidding, Rusty," I said, completely taken aback. "We couldn't possibly accept those."

"You been like a brother to me, ever since we was in boot camp. I insist."

After a moment, I realized how much Alex would be touched by the gesture. "For Alex's sake, I'll accept. Thanks, man."

"You better get on over to your boat and get changed," he said. "Unless you wanna get married in fishing shorts and boat shoes."

I picked up the little box and walked out to my boat. The dog was curled up on the deck of the cockpit, sleeping. He lifted his head as I stepped aboard.

"Pescador, go get on the skiff." To my surprise, he bounded off the deck and trotted down the dock to my Maverick, where he sat down on the casting deck. I yelled at him, "Stay there for a while."

I wanted him with me when I left, hopefully with Lester. After making my way to my stateroom, I opened the hanging closet and surveyed my options. Then I sat down on the bunk and called Alex.

When the connection was made, she said, "A bit overwhelmed, Captain?"

I chuckled. "Rusty gave us his and Juliet's rings as a wedding gift. Can you believe that?"

"Yeah," she said, "Julie told me he was going to. I just love that guy."

"What are you wearing? I'm sitting in the stateroom, staring into my hanging locker, and my choices are severely limited."

"Julie wants me to wear this little white dress she has. It fits well and looks nice, but it's not me, Jesse. Can we keep it simple, before things get too out of hand?"

"God, I love you," I said. "Jeans okay?"

"Perfect. I have a nice pair of designer jeans that look great. I can wear a white blouse along with it."

"Okay, jeans I have an abundance of. Hang on." I sorted through the hanging locker. "Yeah, I have a decent white long-sleeve shirt."

"Okay," she said. "Let's do this."

I ended the call, stripped, and got in the shower. Five minutes later, I stepped out, toweled off and shaved. I could use a haircut, but what the hell? Another five minutes and I was sitting on the bench by the dock, slipping on my black loafers. I didn't like black-soled shoes on the boat. They left scuff marks.

Jimmy was walking down the driveway when I got back to the bar. He said, "Everyone's here that's coming. You ready, Skipper?"

"Yeah," I replied.

"This ain't your first time, is it?" he said, as we approached the door.

"This'll be the third time for me."

Together, we walked into the bar, where everyone was still congregated. Rusty waved me over to the bar and set two shot glasses down, then poured us both a shot of Pusser's Navy rum. Lifting his glass, he said in a loud voice, "Here's to the wind that blows, the ship that goes, and the lass who loves a sailor."

We both tossed back the rum and Rusty added, "Let's get on with this before I get cold feet."

Everyone followed us out of the bar. All Alex's and my friends were there. Aaron and Art came through the woods and came over to Deuce and me. As Aaron handed me Rusty's necklace, he said, "Those guys on the boat? They left just after sunrise. All but the Hispanic guy. They must have rented a car last night—it's a silver Toyota four-door."

"Thanks, Aaron," I said.

"Lester must be really tired," Art said. "The other three left soon after sunset in a taxi but didn't get back until past midnight in a rental car. He was sitting on the bridge, making passes at every woman who walked by. It was pathetic. Rodriguez is on the bridge now, but it looks like he's even more tired. He's snoring away."

"Odds are they'll show up here in a few hours," Deuce said. "Jesse, I'm not real crazy about doing this, with those guys looking for you."

"*No problemo*, man," Jimmy said, walking up behind me. "I put up a chain across the driveway, with a sign on it saying, 'Open party at noon.' We have two hours."

Angie came around the corner of the bar, carrying her guitar. "We're ready, Jesse," she said. Then she walked back to the corner and sat down.

"Let's do it," Rusty said. "Saturday night, rock and roll."

Rusty led the way, with Deuce and me following. We walked up to the altar and took our places. Then Angie started playing softly on the guitar and Julie came around the corner of the bar, walking down the row between the tables. She came to stand on the opposite side of the altar, across from Deuce and me. Angie started playing the "Wedding March" and everyone stood.

Alex walked around the corner and came down the same aisle. She was wearing a ruffled white blouse and tight jeans, low on her hips. She looked beautiful as she came up to stand next to me.

Rusty said, "Everyone sit down, please." When they had taken their seats, he said, "We're all here today to see two friends marry. This day has been a long time coming. Who gives this woman?"

Jimmy stood and said, "Myself and all her friends."

Alex smiled and nodded at Jimmy, then looked into my eyes. She whispered, "Last chance, Captain Jesse."

I smiled back at her and nodded at Rusty. He said, "Do you have the rings?"

I handed the rings to Rusty and he continued with the service. "By exchanging these here rings, which have no end, you two are promising to love one another to no end. Jesse, place this ring on Alex's finger. Do you take this woman to be your mate, to love, honor, and cherish her, as long as you both live?"

"I do," I said.

"Alex," Rusty said. "Place this ring on Jesse's finger. Do you take this man to be your mate, to love, honor, and cherish him, as long as you both live?"

"I do," she said.

Rusty continued, "By the power given to me by the great State of Florida, I now say y'all are man and wife. Brother, you can kiss your bride."

I took my new wife in my arms and kissed her as Rusty announced, "Folks, allow me to introduce Jesse and Alex McDermitt."

Everyone got to their feet and cheered as we walked between the tables. Once we got to the last table, Rusty yelled out over the crowd, "Now, let's celebrate! No damn hurricane can overcome the Conch spirit!"

The reception continued until noon, and then Jimmy went out and took the chain down. There were a number of cars already waiting on the shoulder of the road.

It was fun celebrating with all our friends, but now it was time for me to be Stretch. Everyone there had already been informed and as more celebrants arrived, Jimmy made sure they knew too. Rusty was down at the docks, helping people tie up and clueing them in, as well. I told Alex that until the bad guys arrived and were out of the way, we had to pretend we weren't together. Just before 1400, when the celebration was really getting under way, my phone rang. It was Jimmy.

"Three non-locals in a silver Toyota coming in, man," he said.

"That's probably them," I said. "Thanks, Jimmy."

"*No problemo*, man," he said. "I even charged 'em forty bucks to get in. Can I keep it?"

"Sure, Jimmy," I said, grinning. "You earned it and more."

I closed the phone, got Deuce's attention, and gave him the go sign. Deuce had said he was going to play me and see how things panned out.

I turned to Alex and before I could say anything, she said, "So how's the fishing been, Stretch?"

I laughed, gave her a peck on the cheek and said, "Thanks, babe. I'll make this up to you."

"You bet you will," she said with a leer.

The Toyota parked in the lot and three men got out. They were obvious outsiders. Lester and Walter O'Hara, we already knew. The other one, we knew from the email Deuce's boss had sent. Tomas Rodriguez. Benjamin Simms was still on the boat.

Deuce was heading toward the parking lot as the three men were coming toward the yard. They walked right past one another, and Deuce turned and hurried around the turning basin toward Rusty's skiff. I moved out to the middle of the yard and was laughing it up with two flats guides. I made sure that I was facing the three men as they came into the yard looking around. Tomas saw the *Revenge* and pointed it out to the other three and they started heading that way. Perfect, I thought, they'd have to walk right past me.

"Hey, guys," I said. "Did you find McDermitt?"

They stopped, and then Walt recognized me from Aaron's office. Lester did a doubletake and stared at the doubloon hanging around my neck. I'd changed into fishing pants and a work shirt. Walter said, "Hey, man. We were just going over to his boat to say hi. Big party here, huh?"

"Yeah," I said, "good time. But hey, you just walked right past him. Guess you missed him in the crowd. There he is over there, getting in his skiff."

The three men looked across the canal and watched as Deuce tossed the lines and looked straight at them before cranking the engine and heading down the canal.

"Damn," Lester said. "He's gettin' away. I mean, um, he's leavin'."

The two guides took the hint when I nodded at them and walked away. The three men watched as Deuce disappeared around the end of the canal, headed west.

"You guys don't even know McDermitt, do you?" I said.

"Sure, we do," Walter said.

"No," I said, "I don't believe you. You almost rubbed shoulders walking past him. What is it you want the son-of-a-bitch for?"

That surprised Walter. I'm sure he'd noticed that everyone he'd talked to down here was less than helpful. "He owe you money, too?" I asked. "Owes me a hundred bucks. I just confronted him about it and he basically told me to piss up a rope."

"You know where he's going?" Walter asked. "What's your name, anyway?"

"Will, but my friends call me Stretch. He's probably headed home. His charter for the afternoon canceled to be at the party here."

"Where's he live, Stretch?" Walter asked. "My name's Walt, by the way. This is Les and Tomas. Yeah, he owes me some money."

"Nice to meet you guys," I said. "He lives up in the Content Keys, north of Big Pine."

"Thanks. How far a drive is that? You know his address?"

I was taking a drink from a beer can full of water and laughed so hard, I nearly choked. "You guys really aren't from around here, are ya? You can't drive there, and there ain't no address. I can take one of ya there, though."

"Watta ya mean, we can't drive there?" Lester asked.

"It's an island, Les," I said. "No roads. But, like I said, I can take one of ya there. For a price."

"Everyone on this island is tight as a clam," Walt said, suspiciously. "How come you want to help us?"

I looked at him hard and said, "Asshole owes me money. And just blew me off, right here in front of clients. You cover his debt and I'll take you to him."

Lester was still staring at the necklace as Walt said, "How come only one of us?"

"Boat's small," I said. "And there's some really skinny water between here and his house. That means shallow water. Any more than about 600 pounds and we'd never get across the flats. I weigh 230 pounds and my dog weighs 100. That leaves two 270 pounds. So, unless two of you guys are less than a buck thirty-five each, it's only one guy."

"What dog?" Walt asked.

"He's on the boat," I said, "taking a nap. Don't go anywhere without him."

"I'll go," said Lester, puffing up a little. "He's a pretty big dude, Walt."

"He ain't all that tough," I said. This seemed to puff Lester up even more.

"Okay," Walt said. "You go and we'll wait at the boat. Call me when you get there."

"Mine's the Maverick in front of Jesse's boat," I told Lester. "I'll be a minute—need to get some bottled water and a thermos of coffee."

I went inside the bar and left the three of them outside. Julie was behind the bar and Alex and Angie were helping with the serving. I went behind the bar and grabbed Rusty's thermos, which I knew he kept there, filled it with coffee, and took four bottles of water from the cooler.

"Everything's going as planned," I told Alex. "I should be back in a few hours and we can start that honeymoon. Where did you want to go?"

"Up to the house," she replied, "and do a little fishing."

"You sure?" I asked. "The *Revenge* has a 300-mile range. We could go just about anywhere in the Caribbean."

"Maybe later in the winter," she said. "Right now, I want to be in our home."

"I like the way you say *our* home," I said. "Be back before supper."

I walked back out to the yard, where the three men were talking. They stopped as I approached and told them, "That'll be cash. Up front."

Walt pulled a money clip out of his pocket, peeled off five twenty-dollar bills and said, "You better be right about where that guy's going, Stretch."

"Where else would he go?" I said. "Everyone's here and his boat's here."

"Why would he just leave his boat like that?" Lester asked.

"It's secure here," I replied. "People don't board someone's boat down here without permission. Probably locked up tighter than Fort Knox, and I'm pretty sure he has an alarm system on board."

"Okay," Walt said, "You and the guys get going, Les. We'll head over to the boat. Don't forget to call me when you get there. And remember our timetable for tomorrow."

He must mean the job that Beech had accepted, I thought. To smuggle the four terrorists from the Bahamas. The two men walked toward the parking lot as Lester and I headed down the dock to my skiff. The dog was sitting right where he'd been when I'd gone into the cabin a couple hours ago. Someone, probably Julie, had placed bowls of water and dog food on the casting deck for him.

As we walked up, Lester asked, "Does it bite?"

"Yeah," I said. "But only if I let him." The dog stood up and bared his teeth at Lester, the hair on his neck and back standing straight up.

"Tell it I'm okay, man." Lester said.

"He thinks it's his boat," I said. "Like I told you, nobody boards another person's boat down here without permission. You'll have to ask him if you can board."

"You gotta be kiddin'," he said. "Ask a freakin' dog for permission?"

"He won't let ya board till you do," I replied.

Lester looked at the dog, looked at me, then back at the dog. It was obvious he had a fear of dogs. I was enjoying it a bit too much.

"Can I get on the boat?" he asked the dog.

The dog growled at him, menacingly. I laughed and said, "You gotta ask permission to come aboard."

"This is ridiculous," Lester said. Then he looked at the dog again and said, "Can I have permission to come aboard?"

To my surprise, the dog barked once and sat down, looking from me to his food bowl, which didn't look as if it'd been touched.

"Go ahead," I said, and he started wolfing it down.

Then to Lester, I said, "Just don't get near him while he's eating. He might mistake your balls for clams, and he really likes clams." Lester's hands subconsciously went to his groin.

I untied the bowline, stepped down onto the boat and told Lester to get in, then started the engine. Indicating the second seat, I said, "Sit there."

Then I untied the stern cleat and pushed us away from the dock. Once we were clear of Alex's boat, I pushed the throttle into forward and headed down the canal.

"We should be able to see McDermitt's trail once we clear the canal," I said. "That way, we'll know for sure he's headed to his house."

"His trail?" Lester asked. "You can't follow a trail on water. Even I ain't that dumb."

"Sure, ya can," I said. "You'll see, once we hit open water."

"That's a nice necklace ya got there, Stretch," Lester said. "I got one just like it." He pulled Russ's doubloon out of his shirt and it was all I could do to keep from strangling him right there. "That's the second one I seen down here. Everybody wear them?"

"Only the ones who can afford it," I said. "This one, I found myself and had it made."

A minute later, we left the canal and I brought the skiff up on plane and turned westward toward the Seven Mile Bridge. Sure enough, the disturbed water where Deuce had passed was still visible.

"There," I said, "see how the water looks different heading around Sister Rock? See the bubbles? That came from McDermitt's prop."

"I'll be damned," Lester said. "A freakin' trail in the water."

We followed Deuce's trail under the Seven Mile Bridge where it was visible, going straight as an arrow to the northwest, up toward Horseshoe Key. I turned almost due west, toward the southern tip of Little Pine

Key. "Hey, what the hell ya doin', Stretch? He went that way," Lester said, pointing toward Horseshoe.

"Yeah, he did," I said. "He's headed to his house. It's the only thing up that way and he's taking the only deep-water way to get there. His boat can't cross the flats like mine, and he damned sure don't know the flats like I do. Water's too shallow, so he has to go up and around. We can just hook around Little Pine Key, and head north up Big Spanish Channel. Don't worry—his place is the only thing out that way and I know these waters better than him. I was born here. He's only been here a few years."

That seemed to calm the muscle head. I was worried he was one of those steroid users. Those guys had really short fuses and could blow up over the smallest things. We rode on in silence for ten minutes and then turned north into Big Spanish. I figured with the head start that Deuce had at the docks, the extra ten miles I was running and my going a little slower than normal, Deuce should have at least twenty minutes to tie up the skiff, get up to the deck, uncase the rifle, and get comfortable.

CHAPTER TWENTY-NINE

Well past sunrise, Walt had woken the other three men. It was cramped on the boat with all four of them. It had been a long night, Lester manning the boat and the rest of them going from one marina to another, all over the island and the next couple of islands to the north, until nearly midnight. It didn't seem necessary to have a lookout all night, so they all got about five hours sleep. Tomas was nodding off in the car on the way back because he'd been up for more than 24 hours already.

They hadn't seen the big fishing boat anywhere. Who would think there'd be so many marinas and docks in such a small area, or that a big fishing boat like that could be hidden so easy?

The plan for the day was to drive across the big bridge and check the marinas on the larger island to the south. But they'd have to work fast to be able to get to the party the marina manager had told them about.

Leaving *Dockside*, they'd driven by the place where the party was supposed to be, but there was a chain across the driveway, so they turned around and headed across the big bridge to w, r next island, called Big Pine Key.

After an uneventful morning, checking a bunch of marinas and docks, they'd headed back across the bridge to where the party would be. The manager was certain he'd show up there. Maybe not in his big fishing boat, but he'd be there. Walt had really hoped to find him at a marina, not a party where there'd be a lot of people. They'd just have to play it by ear, if and when they found the guy.

Early in the afternoon, they'd turned into the driveway where the party was supposed to be. The chain was gone, but there was a skinny, long-haired guy there, talking to everyone who was lined up to pull in. When Benny pulled the car up to the guy, he rolled the window down and Walt leaned over.

"Three people?" the long-haired guy asked. "That'll be thirty dollars, plus ten to park the car. You guys were smart to carpool."

"Forty bucks?" Walt asked. "We're just stopping by to see if a friend's here."

The guy laughed and said, "Yeah, I haven't heard that line yet today. Only like a dozen times, man. Forty bucks. The food'll be worth it, plus it's an open bar. Who's your friend? I know just about everyone—maybe I can save ya the trouble."

"Jesse McDermitt," Walt said from the front passenger seat.

"Jesse?" the guy asked. "Yeah, he's here, dude. Well, at least his boat is. I been stuck out here since I got here, so I couldn't tell ya for sure that he didn't wander off somewhere in his skiff."

"That's good enough," Walt said, and handed the guy forty dollars.

Benny drove on through the overhanging trees into a parking area that was nearly full, with many cars and trucks parked on the grass. Benny maneuvered the little rental car into a space and the three men got out. Just like everywhere else they went, people turned and stared.

Walt said to Tomas, "These people don't seem to like outsiders much."

Tomas simply nodded as they walked past a guy who looked vaguely familiar and continued toward the large group of people around the tables. A fisherman said something to Walt, and they stopped. Walt recognized him as the guy they'd met a few days ago who'd told them where to find McDermitt. They struck up a conversation and the guy pointed McDermitt out. It turned out that McDermitt and the guy, who called himself Stretch, weren't close friends and the guy offered to take one of them to the McDermitt's house. Apparently, McDermitt owed Stretch $100 and he'd help them if Walt would cover the debt.

A deal was made, and Lester was picked to go with the guy since his boat would only hold two people. The guy went into the bar to get water and coffee and Walt said, "Les, once you get near McDermitt's house, think you can take him out? Get my money back? We can't have any witnesses to a kidnapping."

Lester said, "Yeah, I can do that. Done it before."

Walt eyed Lester and said, "When did you ever punch someone's ticket?"

"A few weeks ago," Lester said proudly. He knew that Walt had killed a few men and wanted to measure up. "Stole this from him, too," he said, showing off the doubloon necklace. "Some big shot scuba diver I was working for. He dove down to pull up a stuck anchor and I went down, pulled his regulator out, and grabbed him from behind with my legs and arms until he drowned. Then I wrapped the anchor line around his regulator, dumped the air outta his tanks, and swam over a mile to shore. Stole his truck, too."

"Whyn't ya steal his boat, too?" Walt asked.

"Wanted it to look like a accident," Lester replied. "When they found him the next day, that's just what they figured it was, too. I wrapped the anchor rope around his regulator."

"Pretty smart thinkin', kid," Walt said, watching Stretch talking to a blond waitress inside. He turned back to Lester and looked at the chain around his neck. "So, what's that necklace worth?"

"Just a few hundred, from what I found out," Lester said, not wanting Walt to think it was worth enough for him to try to take him out.

When Stretch came back, he and Lester went off in the guy's boat, while Benny and Walt headed to the car. They would return to the marina and wait. As they were walking toward the car, Walt noticed one of the waitresses, a really hot-looking blonde, carrying a platter of food to one of the tables. He eyed her from behind before heading to the car. Then suddenly, he stopped halfway and turned around, looking for her again. She was gone, but he could have sworn she was the same woman he had seen on the docks up in Miami a couple days ago.

Benny drove the car back to the docks and Walt found Tomas sleeping in the chair behind the steering wheel. "Wake up, Rodriguez!" Walt shouted as they climbed aboard.

"Huh," Tomas mumbled, startled. "*Donde está Les?*"

"We just missed McDermitt at the party. His boat's been there all along. He musta recognized us somehow and spooked. The guy that tipped us off that he'd be in Miami was at the party and offered to take one of us to his house. Les went with him. I hope he can take the guy by himself."

"What about the guy driving him?" Tomas said. "Think he'd try to stop Les?"

"Les guh keel him, when dey get close to di mon's house," Benny said.

"Lester?" Tomas asked.

"Yeah," Walt said. "Turns out our new boy has already got his hands dirty."

"I watch di boat, mon," Benny said. "Guh get some sleep."

"*Gracias*," Tomas said. "I am muy sleepy."

Walt was thinking about the blonde. Could she really be the same one he and Lester had seen? Les had gotten a better look at her. All Walt had seen was her walking away. But, in his opinion, a woman's ass was as individual as her face and that blonde had an ass to remember. If it was the same woman, what was she doing waitressing down here? If she lived here, what was she doing strolling on a Miami dock two days ago? He decided to think on it some more and get a nap. He was having trouble concentrating.

"Here," Walt said, handing Benny his phone. "Les should call within the hour. I'm gonna get forty winks."

"Guh rest, mon. Everting is irie."

CHAPTER THIRTY

Sonny was waiting but growing more and more impatient. Walt had called two hours ago to say they nearly had McDermitt, but he'd left in a smaller boat. They'd found a local guy that had a grudge against McDermitt and was willing to take Lester to his hideout on a deserted island about thirty miles north of Marathon. Sonny had really hoped to have McDermitt on ice by now, getting information from him about other treasure. He knew how these guys worked. Sometimes they'd work together and sometimes solo, but never really apart. And they were tight, keeping others at arm's length.

He also had the other job for the Arab guy to consider. From where the boat was now in Marathon, it was a good six or seven hours to Brown's Cay. Further, if they had to come to Palm Beach first to drop McDermitt off.

Lester had finally told Sonny how he'd come into possession of the gold bar, and Sonny had been impressed that the kid could think quick and take advantage of a situation, even if it meant killing someone. He shouldn't have any problem with McDermitt; he was just a fisherman, and Sonny had seen firsthand just how strong the kid was. He was even having second thoughts about having taken advantage of him on the treasure he'd stolen from the old diver.

Sonny's cell phone rang, and he picked it up. It was Lester, hopefully calling to say he had the guy and was headed back to the boat.

"About damn time, Les," Sonny said into the phone. "I was starting to worry about you. Thought maybe you decided to go solo."

"I had him, Boss," Lester said. "They tried to pull a fast one. The guy called Stretch that was taking me up to McDermitt's place was McDermitt himself. They been on to us from the start."

"Wait, slow down," Sonny said. "Who the hell is Stretch?"

"We met a guy at the party," Lester said. "His name was Stretch something. Walt paid him a hundred bucks to bring me out to McDermitt's house. But it was McDermitt his self."

"Wait," Walt said, not believing his ears. "McDermitt pretended to be someone else and Walt hired him to take you *to* himself? Is that what you're tellin' me?"

"Yeah, but I figured it out."

"So, whatta ya mean you had him?"

"He got away, Boss. I played like I didn't know it was him, but I did, and I was sure he was taking me into a trap. He said it'd take about thirty minutes to get up there, still pretending to be Stretch. So, when twenty minutes passed, I made out like I was seasick, ya know. He stopped on a little sandbar and I pretended to be puking over the side. When he stood up and came at me, I grabbed him, and we wrestled. My phone musta fell outta my pocket, 'cause I just found it."

"What happened to McDermitt, dammit?" Sonny asked impatiently.

"I caught him with an elbow and we both went over the side. I clobbered him good in the water and we went under. I went after him and figured I'd have to do him, like I did the old guy a few weeks ago. But he broke loose under the water. It was deep, and he just disappeared. I got back on the boat and had my gun ready, but he never came back up. His dog grabbed my leg and I'm bleedin' pretty bad. I knocked the dog loose and he was yappin' at me, then all a the sudden, the dog jumped off the boat and swam to an island a long ways off and he disappeared, too."

"McDermitt drowned?" Sonny asked.

"I guess so, Boss," Lester replied. "But I never saw his body come up."

"Okay, don't beat yourself up, kid. Things just went sour. Think you can find his house by yourself? See if there's any treasure there?"

"I dunno, Boss," Lester said. "Everything out here looks exactly da same. Pretty sure we were headin' northwest. If I can get da boat started, I might be able to find it. But the other guy we were chasin' is probly there."

"What other guy?"

"The guy pretending to be McDermitt," Lester replied.

"You do that, Les. Try to find his house and keep me posted. I'm gonna have the other guys get back here with the boat. You can drive back in the rental, once you check the house."

"Okay, Boss," Lester said, sounding less than enthusiastic.

Sonny was dejected. He was hoping to have McDermitt long before today and beat the location of his cut of the treasure out of him. He was certain there was more. He'd even planned to force the guy to dive the last location listed in the leather journal Les stole, to find the other gold bars Les had told him about. He called Walt.

"McDermitt got away," Sonny said. "You guys need to get the hell back up to Miami."

"You gotta be shittin' me," Walt said. "How'd he get the drop on Les?"

"The guy you hired *was* McDermitt, you idiot. Les figured it out and played along, then tried to jump him. Les thinks he drowned when he went overboard. This job's on hold till we can find out if he's still alive and where he's at. You guys need to get back up here and get the boat over to Brown's Cay by tomorrow night. Les'll drive back in the rental. You got enough daylight to get part of the way. Just get moving and find a place to hole up for the night, away from there."

Sonny closed the phone and plopped down in his chair.

At *Dockside*, Walt rousted Tomas. "We gotta get going," Walt said. "McDermitt got Les." Then he stuck his head out of the cabin and told Benny, "Untie the lines. We're leaving."

Benny jumped up, noting the urgency in Walt's voice, and went to untie the boat while Tomas headed over to sit in the driver's seat and start the engines. Walt came out of the cabin, clearly anxious. "You guys hurry up. We need to get as far north as we can before it gets too dark to see."

Eyeing the boat ramp, Tomas remarked, "I seen dat car and boat before. At da dock in Miami."

When Benny glanced over to where Tomas was pointing, he agreed. "Ya, mon. I seen di cah and boat befoe, too. At dat jump up dis aftahnoon."

Finally, Walt checked out the ramp, where a yellow Jeep Cherokee was about to back a boat into the water. Two women had just climbed out to release the straps.

"And I seen that ass before," Walt said. "That's the woman me and Les seen on the dock, up in Miami, checking out the boats. Seen her at the party, too. She was hanging on that Stretch guy inside the bar. Turns out Stretch is McDermitt. He pulled a fast one on us, guys."

Benny climbed back on the boat and said, "We all irie, Walt."

"Not quite yet," Walt said. "Pull out, and then come up to the end of that last dock. Be ready when I get there. We're grabbing the blonde." He jumped out of the boat onto the dock and casually walked over toward the boat ramp.

As he got near the ramp, he heard the dark-haired girl say, "Jesse's gonna be really surprised when he finds out Deuce gave y'all the boat for a wedding present."

Jesse? So, Stretch really was McDermitt, and he was married to the tall blonde. No wonder he got the drop on Les. He got behind the woman, pulled his Colt from the back of his jeans, and grabbed her around the waist with his left hand. Putting the Colt to her head, he murmured, "Nothing funny, sweet cheeks."

From across the tongue of the trailer, the other woman could see what was happening. "Don't you go gettin' any ideas, girl. I'll blow her head off, quick as lookin' at ya."

He pulled the blonde out onto the first dock just as their boat glided up to it. Benny helped wrestle her aboard, and then Tomas hit the throttles, ignoring the *no wake* signs. The boat roared down the row of docks and into Sister Creek, belching blue smoke.

They wound through the creek at full throttle, rocking the boats tied to piers all along the creek. Once they hit open water, Tomas made a wide turn around a small island with a single house on it and headed east-northeast toward a lighted tower.

Looking at the radar, Walt could see that there were quite a few other boats going the same direction. *Headed home to Miami*, he thought, *after a weekend of fishing in the Keys, or partying in Key West.*

Most of the boats were further away from the island chain than they were, so he angled farther out, hoping that he could lose any police vessels that were sure to be in pursuit pretty soon.

It was nearly sunset, maybe an hour of daylight left. It would take them eight or nine hours to get to Palm Beach. And they were all tired. He didn't want to be out here at night, but they didn't seem to have much choice now.

Benny tied the blonde up and put her in the forward berth. She was a handful but calmed right down after he backhanded her.

Back up on deck, he told Walt, "She be quiet now. Weh we guh stop tonight, mon?"

Tomas answered, "No stopping. Look at dis radar. Muy boats headin' to Miami. Be safer if we keep goin'."

"Tomas is right," Walt said, looking at the radar screen. It was covered with dozens of little white spots and off to the right, further from shore, he could make out at least ten boats, all headed the same direction. "Get out there, Tomas. Lose us in the crowd of boats. Time to call the boss." He opened his phone and punched in Sonny's number.

When Sonny answered, he said, "Change of plans, Boss. Just as we were leaving the dock, McDermitt's wife showed up. We got her aboard and headed to Palm Beach."

"His wife?" Sonny asked. "That's perfect. But don't come here. How much gas is in the boat?"

"We topped the tanks. They're full."

"That's great. Good thinking, Walt. Let me talk to Tomas."

Walt handed the phone to Tomas, "Si, Jefe?"

"Tomas," Sonny said, "You know the waters between Key Largo and Brown's Cay?"

"Very well, Jefe."

"Good. Look for it on the GPS. Ever been there?"

"Many times, Jefe. I have a cousin; he lives there with his fat wife. They fish and have a dock."

"Better than I'd planned on, Tomas. Will your cousin let you dock there without anyone knowing? Like about midnight?"

"His wife be muy pissed off, Jefe. But he will do it."

"Take your time getting there, so you arrive after midnight. Stay at your cousin's house until early Tuesday morning, then head over to pick them up. I'll text you the location. They're bringing gas for the return trip and will meet you there before sunrise. You'll be in Palm Beach by the afternoon. You did good, grabbing McDermitt's wife."

"Gracias, Jefe. I got it."

"I'll call Mutt," Sonny said, "and tell him to get the Cigarette ready to go. We'll pick up your package on the way in."

CHAPTER THIRTY-ONE

Julie had been able to spend a little time alone with Deuce during the reception. He'd let her in on most of what they were planning to do, and Julie was able to fill in the missing pieces. Rusty had mentioned earlier that morning that Jesse was planning to make Deuce an offer on the boat and while she was talking to Deuce, she'd told him about it.

"Hell, I'll do better than that," Deuce had said. "I've grown to like Jesse and Alex a lot. They're good people. Think they'd accept the boat and trailer as a wedding gift?"

"That'd be really nice, Russell," Julie had commented. "I'm sure they'd be thrilled to death."

"Then let's do it," he'd said. He'd liked the way that had sounded. The two of them giving Jesse and Alex the boat, instead of it just coming from him. "If things work out like we're hoping, Jesse and I will leave some time this afternoon to go up to his house. While we're gone, why don't you tell Alex that we're giving them the boat and you and her can take it over to the boat ramp, put it in the water, and bring it over here? That way, when we get back, it'll be all set for them."

"*We're* giving it to them?" she'd asked, coyly.

"Maybe I'm overstepping myself," he'd said as his cheeks flushed. "I just meant, you know, we're kind of, well, you know."

Julie was touched that this man, who'd fought so bravely in both Afghanistan and Iraq, became flustered when it came to verbalizing his feelings for her. "Yeah," she'd said, "I feel the same way. Even if you can't express it." He'd smiled and kissed her before Jesse had gotten his attention and they'd moved ahead with their plans.

Now, the whole world was crumbling. Julie had watched as the bald guy Jesse had been talking to an hour earlier had forced Alex aboard his boat. At first, she couldn't think what to do. Then she ran to the Jeep, grabbed her cell phone and dialed 911.

"There's been a kidnapping," she'd told them urgently, then explained to the dispatcher what had happened. The dispatcher promised they'd get someone there right away. She hung up the phone and called her dad, frantic.

"Dad, that bald guy just took Alex," she said.

"What?" Rusty exclaimed. "Where are you? Are you all right?"

"I'm okay, Dad. We came over to *Dockside* to launch the boat. We're giving it to Jesse and Alex as a wedding gift. Dad, she's gone. They just roared off down Sister Creek in a Carver."

"Did you call the police? I'll be there in three minutes."

"Yeah," she replied. "I called them. Dad, hurry."

She disconnected just as Art trotted up and said, "I saw it happen, Julie, but couldn't get to him in time. Are the cops on the way?"

"Yeah," she replied. "And Dad, too." They could hear sirens in the distance as Rusty came sliding to a stop in his old Chevy pickup. He and Tony both had the doors open before the truck stopped and came running. Minutes later the first police car arrived, followed seconds later by another. Since Art and Julie had both witnessed the abduction, two cops took their statements.

Tony and Rusty stood off to the side, listening. The first cop got on his radio, reported the direction and description of the boat, and asked to be connected to the Sheriff's Department patrol boat on duty. To Rusty, he said, "Don't worry, sir. The Sheriff's Department has a boat on duty 24/7, and it'll be moving in minutes. He'll be able to find them on radar once he's in open water."

"Son," Rusty said to the officer, "you do know what day and time of the month it is, don't you?" The cop looked confused, so Rusty explained, "It's Sunday, the last weekend of October. Today's the last day of Fantasy Fest, down on Key Weird. There's probably a thousand boats headed up the reef line right about now."

"Oh, jeez," the cop said. "You're right. A lot of people go down there by boat." Then the sheriff's patrol boat came over his radio and he relayed the information.

Tony approached Art and motioned for him to follow his lead. Once they were out of earshot of the others,

Tony said, "What do you think? Should we identify our-selves?"

"I don't know, Tony. Maybe we should call ADD Smith first and see what he says."

"Okay," Tony said, "Get back over there. I'll give him a call."

Art rejoined the now-growing group, while Tony made the call. He explained the situation, then waited while the ADD mulled the options, then gave Tony instructions. Once he'd disconnected, Tony walked straight up to the sergeant, who had just arrived.

"Sergeant," he said, pulling out his wallet and showing him his credentials, "I'm Agent Anthony Jacobs, Department of Homeland Security, Caribbean Command. This is Agent Arthur Newman. Can we have a word with you?"

The sergeant was stunned. He didn't like Feds but knew better than to piss off two DHS guys. The three walked out to the end of the dock Alex had been taken from.

"What are Feds doing down here?" the sergeant asked. "Especially Homeland Security?"

Tony smiled and replied, "That's above your pay grade, sergeant. Moreover, before you make the call, you're thinking of making, it's above the sheriff's pay grade also. This kidnapping may have national security implications. Your sheriff will call you shortly."

Seeing where Tony was going, Art added, "We have reason to believe that the men who abducted Alexis Mc-

Dermitt are linked to suspected al Qaeda sympathizers involved in smuggling terrorists into the country."

"Terrorists?" the sergeant asked. "Here? In the Keys? Wait, you said Alexis McDermitt? I thought her name is Alex DuBois."

Art said, "She married Jesse McDermitt this morning."

"That's right," Tony said, "and the boat they took her on will be picking up four terrorists on Brown's Cay in the Bahamas in about 36 hours. What I'm about to tell you is classified. Do you understand?"

The sergeant nodded

"We think this abduction is linked to the smuggling," Tony said. "Mr. McDermitt is one of our operatives."

"Jesse McDermitt is DHS?" the sergeant asked, obviously flustered. "I've known Jesse for five years. I find that hard to believe."

Art said, "He's a contractor for us."

"So, what do you want us to do?" the sergeant asked.

"We need eyes in the sky," Tony said. "Like, about ten minutes ago. Does the Sheriff's Department here have a helicopter?"

"Sure, it's less than a mile away," replied the sergeant.

"Good," Art said. "Contact their office and have them get the pilot ready. The sheriff should be getting a phone call right about now to confirm. Time's of the essence."

The sergeant did as he was instructed, then told Tony, "The pilot's already in the air. At the sheriff's orders. You guys have some major strings."

"Contact the pilot and tell him to set down in that clearing over there," Tony said, pointing to a park across the street. "Get two of your men over there and clear a landing zone. Agent Newman is going up with him."

Within minutes, the sheriff's chopper set down in the park and Art ran over and boarded it. Putting on a headset, he showed his ID to the pilot and said, "Take me out over the reef. We're looking for a 32-foot Carver aft cabin. It left here twenty minutes ago, probably headed toward Miami." The pilot nodded and pulled on the collective while adding throttle. The chopper lifted quickly and once clear of the trees, he pushed forward on the cyclic stick and the chopper nosed down, accelerating forward out over the water.

"Take me up to about 2000 feet; if that boat's out past the reef, there are probably a lot of other boats out there to hide among."

Tony watched the chopper disappear over the trees and then turned to a deputy who had just arrived. "I need a radio with the chopper's frequency."

The deputy gave Tony the once-over. "And just who the hell are you?"

"Don't mess with him, Ben," the sergeant told him. "He's freaking DHS."

Tony flashed his ID and badge to the deputy, who quickly responded with, "Just a second, sir. Got one in the patrol car you can have."

He ran back to his cruiser and returned with a hand-held radio for Tony. "Already on the chopper's freq. He's standing by."

Tony put the radio to his mouth. "Art, do you copy? It's Tony."

Art's voice came back over the speaker. "We're out over the reef, Tony. I have a visual on no fewer than 50 boats, all headed east-northeast. Not enough light to pick out the right one. We're going to go boat to boat and look closer, but we're running out of light."

"ADD Smith said to consider both Jesse and Alex as one of our own," Tony told him. "Do what you can. I'm going to call Deuce so he can tell Jesse. They should be together by now. Good luck and contact me on this frequency if you find them."

CHAPTER
THIRTY-TWO

Deuce had made it to Jesse's house with no problem. Still a half mile out, he knew where it was, because of the barge and backhoe anchored beside the channel. Several pelicans were perched on the barge and took flight as he motored up the narrow channel. The deck and roof were visible from about 200 yards out, just as Jesse had said, but completely disappeared once he got closer and the trees blocked the house. He motored slowly through the overhanging mangroves and saw that the channel had been dug completely into the island itself.

The house sat on large concrete piers sunk into dry land. Just before he drove underneath the house, he noticed a larger area had been dug out enough to turn a boat around. He took the time to turn Rusty's skiff around, backing it under the house in case he needed to leave in a hurry.

Jesse had told him that he'd dug the channel, turning basin and the area under the house by hand, using nothing more than a large pole, a pick and a shovel.

Quite a feat, Deuce thought.

He tied off the skiff, opened the fish box with a key on the key ring, and removed the long fly rod case. Climbing the steps to the deck, he was impressed with the workmanship that had gone into building the house. The docks, steps, deck, and everything else looked and felt extremely sturdy. Once on the deck, he used a key that Jesse had given him and let himself inside. It was obviously a single man's home, but here and there, he could see that Jesse had taken pains to make a woman feel at ease in it, too. After grabbing a bottle of water from the fridge, he'd gone back out to the deck. There, he set the case on the south-facing part of the deck, went back around the side, retrieved one of the patio chairs and a small table, and moved them to the center of the deck near the rail, facing the direction Jesse and Lester would come. He placed the case on the little table and opened it.

Jesse was meticulous about his weaponry—that was obvious. The rifle was completely free of any dirt or rust but was well-worn. Clearly, many rounds had passed through the barrel. He removed the rifle and closed the case. He'd have preferred to have a sandbag to rest the stock on but settled for placing his left arm on the rail and setting the stock in the crook of his elbow. Removing the covers from the front and rear of the scope, he looked through it and sighted in on a small island about 300 yards away. The scope brought the northern shore of the island into clear focus and he could easily make out several shells, a coconut, and two crab trap floats. He really needed to try it out before taking a shot through a cold barrel at something as small as an oar close to Jesse's head. But they were probably too close. He knew that sound carried further and better over water than on land, and the report of a rifle would be heard five miles away, or further.

He wasn't real crazy about the MST-100 scope. Zeroing the damn thing required adjusting the elevation knob with an Allen wrench. But once it was zeroed, elevation changes could be made simply by turning the elevation knob. At least, he was familiar with it. Marines seemed to love that damn scope. Since it was zeroed for a 200-meter shot, he didn't have to worry about anything but windage.

Sighting in on the little island again, Deuce checked the wispy grass close to the water's edge, then checked the fronds on a palm tree in the center of the island. Fortunately, there was no wind blowing on either the grass or the higher palm tree. Looking further past the east side of the island, he couldn't see any ripples in the water, nor were there any ripples between him and the island. He was satisfied that for the moment the air on the surface of the water was still, all the way up to the twenty-foot-tall palm tree. Now all he had to do was wait.

After twenty minutes had gone by, he was starting to worry. Maybe Jesse was just taking it slow to give him more time to set up. Maybe Jesse thought he might get lost. Without the GPS, that would have been a good assumption. The islands all around him looked identical, except for size. He let another ten minutes tick by, scouring the water to the south. That's when he saw a man walking in knee-deep water. More of a slow jog than a walk, and a dog was half swimming and half leaping alongside him. Jesse.

In the gathering darkness, Deuce put the rifle back into its case and started down the steps to the skiff. His phone vibrated in his pocket. He saw on the screen that it was Tony.

"Yeah," he said.

"Deuce," Tony said, "Alex was kidnapped ten minutes ago. It was Walter O'Hara and the other two."

"Oh, shit," Deuce said. "That's bad. Lester must have gotten the drop on Jesse. I just spotted him wading through the water, headed this way. I was just about to go pick him up. What's the status there?"

"They left Boot Key Harbor in the Carver," Tony said. "Art just went up in a Sheriff's Department chopper and the sheriff's patrol boat is already heading out to search. But it doesn't look good. According to Rusty, there'll be hundreds of boats moving along the reef tonight, leaving Fantasy Fest in Key West. Art's already confirmed dozens in the area and with reduced light, he's having to go boat to boat."

"Double bad," Deuce said. "I'll let Jesse know. You might want to evacuate Marathon. He's gonna go off like a nuclear bomb."

After securing the fly rod case in the fish box, Deuce untied the skiff, jumped aboard, and started it up. Then he idled out the channel and brought the skiff up on plane, heading due south, to where Jesse was slogging through the shallows nearly a mile away.

Tony was on the phone with ADD. Smith again. He moved away from the crowd of people.

"Since it's a kidnapping," Smith said, "the FBI had to be contacted. An agent should be arriving there shortly from Key West. Director Goss has already informed Director Mueller that Captain McDermitt is one of our contractors and we have the lead in the investigation."

"Just one agent?" Tony asked.

"I'm sure there'll be more. Besides Key West, the nearest field office is in Homestead. Jim Franklin's on his way down, too. Should be there in two hours. Our takedown team is being split up. Half are on their way down to you in a Gulfstream and the other half will stay in Miami. They will carry out the takedown when Beech's boat returns from Brown's Cay. The government there won't allow us to come in on such short notice. How long before Commander Livingston and Captain McDermitt get there?"

"About thirty minutes, sir," Tony replied.

"The Gulfstream will touch down in ten minutes," Smith said. "The agent from the Bureau will be there in twenty and Franklin in two hours. Until Commander Livingston gets there, you're in charge."

"Yes, sir," Tony said. "If I may, sir?"

"Please do," Smith replied.

"I think it might be prudent to keep Franklin on Beech, sir. We don't know if O'Hara is taking Mrs. McDermitt up there, or where. He could pick something up. Besides, he's kinda gruff and he and Captain McDermitt together would be like a flame to a gas can."

"Yes, two very good points, Mr. Jacobs. I'll pull him off and keep him surveilling Beech. Contact me if anything develops and have Commander Livingston call me when he arrives."

CHAPTER THIRTY-THREE

I only had a couple of hours until it got dark, but I was certain that once I got around the southern tip of Water Keys, Deuce would see me, even at two miles. I probably could have gone ashore on Big Torch Key and made my way to one of the many houses there, but most were vacation homes and probably boarded up.

Lester and I had struggled when he'd feigned being seasick, and both of us had gone overboard into the deep channel. We'd wrestled underwater in the channel and I'd barely broken free after he'd caught me with both an elbow and a fist. The man was freakishly strong, and I considered myself lucky. When I reached for my Sig and it wasn't there, I dove deep in the channel and swam with the current until my lungs burned.

Turning out of the deep channel into a small side cut, I'd finally poked just my head above the surface when I was sure I was between Lester and a little mangrove island. I was hoping that he wouldn't see me with the island behind me. Even if he did, I was nearly 100 feet away, much too far for a handgun, which I was sure he was carrying. He might even have my Sig; I wasn't sure when it had fallen out.

I'd watched Lester climb back onto the skiff, pull a gun from his waistband, and look around. Then the dog had lunged, sinking his teeth into the back of Lester's calf and shaking his big head. Lester hit him with the barrel of the gun and the dog let go, but stood defiantly, barking at him from the casting deck. With Lester's back to me, I stood up in knee-deep water and waved both my hands over my head, hoping the dog's sharp eyes would spot me. I was very relieved when he leapt out of the skiff and swam quickly in the current toward me.

I dove under and swam further west in the shallow water until it was too shallow to swim, then lifted my head up. I now had another smaller island between Lester and me and the dog was still swimming in the channel to my right. I rose up on one knee and waved to the dog. He turned and swam up to me. Together we sloshed toward the tiny island and I could hear Lester talking. I guessed he was on a cell phone, either his or mine—I didn't know. After a brief conversation, I heard him start the skiff and back it off the sandbar I'd beached us on.

If he continued to follow the channel, Deuce would see him within minutes. But to my surprise, he headed northwest, between Big Torch and Water Keys. *Good luck*, I thought, *nothing but shallows, mangroves, mosquitos, and heartache that way.*

Once Lester was out of sight, I jogged in the shallow water to the northern tip of Big Torch Key and then swam across the narrow channel to Water Keys. The dog followed obediently as we sloshed along the eastern shallows for about a half mile.

Finally, I could see the barge and backhoe, so Deuce should have been able to see me. After splashing along another 50 yards, I heard Rusty's big Evinrude start up and a few minutes later, I saw Deuce coming out of the channel toward me. As he slowed down and came off plane, I could see the concerned look on his face.

"We're okay," I said, when Deuce shut the engine off and drifted up to me. "Lester surprised me, and he got away in my skiff. He headed up into the flats, between the Water Keys and Raccoon Key. We can catch him, but we gotta move fast. It's getting dark."

After helping the dog into Rusty's skiff, I climbed in after him. I expected Deuce to move over to the second seat, since I knew the water better, but he remained seated at the helm.

"Sit down, Jesse," he said flatly. I didn't like the sound of his voice, so I sat down in the second seat. He looked at me and said, "O'Hara got Alex. Tony and Art are looking for them, with help from the Sheriff's Department. They took off in the Carver."

"Alex?" I asked, unwilling to believe what he was saying. "What do you mean, he got her?"

"Alex and Julie were at the boat ramp at *Dockside*. I don't know how, but Lester and his guys must have figured out what was going on and grabbed her. We'll get her back, Jesse. You have my word on it."

He started the skiff and backed away from the shallows into the channel. "Get up," I said. "I'm driving."

"Are you sure?" he asked.

"Yeah, get up," I repeated.

This was going to be a high-speed run in the dark and I didn't trust anyone's instincts but mine. Deuce and I switched seats and I shoved the throttle to the stops, dragging the skeg on the outboard in the shallows for a second before the skiff lifted on plane. I turned due east and took the skiff across the shallows north of Howe Key, then threaded the narrow cut between Cutoe Key and Annette Key and into Big Spanish Channel. I continued threading cuts and channels following milk jug markers between Little Pine Key and the Johnson Keys, then cut sharply east and crossed Friend Key Bank, running wide open.

Lights from cars crossing the Seven Mile Bridge were in view and ten miles east, we could make out the glow of Marathon. I trimmed the tabs and got a little more speed out of the old Evinrude as we shot toward the far end of the Seven Mile Bridge.

"Where're Tony and Art?" I asked, surprising myself with the calmness in my voice.

"Art's up in the sheriff's chopper and Tony is running things at *Dockside* until we get there."

I knew Rusty had a VHF radio under the console, so I gave Deuce the frequency for the chopper. He dialed it in, picked up the mic, and spoke into it. "Art, this is Deuce, do you copy?"

Art's voice came over the speaker, "Affirmative, Commander. We're searching boat to boat out here beyond the reef. But there are a lot of boats. Agent Jacobs has set up command and control at *Dockside*."

I realized immediately what he meant. Hundreds of revelers would be heading back up the Keys in boats from Key West's Fantasy Fest celebration. I explained this to Deuce. But why was Art being so formal?

"Tony and Art must have identified themselves as DHS," Deuce yelled over the screaming outboard. "To expedite the search. That means one of them, probably Tony, must have contacted the deputy director. There'll be more agents helping soon and the FBI will probably have already been called in. It also means the DHS director himself has contacted the FBI director and probably told him you are one of us."

I continued driving the boat at breakneck speed. Much faster than was safe at this time of day. The sun had just slipped below the horizon behind us and nothing, but darkness lay ahead. I wasn't worried about shallows. We had twenty or more feet of water below us all the way to the harbor entrance. Boats were the big concern, especially rental boats, whose operators often neglected to turn on their navigation lights before twilight.

I switched on the big spotlight Rusty had mounted to the bow and it instantly illuminated a party barge anchored right in front of us. I turned the wheel sharply and the skiff responded, skidding to the right on the starboard chine. I brought her back to the left and lined up on the southernmost marker to Moser Channel. I was going to cross the channel and cut under the bridges between it and Pigeon Key.

Minutes later, we were south of the bridge and running wide open toward the mouth of Boot Key Harbor. I could just make out three boats with blue flashing lights, moving east on the south side of Boot Key toward the reef.

I slowed down a little as we came into the harbor, but never came down off plane, weaving in and out of boats and mooring balls, until I was 100 feet from the boat ramp. Only then did I bring the boat down off plane.

Deuce scrambled forward and grabbed the bow line, tossing it to a uniformed deputy standing on the dock where I used to moor the *Revenge*. Deuce and I climbed up onto the dock, but the dog took a more direct route, leaping from the bow and swimming to shore, meeting us at the end of the dock. Tony stood waiting with three uniformed officers, one man in a suit, and three men who were obvious door kickers, dressed in black, with large packs slung over their shoulders.

"Sit rep!" Deuce demanded as he handed the fly rod case from the fish box to one of the door kickers.

"Agent Newman is airborne and has visually checked eleven small craft, headed northeast," Tony reported. "All negative, sir. There're dozens more, he says, but it's getting too dark to see. The associate deputy director has brought the Bureau on board, but we're lead, since Captain McDermitt is one of ours. This is Agent Binkowski, of the Key West field office." Tony nodded toward the suit and continued, "ADD Smith has also contacted the local LEOs, who have provided the chopper and a patrol boat. Deputy Sergeant Pollard here contacted the Coasties. They've dispatched two more patrol boats, one out of Islamorada and another out of Boca Chica. A cutter will be underway out of Windley Key within a few minutes. The ADD has put you in charge of the investigation, sir." Turning to me, he said, "No sign yet, Jesse. But we'll get her back."

Deuce turned to me and asked, "Is the *Revenge* fueled up?"

I knew where he was going and was already a step ahead. "I'm leaving the dock at Rusty's in five minutes. I can catch that Carver before she makes Key Largo. I need a boarding party."

Deuce nodded toward the three men to his left and announced, "This is part of my team—we're going with you." Then he turned to Tony and ordered, "Agent Jacobs, remain here and coordinate the search. We're going to take a more unorthodox approach."

CHAPTER THIRTY-FOUR

Tomas kept looking back at the chopper flying low, going from one boat to another, illuminating each with a powerful spotlight. There were at least 30 boats in this group and the chopper was still a mile back. The sun had already set, and he was doing his best to match the speed of the other boats, while keeping several hundred yards of separation. He hoped the chopper would give up or run low on fuel.

"They just lit up another one," Walt said. "How long before we get to Key Largo?"

"'Bout an hour," Tomas replied.

"Any idea how far one of those things can fly?" he asked.

"Not far, I think," Tomas responded. "Least not da way dey flying from boat to boat."

"Hey look pon dat," Benny said, pointing astern.

All three men watched as the chopper descended on yet another boat. But this time, instead of illuminating it and flying on to the next one, it kept the searchlight on the boat and flew alongside it. After a minute, it moved in front of the boat and dropped lower, blinding the driver. The boat slowed, and the chopper took up a position above it. The boat finally stopped and far behind, they could see boats with blue flashing lights.

"Wha yuh tink 'bout dat?" Benny asked.

"No idea," Walt said. "But it looks like we're safe for now."

The chopper was falling back fast, and the three men breathed a collective sigh of relief. Tomas was calculating the range of the Carver. They'd made it from Miami to Marathon without running out of gas and it was nearly the same distance to Brown's Cay. He turned to Walt. "Call de boss. We can make Brown's Cay without stopping in Key Largo, if we go slower."

"You sure?" Walt asked.

"*Sí*. It only 'bout twenty miles further than what we did from Miami to here and that was going fast."

"Okay," Walt said, after thinking it over. "Turn slowly out to sea and slow down a little once we get clear of these other boats. Then make a beeline for Brown's Cay. I'll call the boss and let him know what we're doing."

Walt went below to call Sonny. He also wanted to check on the woman. When he opened the door to the forward berth, he found her as they'd left her, lying on the bunk, her mouth gagged, hands tied behind her back and feet tied together. Her eyes were open.

Yeah, he thought, *she's hot*. He knelt beside the bunk and stroked her face where Benny had backhanded her, leaving a big, red welt. Her eyes were like fire and she struggled against the knots. Reaching down, Walt grabbed the front of her white blouse and tore it partly open, the top three buttons flying across the cabin. She was wearing a lacy white bra. He grabbed one of her breasts and kneaded it through the soft material, then stood up and stared down at her.

"Yeah, we're gonna have us a party, later," he growled. Then Walt called Sonny from the main cabin to let him know the change in plans.

When he came back up to the deck, he looked back to find the chopper nearly out of sight. The line of boats they'd been running with were now more than two miles off to the north. "Anyone following us?" he asked Tomas.

Tomas studied the radar for a minute. "No, *esé*, I think we clear."

Walt checked the speedometer and noted they had slowed down to just fifteen knots. He wasn't sure, but figured a knot was what boat people called a mile per hour. "You sure we can make it to Brown's Cay with the gas we have?"

"*Sí, no problemo*. And we look more innocent, going so slow."

"What time will we get there?"

"Bout one o'clock."

"Good," Walt said. "Benny, you go on down to the rear cabin and get some rest, then come up and spell Tomas in two hours."

"Wah will yuh be doin'?" Benny asked with a leer.

"I'm going to entertain our guest for a while, then get some sleep myself," Walt replied.

Benny grinned and said, "How bout yuh wake mi afore yuh guh ta sleep. I can dance wid har fah a while."

Benny headed down to the rear cabin and tried to go to sleep, but the sounds coming from the forward cabin made that nearly impossible.

CHAPTER THIRTY-FIVE

Rusty stood with Julie next to his old Chevy as I approached with Deuce and his door kickers.

"We'll get her back," Rusty said.

"Take us to the *Anchor*," I said.

Julie slid to the middle of the bench seat and I moved into the passenger seat beside her as Deuce and his three men climbed in the back.

"What're you going to do, Jesse?" Julie asked.

I stared straight ahead and didn't answer. Rusty started the truck and took off down Sombrero Boulevard. When Deuce tapped on the glass between the cab and the bed, I slid the little window open. "Mind if Hinkle here hangs on to your fly rod?" he asked.

"No problem," I replied. "I have another just like it on board. And a few other things."

Minutes later, we were boarding the *Revenge* while Rusty and Julie cast off the lines. Rusty stepped down into the cockpit, looked up to me on the bridge and said simply, "I'm going."

"Then come up and take the helm," I said. "Deuce, you and them door kickers come with me." Deuce and I went forward as Rusty got the engines fired up and started down the canal. The three men from the take-down team joined us in the salon.

Deuce looked around at his team and said, "Rather than use names on the comm, I'm Alpha One, Jesse's Alpha Two and Rusty, up on the bridge, is Alpha Three." He went on around the salon, assigning numbers to the others. The shooter with my fly rod case was four and the other two were five and six. I'm sure he did this for my benefit, rather than make me try to remember names.

"What're your orders?" I asked Deuce.

"Seems like this is your ball game, Jesse," Deuce replied as he handed me two earwigs. "One's for Rusty."

"No," I said. "I meant, what orders did Smith give you?"

"The rest of our team is standing by in Miami, along with our surveillance team. Our plan was to take them all down simultaneously when they brought the terrorists ashore. But, like all plans, that's out the window now. I'm superseding his order and we'll attempt to take down the Carver at sea."

"Run that past him," I said. "I don't want you to get in trouble. But make no mistake, Deuce. This is my vessel and I give the orders. When we catch that Carver, I intend to get my wife off by any means necessary. If she's been hurt, I intend to send it and the crew to the bottom."

Then I looked at each of the men in turn and said, "If that bothers anyone, we're still in the canal and it's a short swim to shore, because if anyone gets in my way, I'll put you off the boat then and there." To a man, they all nodded.

Rusty's voice came over the intercom. "Jesse, get up here."

Deuce and I climbed up to the bridge just as we were clearing the channel. Rusty moved over to the second seat and I took over the helm. Rusty said, "Art found the Carver. They have it stopped, and the patrol boats are closing in."

I brought the *Revenge* up on plane, then pushed the throttles to the stops and headed south-southeast toward the deep cut through the reef, just east of Delta Shoal. I slowed to twenty knots as we neared the cut, checking the forward sonar for any obstruction. Not seeing anything, I nailed the throttles and shot through the cut at 40 knots, turning east-northeast toward Tennessee Reef.

I handed the earwig to Rusty and said, "You're Alpha Three. Turn the VHF to the chopper's freq." Rusty made the channel adjustment and handed me the mic. "This is *MV Gaspar's Revenge* to sheriff's helo, do you copy?"

Art's voice came over the headset saying, "Loud and clear, Jesse. We have the Carver heaved to and the patrol boats are about three miles out. ETA to boarding is five minutes."

I checked the radar and found the chopper easy enough. "I have you about a mile south of Alligator Reef," I said.

"That's affirmative," Art replied.

"I'll be there in twenty-five minutes," I said. Then turning to Deuce and pointing to my ear, I asked, "How the hell you turn these things on?"

Deuce nodded to one of his men, who opened a small black tactical computer case and punched a few keys. Then he nodded to Deuce and I heard him over the headset, saying, "Comm check, Alpha One."

I nodded and said, "Alpha Two." Then Rusty responded, followed by the three men on the deck.

I said, "Alpha Four, leave the case on one of the seats in the salon and take what's in it up on the foredeck— and keep your eyes peeled."

"Roger," he said. I noticed he had an Australian accent.

"And never mind the dog— that's his usual position," I added. "Alpha Five, take the starboard rail, Alpha Six, the port rail."

"They have them, Jesse," Deuce said. "Alex will be safe in just a few minutes."

"I'll relax when she's aboard the *Revenge*," I said.

A couple minutes later, Art's voice came over the loudspeaker on the boat's radio. "Jesse, they're boarding the Carver now."

"Let me know when Alex is aboard the patrol boat," I said. The next few minutes ticked by, seeming like hours.

I nudged the throttles again, but they were already wide open.

"Jesse, it's the wrong boat. Repeat, it's the wrong boat!"

"Damn," I said to nobody and again pushed the throttles harder.

Deuce's phone rang and when he looked at it, he said, "It's the ADD." He answered it, listened for a minute, and then disconnected and closed the phone.

"He said they just got the okay an hour ago for a phone tap on Beech's phone," Deuce said. "O'Hara just called Beech to say they were changing their plan and heading straight out to Brown's Cay. Beech is going to meet them in open water to take Alex before they get to Brown's Cay."

"He has another boat?" I asked.

"That's the bad news. His other boat is a Cigarette 42x," Deuce said. "Top speed is in excess of 90 knots. Registered as *Beeches, Knot Cream.*"

Rusty had been studying the radar screen and had pushed the setting to its max range of 36 nautical miles. "Jesse," he said, "take a look at this. I been watching the screen since we left the channel. See this blip here?" he said, pointing to the screen. "It left the line of boats heading along the reef about ten minutes ago. Its course looks to be about 055 degrees. Lemme see your big chart."

I switched on the autopilot, pulled a chart out of the chart cabinet and unrolled it over the wheel. Rusty pulled a compass from the door of the cabinet. "Here," he said, pointing at Alligator Reef. "This is about where that boat deviated from the others. On a heading of 055, it's headed straight for Brown's Cay."

Deuce said, "They have about a 90-minute head start on us. The chopper will be running low on fuel and the patrol boats don't have the range to make Brown's Cay. The cutter out of Windley will be able to catch it before it makes Brown's, but if they make the exchange at sea, she'll never catch a Cigarette."

"We need to know where that Cigarette goes after they make the exchange," Rusty said. "Probably back to the coast, but where? Miami? West Palm? A go-fast boat like that probably only has a range of a couple hundred miles."

"They don't know we're onto them," Deuce said. "They have to know we're searching, though. They don't seem to be real boat-savvy. If the cutter continues toward Brown's Cay, they can keep track of them and the go-fast boat at the same time. We can refuel in Biscayne Bay, put back out to sea and use the radar to locate a fast mover as it comes back closer to shore. With a little luck, we can take him down as he comes back in."

"Make the call," I said. "Make it happen. But I have a call to make, too. And a slight change in that plan. Rusty, can I talk to you in the salon?"

CHAPTER THIRTY-SIX

J ulie was beside herself, waiting at *Dockside*. Aaron had brought food and drinks out to the cops and everyone else involved in the search, but she couldn't eat anything. She felt responsible, because she'd brought Alex to the docks and didn't do anything to stop the guy from taking her. At just after eight o'clock, her phone rang and when she looked at the caller ID, she saw it was her dad.

"Dad, what's going on? Nobody here will tell me anything."

"Is Tony close by?" Rusty asked.

"Yeah, he's talking to the FBI guy."

"Get him. We need both of you. Don't let the FBI guy know. My keys are in the truck. Get Tony in it, so we can tell both of you what to do."

"Okay," Julie said. She was already sitting in the truck, so she tapped the horn and when Tony looked her way, she waved him over. Once he'd climbed in the passenger side, she said, "Okay, Dad, he's here. I'll put the phone on speaker."

Deuce's voice came over the speaker saying, "Tony, you're on speaker here with Rusty and Jesse. Did the ADD clue you in about Alex being transferred to a second boat?"

"Yeah, I was just telling Special Agent Binkowski about it."

Rusty broke in, "Julie, do you have Alex's purse?"

"Yeah," she replied, "it's right here on the seat, where she left it."

"Look in it," I said. "Are the keys to her skiff in it?"

"Yeah, they're here."

"Good," I said. "We need you and Tony to take Alex's skiff and cut across the flats as fast as you can. We need you in Biscayne Bay in less than two hours. Tide's nearly peaking in the bay; you can run flat out the whole way. Her boat'll do almost 65 knots. Keep it under 60 and you'll get there in plenty of time. There're two full gas cans in Jimmy's skiff at the *Anchor*. Take them and you won't have to stop for gas until you get there."

"Got it, Jesse," Tony said. "What do you want us to do when we get there?"

Deuce answered for me. "You're going to be our eyes. We'll track the Cigarette with radar and let you know where she's going to make landfall. Once it's inside the Intracoastal, you'll have to follow her visually. Find out where it docks, and we'll arrive within thirty minutes, if all goes well."

"It's gonna be just us?" Tony asked. "No Coasties or FBI?"

"Just us," Deuce said. "But we have no idea where Beech will head after the exchange. If he heads to Palm Beach, you'll have to move fast to get up the coast on the inside before he gets there. Get gas in Key Biscayne and be ready."

As Tony pointed ahead of the truck to indicate they should get going, Julie started it up and kicked up gravel as she headed to the *Anchor*. "Okay," Tony said, "we're on the way. I'll check in with you in an hour."

They were in Alex's skiff within five minutes, speeding down the canal to open water. Once clear of the canal, Julie turned sharply left and headed through Vaca Cut into Florida Bay, with Tony hanging on to his seat.

"You sure you know where you're going?" he shouted.

"I grew up fishing these flats," she said. "I know every hole and sandbar in the bay. I've been dying to get involved in this, somehow. It's my fault Alex was taken. I'm not gonna let her down."

She switched on the bright spotlights mounted below the gunwales on either side of the bow, illuminating a heron wading in the water just ahead and to the right.

"What the hell's that bird standing on?" Tony asked.

"The bottom," Julie replied.

"The bottom?" Tony exclaimed.

"Don't worry. We're in a natural cut called Smuggler's Run. It'll take us out to deeper water. We'll have to run through a few other cuts up near Key Largo. But mostly, we'll be running about 60 knots, in six or seven feet of water."

Tony looked at the digital dash and was amazed at how fast they were going already. Julie weaved now and then as she made her way to deeper water north of Grassy Key, then she pushed the throttle to its limit and the little skiff responded like a rocket sled on rails. When the knot meter pushed up above 60, she backed it down a little. Julie was behind the windscreen, but Tony was in open air. By bending down a little, he was able to get into the slipstream created by the bow. They maintained that speed for 40 minutes before Julie slowed the skiff. The spotlights illuminated a seemingly unbroken line of mangroves.

"There's a handheld spotlight under your seat, Tony."

Tony stood up and got the big light out. Plugging it into an outlet on the dash, he turned it toward the mangroves in front of them and switched it on.

"Shine it northward," Julie said. "Look for two red milk jugs near the waterline."

He swept the light back and forth along the shore, and then saw them. "Over there," he said, pointing slightly north of where they were heading.

Julie spun the wheel and headed due north for 100 yards, then spun it back toward where the milk jugs were, heading southeast. Tony kept the spotlight on the jugs and then he saw the opening between them. The lights from Key Largo were glowing through the trees and reflecting off the water beyond. The cut through the mangroves was not much wider than the skiff, with branches hanging down to within five feet of the water.

"You do know these waters," he said. "If they allowed women, you'd make a good SEAL. No wonder Deuce likes you so much."

"He say that?" she asked.

"Well, no, not exactly. I've served with Deuce and Art for over six years now. We can almost read one another's minds."

Once clear of the narrow, winding cut, Julie told him, "This is Blackwater Sound." She pushed the throttle and brought the skiff back up on plane, heading due east toward the city, then turned the skiff to the left near a small point of land and threaded through a slightly wider cut, then under a low bridge. "And that's US1," she added.

She accelerated across Barnes Sound, keeping the skiff at 40 knots, and passed under the high arch of the Card Sound Bridge into Card Sound itself. "If you ever get a chance, that place over there has the best blackened grouper sandwich in the Keys. Well, maybe second best, next to Rufus's. It's called Alabama Jack's. They filmed part of the movie *Drop Zone* there."

Pushing the throttles further, they rocketed across Card Sound and into Biscayne Bay. Then the engine started to sputter.

Julie pulled back on the throttle and said, "Time to switch tanks. We're outta gas."

Tony already had the gas line from the first spare tank threaded between them. Turning around, he disconnected the main tank's gas line and connected the spare line to the engine. After he primed the line with the squeeze pump, the engine settled into a steady hum and Julie pushed the throttles forward. She pointed the bow toward Cape Florida Lighthouse and the Key Biscayne Yacht Club.

Once they'd tied up to the gas dock, Tony called Deuce on his cell phone. When Deuce answered, he said, "We're getting gas at the Key Biscayne Yacht Club now. Damn, this girl can drive a boat."

Julie smiled at the compliment as she filled the main gas tank of Alex's skiff to the brim, and then topped off both spares, too. She paid the dock attendant as Tony ended his call.

When she stepped back into the skiff and untied from the dock, Tony said, "Deuce told me that the cutter is only about twenty miles from the Carver, and the Cigarette boat is closing on them now. The Coasties are going to keep both boats on radar until they transfer Alex to the Cigarette. The *Revenge* is only a few miles behind us and they'll refuel here and be back out on the water, heading up the coast on the outside within twenty minutes. With luck, they can be off Miami Beach in plenty of time to pick up the Cigarette coming back in and let us know if it's headed to Miami or Palm Beach."

"God, I hope Alex is all right," Julie said.

"Me too," Tony said. "I'd sure hate to be those guys if she has even one hair out of place. Deuce said for us to go up to Rickenbacker and wait for their call."

Julie started the big outboard and motored back out to the channel at a much slower pace. There were a number of boats out on the bay, even at this late hour. Once they passed under the Rickenbacker Causeway, she headed toward the Miami Beach skyline and beached the skiff on a small sandbar near the northern tip of Virginia Key.

They didn't have to wait long. Thirty minutes later, Tony's phone chirped, and he put it on speaker. "Yeah, Deuce," he said. "We're at the northern tip of Virginia Key."

"The Coasties said the Cigarette is headed straight toward Miami," Deuce said. "He should be there in fifteen minutes. He's moving at nearly 80 knots right now, but he'll have to slow down once he comes through the inlet. We're drifting about a mile off Miami Beach. We'll follow him through the inlet about two or three miles behind."

"Roger that," Tony said and clicked off. "You really like Deuce, huh?" he asked Julie in the darkness.

"Yeah," she said. "I think Russell's a really special guy."

"Russell?" he asked. "Oh yeah, never mind. His first name slipped my mind. He's always been Lieutenant, Commander or just Deuce to me."

"Is it normal for enlisted men to call officers by their first names?" she asked.

"Not in the regular navy," he said. "But we get to be really close in the SEALs and unless we're around other officers, he prefers Deuce."

"I'm not real big on nicknames," she said.

They sat in silence for a few more minutes, and then Tony's phone chirped again. Once more, he put it on speaker and said, "Go."

Jesse's voice came over the speaker. "He's headed to Government Cut. That's just north of where you are. He's only about fifteen miles out. You need to move due north to the northwest corner of Fisher Island, because once he comes through the cut, he can go three different directions and you can only see one from where you are."

"Roger that," Tony said. "I'll call you when we spot him."

Julie was already backing off the sandbar. She spun the little skiff around and idled due north for about half a mile until they were across the shipping channel from the Port of Miami docks. She beached the skiff on another sandbar west of Fisher Island. From there they could see Government Cut, which was the channel to the Intracoastal going north, the entrance to the shipping port, and the ship channel directly in front of them.

Minutes later, not one but two Cigarette boats came through Government Cut. One turned and headed north, toward Star Island, and the other continued straight ahead into the shipping channel.

"Oh, shit," Tony said. "Do we have any binoculars?"

"Under your seat, I think I saw a case."

Tony stood up and opened the seat. He took the binoculars out of the case and focused on the Cigarette furthest from them. The one going north had four people in the cockpit, two men and two women. He turned to train the binoculars on the other boat just as it was going past them, not 300 yards away. He saw two men in the cockpit and as it went on by, he could see the name on the stern.

"The one going due west is called *Beeches, Knot Cream*," he said. "That's gotta be him."

Julie put the skiff in reverse and backed off the sandbar, then took off after the Cigarette boat about a quarter mile behind it. Tony lifted his phone and punched a number. A second later he said, "He's headed west from the Cut. That is, if the name of the boat is *Beeches, Knot Cream*."

Deuce's voice came over the speaker: "Yeah, that's him. We didn't pick up the other Cigarette until just a few seconds ago. He must have been running the shoreline."

"He's near the end of the loading docks and turning slightly southwest."

"Stay with him, Julie," Rusty said.

"He's heading into a canal," Tony reported.

"There aren't any canals there," Jesse informed him over the speaker. "He's heading up the Miami River."

"Follow him?" Tony asked.

"Yeah," Jesse said. "But hang back a ways. There're only a couple of navigable canals off the river for a few miles. Keep track of the number of bridges you go under and watch out for freighters. There's a lot of shipyards up there."

Julie drifted the skiff for a few minutes, then put it in gear and started up the river. They passed under a busy four-lane surrounded by tall office buildings. Julie guessed it to be US1. Like most islanders she didn't like Miami and rarely came up there.

The river turned to the left and they passed under several more bridges, the Cigarette disappearing and reappearing around the curves in the river. Tony was relaying each bridge as they crossed under them. After twelve bridges and about three miles they crossed under another bridge and just past it, they saw the Cigarette tied up to a dock at a shipping warehouse. There was a canal just before it that fed into the river.

Tony took the phone off speaker and said, "Past the thirteenth bridge, just a hundred yards past a canal on the left, tied to a loading dock at a warehouse on the south side of the river. How far out are you?"

"Just coming into the river's mouth now," Jesse said. "Is it the first building past the canal, or the second?"

"Looks to be the second one," Tony replied.

"I know that place," Jesse said. "Used to be Jacky Shipping. First building's the Trans Global yard. Turn into that canal on the left—they have a dock under the trees immediately to starboard. Tie up there. A buddy of mine runs the place."

"Deuce," Tony heard Jesse say in the background, "do whatever you gotta do; the Fifth Street bridge only has a twelve-foot clearance. We can wait till we get there and call the bridge operator, but we'll lose a lot of time."

CHAPTER THIRTY-SEVEN

O nce we entered the river mouth, I slowly idled under the first few bridges, heading up the river. Bridge clearance wasn't going to be a problem, at least until we got to Fifth Street. There were some good-sized island freighters that went up and down this river to the docks where the Cigarette was tied up and further beyond it. My clearance was thirteen feet and many of those freighters were taller.

Deuce closed his phone and said, "The ADD has contacted Miami-Dade PD. Units are headed to the Fifth Street Bridge and South River Drive. They'll set up road blocks a mile above and below the dock, with lights off."

A few minutes later, we got to the canal and I idled past it, then shifted the starboard engine to reverse and the port engine to neutral and slowly backed into the canal. I could see Julie and Tony standing on the dock next to Alex's skiff.

Rusty said, "Jesse, maybe Julie should stay with the boats, in case someone comes along."

Rusty knew this area, too. Not the best of neighborhoods. I knew he didn't want her to be anywhere near any rough stuff and Deuce, reading both our minds, said, "Yeah, that's a good idea."

"No need," I said. "Get them both aboard—we're going to tie off there and go in on foot. That dock is too open. And Rusty, you stay here with Julie."

"No way, Jesse. I'm going in."

"No, you're not," I said. "You have a kid to worry about and it's been a long time since you were in a firefight. We don't have any idea what we're up against here. You're staying. That's that." I didn't like pulling rank on my old friend, but it was true and he knew it. He'd lost his edge years ago and his added weight could be a problem.

Deuce and I climbed down from the bridge as Julie and Tony boarded. I looked around and noticed that all of Deuce's men had donned lightweight jackets and hats with the letters DHS stenciled on them. The three door kickers, whose names I still didn't know, were carrying MP-5 submachine guns. Deuce had been on the phone with his boss since we'd entered the mouth of the Miami River.

"The director has given the go-ahead for a takedown here," Deuce said. "Both to get Alex out and seize the Cigarette. Here, put this on." He handed me an oversized black windbreaker like the others wore, with DHS in big bold letters on the back.

"Just across the street from the dock is a container yard," I said, shrugging into the windbreaker. "Your shooter can get over the fence easy enough and up on top of those containers. They're usually stacked two or three high. From there, he can control the whole front of the building and the street in both directions."

I pointed toward the overhanging trees that Julie had docked under and turned to the man Deuce had called Hinkle. "Go through those trees, cross the street, and it's the first yard on the left." He shouldered the rifle I'd given him, jumped to the dock, and trotted off.

"The office is on the north end of the warehouse," I said. "There's only one door to the office from the parking lot. The warehouse itself has several big cargo doors on the parking lot side and several more on the river side. The yard is completely fenced from the office to the northeast corner of the warehouse."

Deuce pointed to the other two men and they followed the rifleman with their MP-5s slung across their chests. Deuce said, "They'll go through the office entry and we'll go around the warehouse. They'll report when in position." We climbed up to the dock and I looked back at Rusty and Julie.

"Wait here," I said to them. "Come on, Pescador."

Rusty nodded and grunted, "Get some."

The dog leaped to the dock and trotted along silently beside me as we moved quickly along the dock, close to the back of the first building. There was a large freighter tied up behind it, but the dock area was quiet, and the loading doors were all closed.

Nearing the fence that separated the two shippers' docks, we spotted a rusted hulk of a flatbed truck backed up to the six-foot-tall fence, with a van parked next to it. The three of us climbed into the bed of the truck, then Deuce climbed up onto the roof of the van and held his fist up, signaling us to hold up. There was a light wind blowing out of the east, carrying the mixed smells of diesel fuel and a restaurant across the river.

The other two men checked in that they were at the corner of the office. The sniper said, "Alpha Four. Two cars parked in front of the office. Lights are on inside the office. Warehouse looks dark."

"Roger that," I heard Deuce whisper through my earwig. "Office detail stand by." Then he pumped his fist to us, signaling us to follow as he jumped down to the gravel yard behind the warehouse. Tony and I followed closely behind him. I noticed that Tony was also carrying an MP-5 but didn't see where it came from. One of the door kickers, or maybe all of them, carried an extra in those packs.

There was a light coming from under the far cargo door and the walk-through door next to it. We quickly moved door to door, stopping to listen at each one. When we got to the walk-through door, I gently checked the knob. "It's locked," I whispered.

Deuce's voice came over the earwig as he whispered, "Office detail, count three after you hear our entry, then breach the office door." Then he nodded to Tony, who stepped away from the door and fired a three-round burst at the lock before lunging forward and planting a boot at the mangled dead bolt. The door swung open with a clang and we moved quickly inside, weapons up and ready.

One man was sitting in a chair with his back against the wall to the right. He started to stand up, pulling a gun from a shoulder holster. I grabbed his gun hand at the wrist with my left hand and followed through with a right elbow to the center of his face. The blow toppled him to the floor, knocking him cold. I picked up his pistol, a Glock, and stuck it in the waistband of my fishing shorts behind my back. Tony rolled him over and quickly checked him for other weapons before pulling a nylon zip fastener from a pocket to bind the man's hands behind his back. We fanned out, with me and Deuce headed toward the office door.

A single shot rang out from the area of the office and I heard someone over my headset say, "Office is clear. One tango down, one in custody."

I hurried through the office door from the warehouse, as Deuce and Tony searched the warehouse. I found two of Deuce's men in the shipping office. One went out through the door I'd just entered to help secure the warehouse. A black man lay on the floor, a pool of blood around his head, and a sawed-off Remington shotgun on the floor just beyond his outstretched hand. Another man sat in a chair, with his back to me. It was Baldy.

I spun the chair around, got right up in his face, and growled, "Where is she?"

His reptilian eyes blinked in recognition and he said, "Your whore was a lot of fun for me and Benny there."

I yanked him to his feet while his hand moved in a blur, coming forward with a long blade that appeared from his jacket sleeve. Then I felt a sharp pain in my left side and something warm flowing down from it. There was a snarling sound as a different blur flew past my shoulder, knocking Baldy from my grasp.

I stumbled back, the handle of a switchblade sticking out of my side. O'Hara dropped to the floor with the dog's teeth tearing at his neck. The last thing I heard as it started to get dark was a mixture of snarling, ripping, and gurgling sounds as the dog ripped O'Hara's throat out.

Then, over my earwig, I heard someone say, "We found her," just as everything went black.

CHAPTER THIRTY-EIGHT

I woke up slowly, hearing a dull, continuous beeping on my left. I was in a hospital bed, a tube attached to my left arm and sensors stuck to me everywhere. My knees and left side hurt like hell. The lights were turned down low, but sunlight was trying to come through the heavy drapes over the window. I could just make out Deuce and Rusty sitting in two chairs at the foot of the bed. Deuce was looking down at his phone and Rusty was snoring loudly, his head flung back.

As I tried to sit up, Deuce stood and came over to the side of the bed. "Hey, thought we'd lost you for a minute, Jarhead."

Rusty's head jerked forward and he opened his eyes, looking right at me. As came around to the other side of the bed I moaned, "Where's Alex? Is she okay?"

Deuce looked down at me. He seemed to be debating something in his head. He pushed a button on the side of the bed and said, "She's here, Jesse. She's in another room."

"What happened?" I asked.

Julie's with her," Rusty said. "She was...assaulted."

Just then a nurse came in, followed seconds later by a doctor. The nurse checked the monitors as the doctor looked over a chart at the foot of my bed. "You're at Jackson Memorial, Mr. McDermitt. How do you feel?"

I looked at the doctor and nurse, then back at the doctor. "How's my wife?" I asked.

"Let's be concerned with you right now," the doctor said, coming around to the other side of the bed, and taking my left wrist in his hand.

My right hand shot out, grabbed him by collar of the white smock he was wearing and pulled him down close to my face. "Tell me how she is now, Doc, or I'll snap your fucking neck."

Deuce stepped forward, took my wrist and applied pressure while pushing the doctor away. "Calm down, Jesse. Don't hurt the people here to help you both."

The doctor stepped back and straightened his smock. "Well, by your actions I assume you're not too badly hurt. You came in with a partially collapsed lung. An inch higher and that knife would have gone into your heart."

"Jesse," Rusty said, "Alex was beat up pretty bad. She's in ICU and they're doing everything they can."

I stared up at my old friend in shock. A single tear rolled down my cheek as I croaked, "How bad?"

The doctor said flatly, "She was sexually assaulted. More than once. She has a severe concussion, broken bones in the face, a fractured skull, dislocated jaw, and three broken ribs. She's in a coma."

I looked up at Deuce, then over at the doctor and Rusty. As blackness again came over me, I heard Deuce say, "Both men who did it are dead."

CHAPTER THIRTY-NINE

When I woke up again, the room was nearly dark and the drapes on the window open wide. I could make out the crescent of the rising moon out over the water. But it was a different room, it seemed. The beeping noise was still going on at my left side. But the tube was gone from my forearm and the wires had been removed from my head. Rusty and Julie were talking to Tony and Art near the door and they all turned toward me as I stiffly tried to sit up and lift the covers.

Julie came over and gently pushed me back down. Her eyes were red and there were dark circles under them. "She's gone, Jesse."

I stared up into her face and croaked, "Where'd she go?"

I was confused. I had no idea how long I'd been out, or what day it was, or even where I was.

Julie looked softly down into my eyes as Rusty, Tony and Art came over to stand around my bed. "Alex passed away two days ago, Jesse," she said. "You've been unconscious for three days. They transferred you here yesterday. You're at the VA hospital. We thought we were going to lose you, too."

"Alex? Dead?" I laid my head back and could not control myself as I started to sob. Julie leaned over and cradled my head, holding me tight, and I felt strong hands on my shoulders.

I was released from the VA hospital the next day, a Friday. Deuce visited Thursday afternoon before I was released, to debrief me on the takedown and arrest of the terrorists, al Madani, and Beech. I had been in a daze since the morning, when Julie told me that my wife of only a few days had died. I didn't really hear much of what he said, until he told me about the dog killing O'Hara.

"Where is he?" I'd asked.

"The dog? He's aboard your boat with Rusty and Julie. They moved it to a dock at Norseman Shipbuilding. Miami-Dade wanted to put him down for killing O'Hara, but I told them he was federal government property."

The days that followed were like walking through a fog. I slept when I was tired, ate when I was hungry and worked when I was neither tired, nor hungry. With Rusty, Julie and Jimmy's help, I moved the *Revenge*, Alex's skiff, and the Grady White that Deuce had given us up to my house in the Content Keys. My skiff and Lester were still missing. Jimmy showed me how to operate the backhoe and I spent a week digging my channel deeper and wider.

On November 10th, Rusty came up and we celebrated the Marine Corps birthday, as we'd done every year since I'd retired. I wasn't in much of a celebratory mood, though. Lester was still on the loose somewhere and I hate loose ends. Rusty left before sunset.

That evening, I decided I'd take Alex's skiff, go out into the flats to the west, and practice fly-casting. I knew I could never match her skill and grace. But in her memory, I wanted to try. It felt weird, being in her boat. Deuce had finally given me the details on the interrogation of Sonny Beech. O'Hara had raped her first. Twice. But according to what O'Hara told Beech, she'd fought hard against him. Then the black man, Benjamin Simms, had raped and beaten her savagely. The second time, she was unconscious, but he raped her anyway and beat her again.

The dog was on the casting deck as we rocketed across the flats between Little Crane Key and Raccoon Key. Ahead to the left was Crane Key and beyond that was a cluster of tiny islands called Crane Key Mangrove. They weren't really islands. At low tide, there were some small areas of exposed sand, but at high tide, the water covered all the sand and the mangroves stood in open water. It was a great place for snapper and grunts, and the dog and I both wanted fried grunts for supper. At least, I told him we did.

The dog started barking as I slowed down near the mangroves. The tide was high, but instead of alerting me to fish in the mangrove roots, he was looking south, toward Crane Key. I turned and steered toward the little island, following his nose. I beached the Maverick on the sand on the north end of the island. Since the tide was high, the small bay just to the south was full of water, but only a few inches deep.

The dog was barking in that direction, so I assembled my fly rod, stuck my Beretta in its clip-on holster under my shirt, and got out. Together we waded toward the little bay. The Beretta was a nice weapon, but I missed my Sig.

When we came to the mouth of the narrow opening, I could see a boat shoved way up under the mangroves. We waded slowly forward, and then I recognized it. It was my skiff.

I put the rod in my left hand and pulled the Beretta with my right. We waded further into the little bay, then up onto the beach next to my skiff. I leaned in and checked it out, while keeping a wary eye out around us. The keys were in the ignition and the fish boxes were all open. I shook the twenty-gallon gas tank in the stern; bone dry. There was a tattered green gym bag on the second seat I remembered Lester bringing when we'd come up here. When I looked inside, I found a Raymarine C120 GPS that I recognized. Russ had had one just like it on his boat the last time we'd dived together. Under it was his journal.

I placed the rod on the casting deck, and then whispered to the dog, "Find him."

Pescador trotted farther up onto the beach, sniffing around, then headed into the trees. I followed quickly, moving the Beretta side to side as we slowly crept forward, the dog sniffing the ground.

I found Lester huddled against a fallen palm tree. His skin was burnt raw, his lips cracked and peeling. He was either dead or sleeping. His clothes were shredded and his shoes in tatters. I knew there was no water on this island, or any of the islands around here. But it had rained six days earlier. Maybe that had kept him alive until now, I thought.

He slowly opened his eyes. They were red and swollen. He had insect bites all over his body and several cuts on his legs that looked badly infected. There were welts all over his calves and thighs. Fire ant bites. Anyone who lived in Florida knew to stay away from their mounds. His eyes slowly focused and then he recognized me.

Lester slowly raised a hand and hoarsely whispered, "Water."

I reached down and picked up my Sig, which was sitting on the log beside his head, and stuck it in my waistband. Then I took what was left of his wallet out of his pocket, opened it. I counted 54 bills, all hundreds. I stuck that in my pocket and put the wallet back in his. Then I unhooked the doubloon necklace that he had stolen from Russ and put it in another pocket.

"Fuck you," I snarled. "I wouldn't let you drink my piss."

As I turned and walked away, I added, "Semper Fi, mac."

I walked back to my skiff and pushed it into deeper water. I tied a line to the bow cleat and pulled it over to Alex's skiff, where I tied the other end of the line to a stern cleat and shoved them both into deeper water. The dog and I climbed in and we towed the skiff back to my house, leaving Lester there for the crabs, gulls and buzzards.

No loose ends, I thought.

When I got to the house, I climbed up on the deck and turned on my phone. I found the number I wanted and hit send.

Assistant Deputy Director Jason Smith answered on the first ring and said, "My deepest condolences on the loss of your wife, Captain McDermitt."

I said, "Tell Deuce the palm tree will be cut down in the morning and I have his dad's necklace, if he wants it." Then I disconnected and turned the phone off.

That call and that simple statement probably wouldn't resonate with Smith, but I knew Deuce would understand. The LZ would be ready, his dad's killer was dead, and he had his transporter.

The End

If you'd like to receive my monthly newsletter for specials, book recommendations, and updates on coming books, please sign up on my website:

WWW.WAYNESTINNETT.COM

Jesse McDermitt Series
Fallen Out
Fallen Palm
Fallen Hunter
Fallen Pride
Fallen Mangrove
Fallen King
Fallen Honor
Fallen Tide
Fallen Angel
Fallen Hero
Rising Storm
Rising Fury
Rising Force
Rising Charity

ABOUT THE AUTHOR

Wayne Stinnett is an American novelist and Veteran of the United States Marine Corps. After serving he worked as a deckhand, commercial fisherman, Divemaster, taxi driver, construction manager, and commercial truck driver. He currently lives in the South Carolina Lowcountry on one of the sea islands, with his wife and youngest daughter. They have three other children, four grandchildren, three dogs and a whole flock of parakeets. He's the founder of the Marine Corps League detachment in Greenville, South Carolina, where he met his wife, and rides with the Patriot Guard Riders. He grew up in Melbourne, Florida and has also lived in the fabulous Florida Keys, Andros Island in the Bahamas, Dominica in the Windward Islands, and Cozumel, Mexico.

Wayne began writing in 1988, penning three short stories before setting it aside to deal with life as a new father. He took it up again at the urging of his third wife and youngest daughter, who love to listen to his *sea stories*. Those original short stories formed the basis of his first novel, Fallen Palm. After a year of working on it, he published it in October 2013.

Since then, he's written more novels and now this prequel in the Jesse McDermitt Caribbean Adventure Series and the spinoff Charity Styles Caribbean Thriller Series. These days, he can usually be found in his office above Lady's Island Marina, where he also keeps his boat, working on the next book.

Made in United States
North Haven, CT
22 October 2022